THE **INTRIGUERS**

Also by **Donald Hamilton** and available from Titan Books

DONALD HAMILTON

A *MATT HELM* NOVEL

THE INTRIGUERS

TITAN BOOKS

The Intriguers
Print edition ISBN: 9781783292981
E-book edition ISBN: 9781783292998

Published by Titan Books
A division of Titan Publishing Group Ltd
144 Southwark Street, London SE1 0UP

First edition: February 2015
2 3 4 5 6 7 8 9 10

A CIP catalogue record for this title is available from the British Library.

Printed and bound by CPI Group (UK) Ltd, Croydon, CR0 4YY.

Did you enjoy this book? We love to hear from our readers.
Please email us at readerfeedback@titanemail.com or write to us at
Reader Feedback at the above address.

To receive advance information, news, competitions, and exclusive
offers online, please sign up for the Titan newsletter on our website:
www.titanbooks.com

THE *INTRIGUERS*

1

The morning I got shot at, down there in Mexico, I'd been out fishing in the high-powered little boat Mac had lent me, along with a trailer to carry it and a station wagon to pull it. Generosity with government equipment is not my superior's outstanding characteristic; but he'd explained that the outfit had been assembled by another agent for a job which was now completed. As a reward for years of faithful service and for taking a bad crack on the head in the course of a recent assignment—he put it differently, but that was the general idea—he was willing to let me take the rig on leave with me, since I'd be needing a fishing boat where I was going. When I brought it back, in good condition of course, it would be sold for whatever it would bring. Unfortunately, our departmental budget doesn't cover the maintenance of yachts, even fifteen-foot ones.

That morning, I'd been fishing at an offshore island, an hour's run—some twenty-four miles at my relatively cautious cruising speed—from where I was staying in the little resort village of Bahia San Carlos, just outside Guaymas, a good-sized port on the mainland side of the Gulf of California. I've had to learn a little about boats and oceans in the line of business, but I'm still a landlubber at heart, and from a small boat twenty-four miles of open water looks like a lot of water to me, even when it's calm. When it starts getting rough, I want no part of it, so when the wind began to pick up gustily around ten o'clock, I aborted my day's fishing plans and got out of there in a hurry, leaving the big boats and the real sailors to cope with the waves and the weather without me.

It was a hell of a frustrating way, I reflected, to end what had been a hell of a frustrating vacation. Of course, in a sense it had actually ended a day earlier when the girl had got really mad at last and walked out on me. Never mind her name. She doesn't figure in this, honest. She was just a girl I'd met on a job a few months earlier. It had been a rough and nasty business, and we'd both wound up in the same hospital. One thing had led to another, as it often does, and we'd agreed to do our convalescing together, down in sunny Mexico. Since I'd been more or less responsible for her getting hurt in the first place, I'd been pleased and flattered by her forgiveness.

At least it had seemed flattering at the time. What I hadn't realized was that, having had lots of time to think things over in that hospital bed—to think me over—she'd come to the remarkable conclusion that, in spite of my reprehensible profession, I was really a sweet and gentle guy who just needed a good woman to reform <u>him</u> from his violent ways.

It was too bad. She could have been a lot of fun if she hadn't decided that I needed a conscience and that she was it; she was a tall, slim, blonde kid who, in addition to her indoor talents, which were considerable, could swim and hike and handle a fishing rod adequately, once she got her strength back. We'd done quite a bit of fishing, and she hadn't been at all squeamish about sticking a big, barbed hook through a small, wiggling sardine to be used for bait; but she'd proved to have a thing about other life forms.

I never can figure how they make these distinctions. This one had absolutely no sentimental feelings about fish or fishing, but she bled copiously for all little birds and animals killed by cruel hunters. When, tired of angling for the moment, I innocently suggested borrowing a couple of shotguns and going out after the doves that swarmed locally, she looked at me with shock and horror—and this was, for God's sake, the same girl who'd casually impaled a live baitfish on a hook; the same girl who'd just hungrily cleaned up a large helping of *arroz con pollo*, a rice-and-chicken dish for which a good-sized bird had died. Of course, that bird had been killed by somebody else. She hadn't had to get its blood on her own hands. All she'd had to do was let me pay for the crime.

When I pointed out the hypocrisy of this, or what seemed like hypocrisy to me, and asked how she could possibly reconcile it with her fierce anti-killing convictions, she got very angry. Apparently there was another delicate distinction, too subtle for me to grasp, not only between fish and birds but between birds and birds: between a dead chicken and a dead dove. I said, sure, a dove tastes better, if you like doves. At that she really blew up and said I couldn't possibly be expected to understand, a callous monster, like me, who carried a gun and showed no respect whatever for life, even human life…

As you'll gather, it hadn't been a very restful leave. Being reformed is kind of wearing, even when it doesn't take. After putting her on a plane a week early at her request, I'd decided to spend a final day doing a little angling and exploring alone before heading back to the US to turn in the boat and wind up my leave in other surroundings, but the weather had just put an end to that project. I decided that I might as well use the rest of the day getting the boat back on the trailer and hosing it down thoroughly to wash off three weeks' accumulation of salt and fish scales. Any time I had left over could be used for packing—but first, of course, I had to make it back to the San Carlos marina.

It was a reasonably exciting ride, surfing along before the mounting waves with the wind getting stronger and gustier by the minute. The Gulf is no farm pond or stock tank. At Guaymas, it looks like the ocean—you can't see across to Baja California—and it acts like the ocean, too, upon occasion. The Mexicans call it the Sea of Cortez and treat it with respect. I wanted to get in before things became really rugged, so I kept the 85-horse Johnson blasting—well, as hard as you want to blast in that size boat in that kind of a seaway, actually not much over half-throttle with a mill that large.

It was quite a power plant. I'd only had it wide open once in the weeks I'd been using it, and it had scared hell out of me. I'd thought we'd go into orbit before I could get it shut down again. I've dealt with some fairly potent machinery on land, but speedboating is not my bag, and my only previous experience with outboard motors, to amount to anything, dated back to an era when ten horsepower was considered pretty hot stuff.

Even at half-throttle, the boat was a bit of a handful with the sea astern—I guess they all are. It was a relief to come around the towering rocky point guarding the mouth of San Carlos Bay and feel her stop making like a runaway surfboard and settle down to a steady planing attitude in quiet water. I unfastened my parka and threw back the hood. Being designed for fishing originally, whatever my mysterious predecessor had used her for, the chunky little blue-and-white fiberglass vessel was wide open all around so there'd be nothing to interfere with the rods and lines. You did your steering from an exposed midships console with no windshield to hide behind. If you wanted to stay dry, you put on something waterproof and zipped it up tight, even on a downwind run.

I'd mopped the spray off my face and sunglasses, and I was reaching for the throttle to hasten things along, now that the traveling was smooth and easy, when I saw the seal off to the right—excuse me, to starboard. They're actually sea lions, whatever the technical distinction may be, and they're fairly common down there in the Cortez, but I was just a country boy from the arid inland state of

New Mexico, and I still hadn't seen enough of them to take them for granted.

I was feeling nice and relaxed and a little triumphant at my victory over the wind and the waves, the way Columbus or Leif Ericson must have felt upon reaching America after a stormy Atlantic crossing. I was in no real hurry to get ashore now that I'd made it into sheltered water, so I put the wheel hard over to get a closer look at the swimming animal. You might say the sleek little beast saved my life, since the rifleman up on the point picked that moment to put the final pressure on his trigger.

He must have been aiming well ahead of me, giving plenty of lead to allow for the forward motion of the boat. It wasn't a long shot, only a little over a hundred yards, but even loafing along as she was, the boat was doing at least twenty miles per hour—close to thirty feet per second—and rifle bullets do not travel with the speed of light, although people keep trying to make them. When the hidden marksman's projectile reached the spot where he'd expected me to be, I wasn't there. My sharp turn away from him had thrown his calculations off just enough for a clean miss, but not enough that I didn't hear the bullet go past or catch a glimpse of the characteristic dimpled splash off to the left—excuse me, to port.

I suppose it's a reflection on my life style, as it's currently known, that even before I heard the report of the rifle from the rocks behind me, I didn't doubt that what had passed me was a bullet, not a suicidal bird or bumblebee; and that somebody was trying to kill me. I checked the impulse to dodge left. He'd be anticipating that. The standard naval routine is to chase the splashes made by the enemy's shells in the hope of confusing his attempts to correct his aim. Instead, I kept the wheel hard right, holding the tight turn I'd started through a full hundred and eighty degrees and ninety degrees more. For a moment that aimed me straight at the shore and the hidden rifleman, who wouldn't be expecting me, I hoped, to charge straight at him.

Another bullet cracked past, off to port again. He'd gambled that I'd straighten the boat out the instant she was heading back out to sea and safety, instead of continuing the turn. He'd lost, but all it had cost him was a cartridge worth a few dimes or pesos, depending on nationality. If I lost, I'd have a large hole in my anatomy.

At the shot, I spun the wheel hard left, chasing the splash at last, hoping he wouldn't be ready for it now. He wasn't. A third bullet slapped the water well off to starboard. I caught a glint of glass up among the rocks: a telescopic sight. Well, that figured. It was time to try something new before I got too clever and dodged right into one of his shots. Heading out to sea again wasn't too bad an idea. Under the new circumstances, the weather was by far the least of my worries. When the bow had swung back far enough, I checked the turn and slammed the throttle clear up to the stop. Eighty-five horsepower came in with a roar. The instant acceleration threw me back onto the helmsman's seat, actually the built-in battery box with a cushion on top.

Then my borrowed little seagoing bomb was screaming over the water, practically airborne. I thought I heard a bullet snap past just behind me, as if the would-be assassin, establishing a lead for a target speed of some twenty miles per hour, had been caught flatfooted by the sudden jump to forty and over, but I couldn't be sure because of the racket. Some seconds passed, and it was time to dodge again before he came up with the proper correction, but I didn't dare. We were going too fast. I'd never before held this boat at full throttle for any length of time; I'd never before hit this speed in any boat. I wasn't at all certain she wouldn't just flip if I tried to turn her.

I consoled myself that a high-speed angling target is something few riflemen can hit, and the range was getting longer by the second. I didn't look shorewards; I didn't dare take my attention off the boat that long. She felt very squirrely indeed at this velocity, and if she started to go haywire I wanted to be ready for her. I did risk a glance at the instruments. The tachometer was right at the 5500 rpm redline; the speedometer wasn't registering at all. Apparently, skimming the surface at this speed, the boat rode so high that the little Pitot tube, or sending unit, attached to the lower edge of the transom, off to one side, was practically clear of the water, with nothing to work on but spray…

Concentrating on keeping the flying little vessel under control, I hadn't realized that we were already getting out beyond the shelter of the point. Suddenly, the smooth surface across which we were racing broke up into hills and valleys of tumbling water. A cresting wave came at us, and the boat smashed into it and was hurled skywards. I managed to get the throttle back while she was still aloft. She hit with a shattering crash and plowed headlong into the next wave, which broke green over the bow. At the same time, the wake caught up with us and came surging into the self-bailing splashwell just ahead of the motor, with enough momentum to carry a lot of it over the bulkhead and into the cockpit—a planing boat doesn't go very far when the power quits; she just squats and stops.

For a moment I thought we were swamped; then I sat, still clinging to the wheel, with water around my ankles and the motor idling softly behind me. Another wave came at us, no tidal wave or *tsunami*, but plenty high enough to impress a shorebody like me. The boat rose to it nicely, however, and the wave passed underneath, sending only a ripple of spray aboard. I heard a humming sound and looked astern to see a steady stream of water being ejected by the automatic bilge pump. Already, the cockpit was almost clear as the water we'd shipped streamed aft to the sump in the stern.

She was quite a little ship. I paid my silent respects to the unknown fellow-agent who'd selected the pieces and put them together. He'd probably saved my life. I shoved the lever forward cautiously to get us moving again, working to windward slowly through the confused seas off the point. Glancing towards the rocks to starboard, I saw that we were still within long rifle range, but it didn't matter. We'd turned the corner, so to speak, and this seaward face was too steep for a man to cling to, let alone shoot from. Anyway, at three hundred yards, nobody's going to hit a target bobbing erratically in six-foot waves.

One of the big party boats I'd seen at the island earlier that morning passed a quarter-mile to seaward, rolling heavily, with an imperturbable Mexican skipper at the helm, and a bunch of seasick Yankee fishermen in the cockpit. Making the turn into the bay, they stared at the crazy jerk in the fifteen-foot motorized bathtub who didn't have sense enough to come in out of the spray, but this close to harbor the wind didn't bother me. I knew I could make it in from here, but there was something I had to do first. There was something I had to find.

Then I saw it on the beach at the head of the mailer bay that had opened up beyond the point: a small white boat pulled up on the sand. He'd have come by water, of course. He wouldn't have risked being seen and remembered as he carried that scope-sighted rifle through the hills from the nearest road. A conventional plastic case designed for a couple of husky salt-water fishing rods would, with a little modification, easily accommodate a long gun, and it could be loaded into a boat right at the dock without causing any comment whatever.

I got out the binoculars I'd been using on sea lions, whales, porpoises, and sea birds, and checked the beached craft as carefully as the distance and the motion of my boat would permit. It was a light aluminum skiff with a small motor, probably around ten horsepower. Although only a foot or so shorter than my fiberglass job, it was much narrower, shallower, and lighter; probably less than one-third the weight, with less than one-eighth the horsepower. He might have me outgunned, but I had him out-boated…

2

It took me a while to set it up. First I had to get back into San Carlos Bay, working on the assumption that he'd left from the same marina as I had—there weren't too many to choose from in that corner of Mexico—and would be coming back there eventually. I went far offshore and swung very wide around the point, this time, to emphasize how gun-shy I'd become. Then I had to find a place to lie in wait for him.

He'd seen me going by, I figured; he'd seen me entering the bay once more and disappearing around the next point, steering purposefully in the direction of the sheltered yacht harbor inland. I knew he wouldn't worry about my reporting the shooting to the Mexican authorities. If he knew enough about me to want to kill me, he knew I wasn't the type of citizen who'd ask for police protection. The thing he wouldn't be quite sure about was whether or not I was really slinking ashore with my tail between my legs, satisfied—for the moment, at least—just to be alive, or whether I was being tricky and dangerous, with immediate and violent retaliation in mind.

He had a problem, all right, and it took him most of the day to solve it to his satisfaction. Meanwhile, I'd found the ideal spot in which to wait him out, holding my course until I was well out of his sight, and then swinging over to the north shore of the narrowing bay—his shore—and sneaking back cautiously through the shallows below the cliffs to a little rocky cove just around the promontory that blocked his view. Here I dropped the patent anchor overboard in eight feet of water.

It was, as I said, ideal. The surrounding rocks hid the boat from seaward, but from a standing position I could see over them, out towards the headland from which he'd done his target practice. I doubted that my face would be visible at that range, even through strong glasses. I broke out the bottom-fishing rig, stuck a dead sardine on the hook since by this time I had no bait left alive, threw it overboard, and set the rod into the starboard of the two holders near the stern. This made me, I hoped, as far as passing boats were concerned, just an innocent fisherman who'd been driven off the open gulf by the wind and was trying to find a little action inshore.

Then I opened the cushioned battery box that also served as helmsman's chair, storage bin, and toolchest, containing a little bit of everything from Bandaids to emergency flares. I got out the waterproof packet of instruction books and other informative literature that had come with the boat. Something was bothering me, a discrepancy that I might have investigated earlier if I hadn't had the girl and her missionary attitudes to distract me: the fact that a craft that was, according to a plate attached to the seat, rated for a full ninety horsepower, should be so nervous at high speed with a mere eighty-five. Of course Chrysler, the manufacturer, specialized in fast automobiles. Maybe they just hadn't learned how to build fast boats yet, but it didn't seem likely.

I tipped up the motor so I could look it over carefully. A switch on the console did the job for me hydraulically, since the giant mill weighed over two hundred and fifty pounds. Aside from being larger than any outboard motor with which I'd ever associated, it looked perfectly normal. The horsepower was plainly marked on the cover; it also figured in the model number stamped on a plate attached to the mounting bracket.

Searching for a clue, I frowned down at the big three-bladed propeller, just clear of the water. According to the factory literature I had available, this V-4 motor block came in several different standard configurations ranging from 85 to 125 horsepower, depending on bore and carburetion. The least powerful motor in the series, the one I was presumably looking at, normally turned a prop with a pitch of some fifteen to seventeen inches. The motor at the stratospheric top of the line swung a wheel with considerably more pitch—with that much extra power, you could drive a boat considerably farther with each turn of the screw.

It took some acrobatics to read the figures marked

on my propeller without falling overboard, but when I saw them I had my answer. The pitch was a healthy twenty-one inches, enough to take a real bite of ocean. What was hanging on my transom was apparently not a normal 85-hp motor at all, since such a mild power plant couldn't possibly have got that steeply pitched wheel up to maximum rpm. Either I had a specially souped-up 85 on my hands or, more likely, somebody had simply taken a 125-hp model and switched covers and identification plates. No wonder the little boat had felt squirrely wide open, I reflected grimly, propelled by almost fifty percent more than her rated horsepower…

The wash of a passing vessel made me look up quickly, remembering what I was there for. Several boats were heading into the channel, but they were all larger craft, refugees from the offshore fishing grounds I'd deserted earlier. A fast runabout with some kids on board—a scow-shaped job with an inboard-outboard propulsion unit—came buzzing out from the yacht basin, stuck its blunt nose out into the rough stuff, turned quickly, and came back in again. Each boat that passed sent its wake across the narrows to rock my little vessel and break against the nearby shore.

I reeled in my line and found that something had stolen my sardine. I replaced it and tossed it out again. I lifted the cushion off the bench seat just forward of the steering console and procured beer and sandwiches from the built-in icebox underneath. All the comforts of home, I reflected wryly; all the comforts and conveniences including a reserve of some ten knots that nobody'd expect the little bucket to produce, looking at the markings on the motor—forty camouflaged horsepower that Mac had neglected to mention, describing the craft, over the phone, when I'd called him from the hospital where I'd been sweating out the mild concussion I'd acquired in the line of duty.

"Guaymas, Eric?" he'd said, employing my code name as usual. My real name is Matthew Helm, but it doesn't get much use inside the organization. "What's so attractive about Guaymas, if I may ask?"

"Fish, I hope, sir," I said. "And a nice, warm, sunny beach."

"You can find good fishing and warm sunny beaches in this country. I should think you'd be a little tired of Mexico. You've been spending quite a bit of time there recently."

I frowned at the wall of the hospital room from which I was being evicted for being too healthy. Mac had promised me a month's convalescent leave, but he has a sneaky habit of trying to get a little government mileage out of our vacations by spotting us where we'll be handy in case he needs us.

I said, "Would you rather have me in California, sir? Or Texas, or Florida, or the Sea Islands of Georgia?" I mean, the only way to stop him when he starts getting subtle is by direct frontal attack. "Just name the spot, sir, and I'll be on my way. Of course, I'll expect to get my month's *leave* later, when you don't require my services any longer."

"Oh, no, you misunderstand me, Eric," he said hastily, two thousand miles away in Washington, D.C. I could visualize him sitting at his desk in front of the bright window he liked to make us squint at: a lean, gray-clad, gray-haired man with bushy black eyebrows. He went on, "No, indeed, I have no special place in mind. I was just curious about the fascination Mexico seems to hold for you. You say you plan to do some saltwater fishing?"

"Yes, sir."

"Then you'll be needing a boat, won't you?"

"I was planning to rent one when I got down there."

"Rental boats are seldom very satisfactory. As it happens, we have a fairly expensive little fishing craft lying idle in Tucson, Arizona, not very far from where you are. We're going to have to dispose of it soon, since it has served its purpose. In the meantime, you might as well get some use out of it."

In one of the clumsy rented tubs from the marina, with a rusty old kicker on the stern, I'd have been a helpless target just now, I reminded myself. I'd had some luck, sure, but essentially it was the speed and maneuverability of my borrowed vessel that had saved me. It was an interesting coincidence. I didn't believe it for a moment.

I didn't even try to sell myself the foolish notion that, when an attempt was made to murder me, I'd just accidentally been sitting at the controls of a boat lent me by Mac that just accidentally happened to have the power and agility to get me away unharmed. Things like that just didn't happen accidentally when you were dealing with

Mac. I didn't even put it past him—well, not very far past him—to have sent that sea lion to turn me off course at precisely the right moment to save me from a bullet, if he needed me alive and healthy for an impending mission.

All joking aside, I didn't really think he could have known I'd be shot at down here in Mexico. He's not omniscient, not quite. But he had obviously known, I reasoned, that there was trouble brewing at sea, or at least as far out at sea—some sea, somewhere—as you'd want to take a fifteen-foot outboard. He'd hoped to persuade me to spend my leave in the neighborhood of the potential danger spot, wherever it might be, bringing with me the disguised little seagoing rocket the department had just acquired for the job. I was rapidly losing faith in that mysterious agent who was supposed to have used it before me. Thinking back, I realized that there had been a good many indications, which I'd been too preoccupied to take seriously, that neither boat, trailer, nor tow car had seen any strenuous use before I got them.

When my thorny attitude had spoiled his plan—for some reason he'd been reluctant to give me direct orders over the phone—Mac had lent me the boat anyway and let me take it down here and play with it so I'd at least know how to handle it when the time came for him to summon me to action. And somebody had come clear down into Mexico to take care of, me with a scope-sighted rifle before that summons could reach me…

I could be reading too much into a simple little murder attempt and a camouflaged 125-hp motor. Nevertheless, the safest course was to act on the assumption that I was entangled in one of Mac's complicated spiderwebs of intrigue, and figure out, since my vacation was all washed up anyway, what he'd want me to do next. That wasn't hard. I was already working at it. Obviously, the first thing required was to deal with any would-be murderers in such a way that they couldn't hamper my future activities.

By the end of the day, I'd finished the beer and the bait and was fishing, if you want to call it that, with a bare hook. It was a long, dull afternoon in one way; but they're never really dull when you're waiting like that in a duck blind, or by a deer trail, or in a promising ambush. There was always the possibility, of course, that my quarry had escaped in some other direction; but the most likely theory was that he'd been working out of San Carlos like me, behaving like just another tourist and keeping an eye on me. And if he'd come out of San Carlos, he'd want to check back in there, because they keep track of the craft using their marina facilities. I considered it a good enough theory that I was willing to wait until sunset and at least an hour longer, if I had to.

I didn't have to. At six-thirty, with the sun just starting to dip behind the spectacular rock formations to the west, his patience ran out, and he came. I first glimpsed a flash of spray well out beyond the point; then I saw the white skiff driving along with the whitecapped waves that threatened to overwhelm it. I was already reeling in my fishing line. This late in the afternoon, I saw, in this weather, we had the whole Sea of Cortez to ourselves.

Laying the rod down, I quickly lowered the motor and turned the key. The big mill began to rumble behind me, shaking the little fiberglass hull. I hauled up the anchor, dumped it aboard, and backed the boat out of its hidey-hole very cautiously: this was no time to bend the propeller on a rock. Then I shoved the go-stick forward, and we took off flying.

He saw me coming. He turned, as soon as the waves would let him, and tried to flee. It was kind of pitiful, actually; just about as pitiful as me innocently chasing seals with his telescope crosshairs tracking me. I shot down the bay at flank speed, mostly airborne; but this time I throttled back in good time before hitting the heavy stuff out past the point. He was plunging through it, or trying to, heading back the way he'd come. Actually, his light boat wasn't making much progress against the waves and the wind. The extra weight and freeboard of my craft, not to mention the extra horsepower, made it no contest. I simply walked up on him as if his little motor had stopped running.

I don't mean to imply that it was smooth and easy. It was a rough, wet chase while it lasted, with a lot of spray flying; but the big crested rollers out of the northwest turned out to be more frightening to look at than dangerous to ride. At fifty yards he went for the rifle. This was ridiculous. He couldn't even hold the thing to his shoulder for managing the boat, and he couldn't have found me in the big sniper's telescope if he had, the way the seas were tossing him around. He fired a couple of times, kind of one-handed and from the hip. I never saw or heard the bullets. While he was working the bolt for a third shot, a wave threw him off balance and he almost fell overboard. The firearm went into the sea as he grabbed the gunwale with both hands to catch himself. So much for that.

The rest was simple. The most vulnerable spot of his boat was the low stern, cut down to accommodate the outboard motor. On larger boats like mine, that motor notch is protected by the splashwell inboard that I've already mentioned, that catches a boarding wave and lets it drain back out again, but his little tub had no such protection. Anything that came through the motor cutout wound up right in the boat with him.

On my first pass, he kicked his stern aside at the last moment by yanking desperately at the motor's control handle. I swung around with him, using all the throttle I dared in that seaway, and he took in some twenty gallons of my wake in spite of his evasive maneuver. The next pass was a clean miss as a rogue wave threw us far apart at the last moment, but I came right around and had a beautiful shot past his stern as he hit the next sea too hard, shipped more water over the bow, and almost lost headway completely, throttling back to keep from driving his little boat clear under.

I had a good look at him as I came up on him fast: a tallish man, not old, not Mexican, clean-shaven, kind of boyishly handsome, with a tanned face and wet brown hair cut short enough to put him well into the ranks of the

squares. It made no difference to me. Square or hip, he'd
tried to kill me. To hell with his haircut.

I gave a quick burst of power and roared past at planing
speed, missing his stern by less than two feet. Looking
back, I saw the white curling wake roll clear over his
motor and transom, right into the boat. An oncoming
wave finished the job. I got my bucking and plunging
little nautical projectile under control, turned her like a
cutting horse between waves, and charged back there.
He was clinging helplessly to the swamped skiff that
was still afloat, of course—they're all loaded with plastic
flotation these days so you can't really sink them—but
when he saw half a ton of speedboat coming at him down
the face of a wave, he kicked himself clear and dove. I
don't know what he thought I was going to do, run him
down, I suppose, or brain him with a boathook. Anyway,
he submerged and presumably swam off, making my job
that much easier.

I didn't even bother to look for him. I simply slowed
down, swung around, and grabbed the braided nylon
painter trailing from the bow of the skiff. Then I headed
for shore, towing the swamped boat with me, leaving him
swimming out there in the oncoming darkness.

3

According to the marina records, his name was Joel W. Patterson. At least that was the name written down opposite the registration number of the boat I'd towed in. He came from San Bernardino, California. He had arrived in San Carlos two days after I had. He'd been staying in a pickup camper at the trailer court across the road.

"Yes, señor, I remember him a little," said the young lady behind the counter in the marina office, where you could buy bait and tackle, arrange for dock space, and hire anything from a single rod-and-reel outfit to a large fishing vessel complete with captain and crew. She went on, "He was expecting to meet a friend here, someone from Arizona, I think. He looked through my book of registration here. But I do not think the friend ever came. I never saw him with anyone. He was quite a handsome young man, but alone, always alone."

He'd undoubtedly been looking for my name and boat number, to make sure I'd arrived so he could get to work on me. I said, "Well, he's still alone, I guess."

"*Si*, señor. It is a terrible thing. I have sent one of the party boats out to search, but in the darkness and in this wind there is not much hope. You did not see him at all?"

"No, I was fishing along the shore and I saw something white drifting off the point," I said. "I went out to have a look and there was the boat full of water with nobody on board. I cruised around it a bit, but I couldn't see anybody swimming, so I just grabbed the rope and brought it in." I rubbed my sore hands together. "It wasn't easy. The damn thing towed like a dead whale."

"You did what you could, Señor Helm." She was a very attractive young lady, and she ran the marina operation very efficiently, but what really impressed me was that she turned up for work each morning in a simple cotton dress. A US female in her job with her figure couldn't have resisted appearing in a ducky little sailor-boy pantsuit plastered all over with cute gold anchors, just to show how nautical she was. "You are staying at the Posada San Carlos? The authorities may wish to ask you some more questions, Señor Helm."

"Sure," I said. "I'll be there until tomorrow morning some time—well, if they insist on my staying on, I suppose I'll have to."

"I do not think that will be necessary."

"In that case," I said, "I'll pay my bill and pick up my boat tomorrow. Is there any chance of getting somebody to wash it down for me after I get it on the trailer?"

"Certainly, señor. The price is six dollars. You had

better come, early while the tide is high so you have plenty of water at the launching ramp... Excuse me."

She turned to take a call on the electronic gizmo behind her, speaking Spanish too rapid and colloquial for me to follow. She put down the microphone and sighed, turning back to me.

"That was the captain of the boat I sent out. He says it is very dark out there, and he has found nothing. I told him to come back in." She moved her shoulders. "If they will insist on taking such little boats out in such bad weather... They cannot be made to understand that this is a big and dangerous body of water, señor. They see it so calm and smooth in the morning and will not believe how it can get rough by evening."

"Sure."

I went back down to the dock to get the tackle I'd left in the boat, although I'd had no trouble with pilferage, and neither had anybody else with whom I'd talked. Gear that would have vanished in an hour from a US parking lot had stayed safely on board week after week, but it seemed unfair to strain some poor Mexican's honesty with a couple of expensive rods and a pair of good binoculars.

After lifting the stuff onto the dock, ready to carry ashore, I checked the lines and rearranged the canvas bumpers so she wouldn't chafe. Then I went over to the aluminum skiff docked astern, still full of water, just the way I'd brought it in but not quite the way I'd found it. I'd taken the precaution, once I'd got it into relatively calm water, to check it over. There had been a soggy

box of 7mm Remington Magnum rifle cartridges, partly
used, tucked under a seat. Lashed to one of the braces
I'd found a long, soft, black plastic fishing rod case that
was arranged a little differently inside from what you'd
expect. I'd slipped the cartridge box into the case, for
weight, zipped up the case, and dropped it overboard in
exactly one hundred and ten feet of water—assuming that
the electronic depth-finder on my fancy little borrowed
ship was properly calibrated.

Now I frowned down at the registration number on
the bow of the skiff, a California number of course,
and debated whether or not to risk a visit to Mr. Joel
Patterson's camper across the road, but I couldn't think
of anything I might find that would be worth the attention
and suspicion I might attract. I found myself wondering
how long he'd lasted out there, and dismissed the thought.

Then I deliberately brought it back out and examined
it, because if you're going to do it you'd damn well better
be able to look it in the eye. I have no respect for these
remote-control killers who can happily push a bomb
release in a high-flying airplane as long as they don't have
to see the blasted bodies hundreds of feet below; but who
can't bear to pull the trigger of a .45 auto and produce one
bloody corpse at ten yards.

There was a chance that he'd made it ashore or would
still make it. I'd known men who could have, but I didn't
think he was one of that select group of amphibious
humans. His specific gravity had been too great, for
one thing: he'd had too much bone and too little fat for

adequate flotation. I've got the same problem myself. He'd looked like a lean, tanned, swimming-pool hero to me, good only for impressing the bikini babes with a couple of smoking-fast laps between drinks, not the chunky, buoyant, durable fish-man type it usually takes to survive in stormy waters a couple of miles offshore.

I stood there a moment longer, feeling baffled and irritable. In my line of work, I have killed several people; in fact you might go so far as to say that is my line of work. However, I'm usually given a few compelling reasons why the touch, as we call it, is necessary for the continued welfare of the human race and the United States of America. In this case I'd been struck at, and had struck back, without having any idea what the hell it was all about.

The sound of a motor made me look up quickly. A boat was coming through the narrow entrance of the yacht basin with running lights on; I'd seen it before. It was the snubnosed I/O runabout that had gone out to test the big waves earlier in the day and come racing back in again. When it came under the marina lights, I saw that spray was crusted on its windshield and that the five kids on board were pretty wet. There was a short-haired girl, two long-haired girls, and two long-haired boys. They were laughing and joking and passing cans of beer around as they coasted up to an empty dock space some distance away.

I picked up my rods and tackle box and carried them up to the station wagon that had been part of the package I'd picked up in Tucson: a big Chevrolet with a monstrous

454-cubic-inch engine. The mill was fairly sluggish for all those cubes; the best that could be said for it was that it worked pretty well on the low-test gas that's all that's readily available in Mexico.

The wagon itself was one of those delectable styling exercises whipped up by the butterfly boys to make the salesmen happy, and to hell with the customers who'll eventually have to live with it. It had a lot of tricky features to generate sales appeal—a vanishing tailgate; vanishing windshield wipers—but big as it was it had no leg-room at all, certainly nowhere near enough for my six feet four. I'd had to have the front seat moved back several inches to make it just marginally inhabitable. Furthermore, although it had seats for six passengers and space for a mountain of luggage, it had springs stolen from a baby carriage designed for very light babies. I'd had to have the rear suspension drastically beefed up to keep the tail from dragging in the road—with a load of just me, one suitcase, a little fishing tackle, and a relatively light boat trailer with a tongue weight of considerably less than two hundred pounds!

Add to these major aberrations various minor, uncorrected new-car ailments that I'd had to have put right, and you can see why I wasn't unreceptive to the idea, once it had occurred to me, that I might be the first person to use the outfit, regardless of what Mac had told me. To be sure, there had been several thousand miles on the odometer when I got the heap, but that can be arranged by the specialists we keep handy, without moving the car out of its tracks. Apparently my superior had gone to some trouble to have the boat and motor checked out—I'd had no trouble with them—but he'd kind of taken for granted that a new car was bound to be satisfactory, which showed how much he knew about modern cars. Well, it was nice to know he wasn't infallible in all areas.

I threw my stuff into the wagon through the trick tailgate and started the thing by fighting the trick starter switch that locked the shift lever, locked the steering wheel, and bawled you out if you left your key behind—it did everything, in fact, except start the car easily. I drove to my hotel a mile away. It was an attractive, rambling collection of low buildings on a beautiful curving beach at the head of a spectacularly beautiful bay. Of course, I couldn't see it in the dark, and I wasn't really in the mood for scenic beauty, anyway.

I stopped by my room to make a quick change from my fishing clothes into something respectable. Then I went into the lounge—the place had no real bar as such—found a big chair near the fireplace in which nothing was burning this late in the spring, and took a grateful slug of the martini that was brought me promptly. Presently I was aware that somebody had sat down in the chair to my left. I looked and saw that it was the short-haired girl from the runabout I'd just seen docking.

She said softly, "So you couldn't leave it alone, Mr. Helm. You couldn't just give thanks for your escape and leave it at that. You had to go after him and drown him!"

4

The Posada San Carlos had only one drawback. The location was lovely, the rooms were comfortable, the food was good, the service was excellent, and the prices were reasonable; but at certain times, of the day the noise, in the lounge and adjoining dining room was almost unbearable due to an electronically amplified group of musicians who didn't seem to feel they were earning their pay unless the big windows facing seawards were rattling in their frames, and the silverware was dancing on the tablecloths. One thing no Mexican band really needs, anyway, is amplification.

They were playing now. I discovered that there was something to be said for them after all. They made conversation possible, if the other party was close enough, without any danger of being overheard by anyone else in the room.

I regarded the girl for a moment, and said, "Naturally, I haven't the faintest idea what you're talking about."

She said, "You're Eric. I'm Nicki. The code is double negative."

I finished my drink and set my glass aside. "Double negative? What does that mean?" I shook my head. "Sorry, Nicki. You've got the wrong guy. My name is Matthew."

"Armageddon," she said.

I'd started to rise. I sank back into the big chair and lifted a finger to summon a waiter. "Another martini, please," I shouted to him over the noise. "Anything for you?" I asked the girl.

"Yes, I'd like a margarita."

My previous female companion had considered margaritas a corny tourist tipple, but then she'd had a lot of screwy ideas. I have no objections to that cactus-juice cocktail myself, although it's not, in my opinion, designed for serious drinking.

"And a margarita for the lady, *por favor*," I yelled, and watched the waiter move away, while the waves of sound from the band washed over me rhythmically. They weren't bad, you understand, they were just too damned loud.

I turned my attention to the girl beside me. She was a reasonably sized, well-proportioned, dark-haired, basically sound specimen of human female, but she was doing her best to hide the fact, at least the female fact. She had a boy's haircut, or what used to a boy's haircut before they all started letting it grow. She also had a boy's pants on, complete with fly—pretty soon nothing will be safe from women's lib, not even our jock-straps.

They were white cotton pants, slightly flaring, and quite

dirty. Her horizontally-striped blue-and-white jersey was pretty dirty, too, as were her frayed white sneakers, not to mention the visible areas of her ankles. She obviously had no brassiere on under the jersey, and it didn't make any difference, not because she wasn't endowed with the customary protuberances, but because she didn't give a damn, and if she didn't, who did?

She was, obviously, a product of years of television commercials, although she'd have hated anybody who told her so. But if enough stupid industrial magnates spend enough million dollars on tastelessly revolting advertising, telling kids that the thing to be is clean and sexy—using product A, of course—the brighter and more rebellious ones are bound to figure out that the only sensible response to make to all this nauseating propaganda is to be dirty and sexless.

Actually, she wasn't a bad-looking girl. She had a nicely rounded young figure inside the grubby pirate costume, and a tanned, slightly snub-nosed face with clear gray eyes. The heavy, dark, eyebrows were, of course, totally unplucked, just as the mouth was totally devoid of lipstick. It was a pretty good mouth, big enough, potentially sensitive, but rather firm and disapproving now. I watched it take a sip of the margarita magically produced by the waiter, as I tasted my own martini.

"You haven't given the countersign, or whatever you call it," the girl said.

"Götterdämmerung," I said, and went on casually: "He's getting doomsday as hell in his old age, isn't he?"

"Oh, he's not so old," the girl said quickly and rather defensively, as if she thought I was trying to trick her into betraying herself, and maybe I was. "Not really."

"So the code is double negative," I said.

"Yes, whatever that may mean."

"If you were supposed to know what it meant, he'd have told you, wouldn't he?" Actually, it was a warning that this young lady, while working for us, was not to be trusted too far; and that therefore any information she supplied should be corrected in certain ways before being used as a basis for action. "What's he called?" I asked.

"I've given you the word. What more do you want?"

"What do we call him?" I asked again, patiently. It was important for me to learn just how much of an outsider I had to deal with.

"He's known as Mac around the office. I never learned why."

"Nobody knows why," I said. "Maybe it's his name."

"Nobody there knows what his real name is."

I said, "You're doing fine. Where's the ranch?"

"What?"

"The ranch, sweetheart. The place we go to have the wrinkles ironed out after a rough assignment. Where is it?"

"Just west of Tucson, Arizona."

"What's behind his desk?"

"A chair, of course. Oh, and a window. A bright window."

"Have I worked for him long?"

"Yes. You were out for a while some years ago but you came back in. You're one of his very senior people."

"Gee, thanks," I said. "I can feel one senior foot slipping into the grave as you say it."

"He has a lot of faith in you, Mr. Helm."

"And you wonder why, don't you?" I grinned as she didn't speak. I asked, "What did I do when I wasn't working for him?"

"You were a photographer; a photographer and journalist."

"Have I ever been married?"

"Once. Three children, two boys and a girl. Your wife's remarried and living on a ranch in Nevada with the kids. Well, the oldest boy is in college somewhere on the West Coast. UCLA, I think."

I hadn't known that. In the business, it's best to stay clear of people you love or somebody'll get the bright idea of using them against you.

"You've done a lot of homework," I said. "If you're Nicki when I'm Eric, who are you when I'm Matthew Helm?"

"Martha," she said. "Martha Borden. No relation to Lizzie with the ax. Do I gather that the inquisition is over, Mr. Helm?"

"For the time being."

"You're a suspicious man." She was silent for a little and went on: "And a vicious one. You didn't have to kill that man."

"That's right," I said. "I didn't have to. He could have lived a long, happy, fruitful life. The choice was his. He chose to shoot at me."

"So you dumped him overboard, towed his boat away,

and left him out there to drown!"

I looked at her grimly. I couldn't get away from them, it seemed. Having just got rid of one who made fine distinctions between birds and birds, I'd acquired one who made fine distinctions between homicides and homicides: shooting was apparently okay but drowning was terrible. Or perhaps it was just unsuccessful shooting that was morally acceptable, while successful drowning wasn't.

"Poor fellow," I said. "If only he'd managed to blow a hole through me with his cute little 7mm Magnum, nobody'd have hurt a hair of his cute little head. My heart bleeds for him. But you didn't come all the way to Mexico just to sympathize with unsuccessful murderers, I presume."

Her lips, innocent of lipstick, were tightly compressed. "Mr. Helm, just because you're shot at doesn't give you the right—"

I said, "Honey, you're getting tiresome. How many times have you been shot at?"

"Well—"

"Wait till somebody takes a crack at you before you start telling people what kind of patient and long-suffering targets they're supposed to be. Anyway, who's talking about rights? It's a practical matter, Nicki. The man shot at me six times today. He missed, but he had quite a few cartridges left. He probably had instructions from somebody—it would be interesting to know who—to keep trying until he got me. But unless he's a hell of a lot better swimmer than I think, he won't be trying anymore. It's as simple as that. Now tell me what I'm supposed to do that I'll be able to do a lot better without an eager rifleman breathing down my back trail."

She drew a long breath. "Well, okay. You're supposed to get to a reasonably safe phone as soon as possible."

I regarded her narrowly. "You were sent all the way down here just to tell me that?"

"You're not supposed to call his special number. Call the office number and ask for him. There's a reason."

"But you can't tell me what it is?"

She shook her head. "I don't really know."

"How soon is as soon as possible? I can't call from here; there's only one phone in the village and one at the hotel desk, and both are too damn public. I either call from somewhere in the city of Guaymas proper, if I can find a phone and get a US connection, or I wait until I'm across the border, a two-hundred-and-fifty-mile drive. And if I head north tonight, I may be stopped by the Mexican authorities who want to ask me questions about an empty boat I found drifting out in the Gulf. Anyway, I don't think I can pick up my boat at the marina this late. I'd have to leave it—"

"No," she said, "don't do that."

I grinned. "I didn't think he'd want me to leave that damned little nautical hotrod after the trouble he went to to plant it on me."

"And you'd better not antagonize the Mexican authorities. I don't think a few hours are critical right now."

"Okay, I'll plan to leave in the morning, then. Tell me

one thing, did he expect an attempt on my life?"

"I don't think he expected it, but he told me to make contact with you at once if I saw one made."

"That,' I said, "is expecting it in my book. I had it figured otherwise, but I'm generally wrong when I try to second-guess him. But he might have warned me."

Her gray eyes were cool. "You're a pro, aren't you, Mr. Helm? Always alert, always prepared, like a Boy Scout? Are you supposed to need a warning to keep your eyes open?"

I grinned. "And if no attempt on my life was made, Miss Borden? What were your instructions then?"

"I was supposed to contact you in another day or two, anyway."

"But if I was shot at or otherwise attacked, you were supposed to move right in with instructions. Well, that figures. He'd know that would change my plans and he'd want you to catch me before I took off to report the incident in the normal manner. How long have you been here?"

"Two weeks."

"Staying where?"

"With some kids. You saw them. I was coming alone, but when I heard they were heading down here I kind of invited myself along, it made a better cover. They've got a converted panel truck to sleep in, over at the trailer court, and one of the boys borrowed his daddy's boat. Sometimes we take our blankets in the boat and sleep on a beach somewhere. Smoke pot. Shoot speed and drop acid. Sniff cocaine. Get high on heroin. Copulate like animals. Real orgies, man." She grimaced. "Actually all they really use, besides a little marijuana, is beer."

"How much do they know?" I asked.

"Nothing."

"How did you work that?"

"I'm an ecological nut, man. Specifically, I'm a birdwatcher concerned about the fate of our feathered friends in this polluted world. I flip over frigate birds and bluefooted boobies, and cormorants and pelicans and stuff. Did you know that the brown pelican is an endangered species, just like the hawks and eagles, all because of DDT? The eggs get so fragile they squash or something." She drew a long breath. "I shouldn't try to be funny about it. It isn't funny."

"No," I said. "So you're a birdwatcher. What does it get you?"

"The privilege of crawling around rocks with binoculars—I was on a hill across the bay when you went racing out to… to meet him. I saw the whole thing through the glasses. And sometime I get this terrible compulsion to go out in the roughest weather to see what the birds are up to—"

"At night?"

"Tonight I talked them into going out to one of the bird islands. You know, those big rocks covered with guano, just outside the harbor. We shone the boat's spotlight on it so I could see the birds roosting, there. Actually… actually I figured that if he'd managed to stay afloat, with the wind the way it was, that's where he'd most likely come ashore. But he wasn't there."

I said, "With a partner like you, I might as well give up homicide as a career. I drown them; you give them artificial respiration. What's the use?"

"That isn't very funny, either," she said coldly. "Anyway, he wasn't there. And I'm not your partner, Mr. Helm. I'm just a messenger girl."

I nodded slowly. "Armageddon," I said. "Götterdämmerung. At the time he switched the identification signals, just recently, I thought Mac was just getting fancy with the vocabulary, but it could be he was trying to tell us something. Like that there's something big and desperate going on." I hesitated. "And the gent who's making like a fish out there was sent by somebody who wanted me put out of action—me and how many others, Nicki? And how many messengers like you have been waiting around to deliver Mac's word to the guys like me whom that mysterious somebody would like to have eliminated?"

Martha Borden licked her pale lips. "You underrate yourself, Mr. Helm."

"What does that mean?"

"As I said, for some reason he has a lot of faith in you. There are some others, yes, but I have the only action message, to be delivered to you. You're supposed to take it from there, once you've been in touch by phone. It all depends on you."

"What does?"

"I wish I knew," she said. "I wish I knew; and I wish

I could believe he'd picked the right man for the job, whatever it is!"

5

In the morning, I got over to the marina about nine to find that I'd missed all the excitement—which was exactly what I'd hoped for and why I'd taken my time packing and eating. I'd figured that with daylight and a calm sea something might be found, and I preferred not to be around when it was.

Now I learned that an early-rising fisherman, leaving the harbor at dawn, had spotted an object washed up on one of the guano-covered rocks off the entrance, and had swung over to investigate. He'd come racing back to report a dead man. The police had brought in the body, sent it into Guaymas, and interrogated its discoverer at considerable length. A khaki-clad officer was waiting to talk with me, although I wasn't considered particularly important. All I'd found was a boat.

Once again, I told where I'd found it, and how I'd done my best to search for the owner in spite of the lousy weather conditions. I was thanked for my trouble and instructed to go on about my business, so I drove over to the trailer parked in the nearby lot, hitched it onto the station wagon, and backed it down the launching ramp into the water. Then I got my boat and ran it over there. With the help of a couple of dockside characters, who earned a US buck apiece for their labors, I eventually got it onto the trailer. The main trouble, I guess, was that I wasn't used to cranking boats onto trailers; but there was also the problem caused by the complicated design of the little craft's bottom: a puzzle of grooves, ridges, and sponsons. You had to get her placed exactly right or the various rollers and supports just wouldn't fit.

After lashing things down, I drove over to the nearby freshwater hose. I was rinsing the salt off the motor when Martha Borden appeared from the direction of the trailer court, dressed as she had been the night before, except that she was barefooted. Apparently the ragged sneakers had been a concession to the formality of the Posada San Carlos. She was carrying a bulging rucksack and a pair of big Japanese binoculars—at least I figured they were Japanese from the beat-up, cardboard-looking case. They've licked the problem of optical glass over there, but they still have a lot to learn about leather.

I said, "Well, they found him, just about where you guessed he'd wind up. He must have drifted a little more slowly than you figured, that's all."

She looked at me for a moment and licked her unpainted lips. "Dead?"

"Very."

"And it doesn't bother you a bit?"

I said, "Sure, it bothers me. I get the shakes every time I think about how it could have been me."

"Damn you," she said. "Where do you want me to put this junk?"

"You're coming with me?"

"You know I am."

I guess I had known it, at that. "Toss your gear in the back of the station wagon," I said. "Then, if you want to be helpful, you can climb up into the boat—use the trailer fender for a step—and grab this hose and rinse things off a bit, particularly the aluminum trim, so it won't corrode. I was going to have a professional job done, but it's getting late and we'd better not waste the time. You'll find a sponge up forward. I've got to go up to the office and take care of the bill."

Twenty minutes later we were on our way, with the official blessings of the marina lady and the police. The paved two-lane road followed the coast for a few miles to an intersection, where a right turn would have taken us to Guaymas and points south. I turned, left instead, towards Hermosillo, Nogales, and the US border.

There's not much between Guaymas and Hermosillo, and for that matter there's only a little more between Hermosillo and Nogales. As we gathered speed across the empty, semi-desert landscape, the girl beside me squirmed a bit, tugged at her pants, and adjusted, her jersey over her unconfined breasts in a gingerly sort of way: she'd managed to get herself pretty wet, hosing down the boat.

Not that it mattered. In that climate she'd be dry shortly, and it wasn't as if she had a pair of sharply creased slacks to worry about, or a crisply ironed blouse, or an expensive, nicely waved hairdo. I suppose in a way it was a relief to get away from such conventional concerns.

"Too much air-conditioning?" I asked politely.

"No, it feels good." She hesitated. "I've got a list for you, you know."

"I figured you had something. Where is it?"

"It's memorized. He didn't want me carrying anything on paper. That's why I had to come along."

"Sure," I said. "When do I get a reading?"

"I can tell you the first name now. There's a woman called Lorna staying at the ranch temporarily. Ostensibly she's resting up between assignments; actually she's there for protection, waiting for word from you."

"And just what am I supposed to do with the lady once I've got her?"

"I don't know," Martha said. "That will be up to you, after you've talked with Washington."

I made a face. "God, aren't we mysterious! Lorna. She's a tough one, I've heard. Won't take orders from any man. Except Mac."

"Why should she? Why should a woman have to work under a man if she's as good as a man?"

I said, "Well, it's the customary reproductive position, but I understand there are others."

Martha gave me a withering glance. "Funny!"

I grinned. "There you sit, wearing a man's zip-up-the-front pants and a man's hairdo, giving me that poor-downtrodden-women line. Just what do you think would happen to me if I started wandering around the countryside in a woman's skirt with my hair clear down my back? What would happen to any man who tried it? You know damn well we'd be locked up as transvestite perverts so fast it would make your head swim. Hell, we poor men can't let our hair grow even a little without half the cops in the country trying to bash in our heads, but you ladies can cut it all off any time you feel like it and nobody bats an eye. Which sex was it you said was being discriminated against?" She gave me another scorching look, obviously unimpressed by my argument. Well, maybe it wasn't much of an argument. I asked, "What's Lorna's real name?"

"I don't know if it's her real name or not, but she's calling herself Helen Holt."

"And judging by her reputation, I don't guess we'll get to call her Nellie for short," I said wryly. "What does she look like?"

"About my height, five-eight, but thinner, say one-twenty. About thirty. She's supposed to be kind of handsome, if you like the lean and bony type. Brown hair, greenish eyes." Martha glanced at me sideways. "You really don't know? You're not just testing me again?"

"That's right," I said. "We're normally kept apart as much as possible, and told as little as possible about each other. That way nobody betrays anybody."

I kept the heavy rig rolling northwards as fast as the

narrow highway permitted. It got a little tricky meeting or passing the big Mexican trucks, mostly christened in the local fashion. One trucker with a literary turn of mind had named his big diesel tractor *Moby Dick*; another had painted *Adios Amor* across his massive front bumper, presumably after a traumatic affair of the heart. We stopped for lunch in Hermosillo and reached the border early in the afternoon.

Here, everything came to a stop while our friendly customs people welcomed us back to our native land with an interminable search of both the station wagon and the boat. At last, they even got a dog and boosted him into the boat—all eighty pounds of him—to sniff out whatever they might have overlooked, which turned out to be nothing at all. The dog looked as if he didn't appreciate the vital importance of his task and would rather have been sleeping in the sun or chasing rabbits. Well, dogs have a lot of sense.

As we drove away from there, I glanced at my watch. It read a few minutes after three-thirty. I passed up three public telephones and settled for the fourth, at a filling station where I also took the opportunity to tank up with US gas.

"Here I go," I said to the girl.

"Remember, call the office, not the special number."

"Yes, ma'am," I said. "I may be senior as hell, but my memory isn't failing me quite yet."

At that, it took me a second or two, once I was in the booth, to remember the office number. Agents of my stratospheric seniority don't use it very often. We generally call Mac direct when we need instructions. I finally dredged the figures out of the sludge at the bottom of my mind, gave them to the operator, and fed enough coins into the machine to play the right music for her. Normally, I'd have reversed the charges, but in this case I had a hunch it was better not to announce who was calling. Mac had wanted to demonstrate something, and I figured I had better find out what it was before I started tossing around names and identifications.

I stood there waiting for the circuits to operate, and watching the girl get out of the car and head for the restroom. Suddenly a voice was speaking in my ear, a female voice with a professional telephone-girl lilt.

"Federal Information Center," the voice said. I said nothing for a moment, and the girl spoke a little less liltingly, almost sharply: "Federal Information Center!"

I hung up slowly. I needed a moment to digest what I'd just heard.

6

Maybe you're accustomed to calling a government office and being greeted with a fancy organizational name. I'm not. Ours isn't that kind of an office and we have no name. At least we hadn't the last time I called Washington, less than a month ago.

Obviously, I'd just learned what Mac had wanted me to learn, or part of it. There had been some kind of a shake-up, the gobbledygook boys and girls had taken over, and we were now something called the Federal Information Center, or a branch thereof. Well, such things happen in Washington. To learn the full extent of the disaster, I drew a long breath and called the same number again. I got a different girl, but she'd learned her lilt at the same school.

"Federal Information Center."

I decided to try the head-on approach and see what happened. "Give me Mac," I said.

"Mac? I'm sorry, sir, without the full name I don't think I can... Oh, yes, of course! You want the Bureau of

Public Safety. I'll connect you."

I waited. Presently another woman's voice came on the line. This was a severe, businesslike, liltless voice. "Bureau of Public Safety, Miss Dodds. With whom did you wish to speak, please?"

I didn't know any Miss Dodds. "Gimme Mac," I said crudely, since that seemed to be the password.

"Who's calling, please?"

"Somebody who wants Mac," I said.

"Really, sir—" She broke off. There was a brief pause; and her voice came again. "I'm sorry, sir. You did say Mac, didn't you?"

"I did."

"Yes, of course. I'll see if I can reach him on the temporary line. His office is still in the old building for the time being, and we haven't been able to make very satisfactory arrangements. You know what telephone service is these days. Please hold."

Normally, calling the office in the old building on a side street where nobody'd expect a government office to be, I'd have got a girl who simply said hello, unless there was a special message for a particular agent who was expected to have to call from a bugged phone or a roomful of people. In that case the girl might tell me I'd reached the residence of Mrs. Amos Aardvark, say, or the home of Mr. Zachariah Xerxes. If the coded message was for me, I'd apologize for dialing the wrong number and hang up. If it wasn't for me, I'd ignore it, say an identifying word or two, and ask to be put through to Godalmighty, the Big Cheese, the Mother Superior, or whatever other facetious name I chose to employ. The whole transaction would generally take considerably less than ten seconds. Obviously, things had changed.

There was a clacking in the phone, and Miss Dodds' prim voice came again. "Sorry to keep you waiting, sir. I'm trying to reach him for you. We've been having some trouble with that connection. It's temporary, you know."

"So you said," I said. "Keep plugging. That's a joke."

"Yes, sir. Ha-ha… here we are now. Go ahead, sir."

The line she'd got me was fairly noisy, but the voice speaking from the other end, while slightly weak, was familiar and reassuring after all the abnormal yak-yak. It spoke three words, mandatory secret-agent-type stuff. I spoke two words in return.

"Eric?"

"Yes, sir," I said. "What the hell's going on in that madhouse city in the Potomac swamps, anyway? The Bureau of Public Safety, for Christ's sake! Wasn't that who chopped off all those heads in the French Revolution?"

"I believe you're thinking of the Committee of Public Safety, Eric."

"Bureau, committee, what's the difference?"

Mac's distant voice said deliberately, "What's going on is, quote, a streamlined reorganization of all governmental intelligence functions, unquote."

I said, "Again? If I remember rightly, a guy tried to pull the same thing a few years back, only he knew so little about intelligence operations that he couldn't even run his own outfit without getting a bunch of communist agents planted on him, so the big deal fell through… Leonard. That was his name. Herbert Leonard."

"You have the right man, Eric. Mr. Leonard is apparently a persistent individual and a skillful politician; and this time he seems to have powerful backing."

"So it's serious, sir?"

"Quite serious. We are going to have to be very circumspect for a while. Mr. Leonard has already given clear indications that he doesn't like us very much. Just a minute. I have another call." I waited until his voice spoke again in my ear. "Eric? What were we talking about?"

"About the way Mr. Leonard doesn't like us, presumably because of the way we helped to lower the boom on him last time. Maybe he's afraid we'll do it again."

"Maybe. What kind of a vacation did you have, Eric?"

"Lousy, sir," I said. "My girl Friday turned out to be a missionary at heart, and somebody tried to shoot me."

"Shoot you? What happened?"

"He missed. Then, unfortunately, he kind of drowned," I said. "They fished him out of San Carlos Bay this morning. His death was strictly accidental, of course."

"Of course. Do you have any clue as to his motive?"

"No, sir. We never really got on speaking terms."

"I see. Well, there are a number of people employed by other nations who have reason not to be particularly fond of you."

"Yes, sir."

"I don't want to seem to dismiss an attempt on your life

lightly, but there are reasons why I'm rather disinterested in would-be murderers at the moment—as long as they are safely dead, of course. We have trouble inside our own ranks. As you'll gather, it couldn't have come at a worse time."

"No, sir. What's the problem?"

"To put it bluntly, one of our people has gone a bit berserk."

"It's an occupational hazard, sir."

"Particularly among agents with families, it seems. Whenever anything happens to their spouses or offspring, their immediate reaction is to employ their training and experience for purposes of vengeance. It's always very awkward, but particularly right now."

"Yes, sir. Who's the current berserker? Do I know him?"

"You did a job with him in Cuba. Agent Carl."

"A big blond guy. Sure, I remember him. What's up with Carl?"

"Let's just say that he received some rather bad news concerning a member of his family. He called immediately afterwards to say that he was resigning to take care of some private business. He said not to send anyone to try to stop him, because anybody who was sent just wouldn't come back." I couldn't help a wry laugh. Mac heard me, two-thirds of a continent away. He spoke in a severe tone of voice: "You seem to find that amusing, Eric. Why?"

"Only because I've used the same line myself upon occasion, as you may remember, sir." I made a face at the phone. "But you *are* sending somebody after Carl, in spite of his warning."

"Yes. You."

"Thanks a whole lot, sir."

"He is presently in Fort Adams, Oklahoma, or somewhere nearby. We don't have his exact address. You'll contact him and take whatever steps necessary to prevent him from involving us in a scandal that could destroy us. I repeat, whatever steps are necessary. Do I make myself clear?"

"Yes, sir," I said. "You always do, sir. But if Carl has resigned, officially, how do his actions reflect on us?"

"Don't be naïve, Eric. Mr. Leonard is just waiting for an excuse to crack down on us. Do you think he'll let a little thing like a resignation stand in his way?"

"It's a point," I admitted. "Well, you'd better give me Carl's current description. These days of long hair and beards I might not recognize him. That Cuba assignment was a long time ago. Oh, and if it isn't too confidential, you might tell me precisely what the news was that sent him off his trolley…"

The girl was back in the station wagon when I returned to it. I signed the charge slip for the gasoline and got behind the wheel. We didn't speak until we were out of Nogales, heading up the four-lane freeway towards Tucson. It's a funny thing, much as I enjoy Mexico, and much as I detest that interminable border hassle, I always feel a sense of relief and relaxation when I'm back in the US with American gas in the tank.

"Well?" Martha said at last.

"What do you know about something called the Federal Information Center?"

"Just what everybody knows," she said. "FINC is the brainchild of a red-faced, white-haired, smoothie political type named Leonard, who's mounted a real slick takeover operation with powerful political support."

"What did you call it?"

She laughed. "Officially, it's abbreviated FIC, but everybody calls it FINC. What else would you call a national collection of snoops and spooks?" After a moment, she glanced at me. "Did you talk to... him? What did he say?"

I reported my conversation with Mac, practically verbatim, and said, "Apparently, we are now the Bureau of Public Safety, operating under said FINC."

"Well, we've got lots of company, Mr. Helm. The CIA's latest overseas booboo and J. Edgar's recent death made it relatively easy for Herbert Leonard. Obviously, it was time for a change, or Congress thought it was, and he's it. The whole ball of wax. All the nation's intelligence agencies wrapped up in one glorious unified package. You must have read about it."

I said, "Hell, I don't read the papers when I'm on leave. Particularly when I'm on leave in Mexico. I don't listen to the radio, either."

"No, all you do is make eyes at skinny blondes." Martha spoke without altering her voice or turning her head. "Tell me, was she really any good in bed? She was tall enough even for you, but it didn't seem to me there was enough of her, crosswise, to give a man any real satisfaction."

I said, "Hush your dirty mouth, Borden. What do you know about an agent of ours with the code name Carl?"

Martha hesitated. "Well," she said after a moment, "his real name is Anders Janssen. He's on the list. There are ten names, eleven including you. He is number six, if that matters, but you were supposed to find him in New Orleans, where he'd been sent to hide out until the right time came, and the right man, meaning you."

I said, "Only now he seems to have resigned and headed for Oklahoma on a private mission of his own. What happened recently in Fort Adams, Oklahoma, Borden?"

"You must have heard—"

"Why make me say it again? I haven't read a paper or listened to a radio for three weeks on purpose. Tell me."

"Well," she said, "well, it was another of those riots, at a small educational institution called Fort Adams State University. The police and deputies opened fire, and three students were killed."

"I see," I said slowly.

"Why did you want to know?" Martha asked curiously. "Has it got something to do with Carl?"

"It's got a lot to do with Carl. One of the kids who got shot was his and he's running amok. My current orders are to do something about it, immediately if not instantly." I frowned at the four-lane highway sliding towards me in the bright Arizona sunshine. "However, I think since we're so close to the ranch, we'd better go have a talk with Lorna first."

7

The ranch is supposed to be absolutely safe, a place where even the most unpopular agent, sought by platoons of professional rub-out men of assorted hostile nationalities, can relax and rest, secure in the knowledge that nobody can reach him. This means, of course, that you don't just drive up to the gate and blow your horn when you want in.

I stopped in Tucson to make the necessary phone call. I got the conditional all-clear, meaning that I could proceed along a specified route out of town, not necessarily in the right direction, until, at a certain specified point, I passed a parked car. The car would indicate, by its open door, that my clearance had been confirmed and I was free to head for my destination in the desolate country west of town. If the door of the vehicle was closed, I'd have to spend a day trying to shake whoever had been spotted tailing me, and call again tomorrow.

When I reached it, it wasn't a car but a pickup truck, but that was a permissible variation. Its hood was up and the driver was performing an invisible and probably unnecessary operation on its insides. The door on the driver's side was open. I drove past and kept going.

At last Martha stirred uneasily and glanced at me. "This isn't the way to the ranch, is it?" she said. "I've never been there, but it's west of Tucson, isn't it? We're heading kind of south and east, aren't we?"

"That's right," I said. "Have you had any training, Borden?"

"Why… why, not very much, yet. Why do you ask?"

"There's a mirror on your door but you haven't even glanced at it once. We've had a tail since about twenty miles north of Nogales." When she started to turn her head to look back, I said, "That's pretty poor technique, too. Not that it matters here, you can't see out the rear window and they can't see in due to that junior-grade ocean liner we have rolling along behind, but it's best to get in the habit of doing things right. Use the mirror if you want to look."

"But who is it? Who'd want to follow us?"

"Who'd want to shoot at me yesterday?" I asked dryly. "All I know is that it's a white Ford Falcon with Arizona plates, kind of old and nondescript, the sort of car nobody looks at twice. Let's hope it's just what it seems, and nobody's stuffed any surprises under the hood. They probably haven't. They probably figure anything with four wheels and a rubber band can keep up with us, the load we're dragging. We hope."

"I… don't understand."

I glanced at her impatiently; she was really pretty slow. I said, "Look, doll, that pickup truck gave us the all-clear, right? He sent us on through to the ranch, *in spite of the fact that we've got a tail on us nobody who was really looking could have missed!*"

"I still don't understand!" she protested. "What are you driving at?"

"It smells," I said. "If you've got company trailing along behind, you just don't get cleared to that place. Hell, that's exactly what all the monkey business is supposed to prevent. But *we* were cleared, tail and all. I think we'd better go on the assumption that something's awfully wrong inside that fancy fence, out there west of Tucson, that's all wired up with bells and whistles and closed-circuit TV. I think we'd better figure that there's a reception committee waiting for us, and that it's not just a bunch of friendly doctors and nurses and trainers concerned with nothing but our welfare. And the boys astern, well, I think we'd better assume they're a pair of sheepdogs assigned to herd us into the right pen and make sure we don't go astray between here and there."

The girl beside me shook her head sharply. "You're imagining things; you must be! From what I've heard, the ranch is the last place in the world where anybody could—"

"The last," I said, "or the first. The one spot I might drive up to, dumb and happy and unprepared for trouble."

"You mean… you mean you really think somebody has gone so far as to take the place over, just to set a trap for you?" She shook her head once more, unbelievingly.

"Aren't you getting delusions of grandeur? Why would anybody consider you that important?"

I said, "We don't know what came first, the takeover or the trap. Maybe they'd already moved in on the ranch for other reasons—maybe they were after Lorna—and when I called, they just decided to let me walk into their arms, a kind of bonus. As for my importance, a certain gent in Washington considered me important enough to send you to me with passwords and secret fists and stuff, remember? And somebody considers me important enough to be shot, and I've got a pair of very persistent shadows astern. Until I find out why all this is happening, I'm going to be the most paranoid character you ever met, seeing murderers and conspirators behind every greasewood bush in Arizona… Ah!"

"What is it?"

I was watching the lefthand mirror as I drove. I said, "It looks as if our friends back there figure I've gone far enough in the wrong direction. Obviously, I'm planning to pass up the opportunity to attend their ranch barbecue as the guest of honor. Now, since I'm being so unsociable, something drastic's got to be done about me and they're just the boys to do it. At least they seem to think they are." We were pretty far out of the city now, and you lose civilization fast in that part of the country. I looked approvingly at the endless, empty landscape studded with sinister-looking dark rocks and weirdly shaped cacti. I said, "Isn't that a lovely hunk of real estate, for people in our situation?"

"What do you mean? It's so bleak and barren it scares

me. There's absolutely nothing there."

"That," I said, "is exactly what I mean, doll. Hang on, now. Here they come. Let's see what they want."

It was a dirt road, but reasonably wide, as they are out there where all it takes to make a road is a bulldozer or grader and a man to run it. When it washes out, the once or twice a year it rains, they just call the guy with the blade and he runs the route again. The little white car was coining up fast in the mirror. I had plenty of room to give it plenty of room, and I did.

"Kneel beside me facing aft, Borden," I said. "Watch them for me. We'll see what they have in mind. We'll give them the benefit of the doubt, first, but if you see a gun aimed this way, holler and duck."

They were pretty childish about it. I mean, I was tooling damn near forty feet of rig, at least three tons total, along that primitive road at a good clip. They put their little compact right alongside that onrushing mass of metal and fiberglass, just as if they didn't have good sense…

"The man in the right hand seat has a gun!"

"Here we go," I said. "Hang on."

I put my right foot all the way down. The big, lazy, 454-cubic-inch engine kicked into second gear and went sluggishly to work, like a sleepy elephant. It didn't have any sudden, exciting urges, but it did have some power if you were willing to wait for it. The little white car stopped gaining and just hung there, approximately level with my trailer hitch.

In the mirror, I could see the strained face of the driver.

I knew he was doing his best to push the pedal through the firewall, as the sickening realization came to him that a lifetime of TV-watching had just led him badly astray. On TV, the guys with the guns just drive up alongside the guys without and start shooting. If they hit, the other car obligingly goes off the road in a harmless direction, but some telepathy—or just plain common sense— was telling the driver behind me that this wasn't going to happen here. First of all, he wasn't going to make it alongside; and if a bullet did hit me, he sensed I was fully prepared to use my last second of consciousness and my last ounce of strength to dump my whole big outfit right into his lap.

The man beside him raised the gun but didn't shoot. At least he was that bright. It was an ordinary .38, as far as I could make out in the mirror, and the ballistics of that cartridge aren't sufficient to drive a bullet through car metal and safety glass at the sharp angle I was carefully maintaining. We thundered down the wide dirt road side by side. The driver got the little Ford up to sixty-five, and then seventy, at which point either his nerve or his power ran out. I held the big rig steady right beside him. I saw him give up and glance over his shoulder to see what his chances were of braking hard and getting out from under.

"Matt, slow down, there's a curve…"

"I see it," I said.

It was what I'd been waiting for. It was a nice, sweeping right-hander with a bunch of the jagged lava rocks out in the desert beyond it. I held the speed to the last possible moment and hit the brakes when the other man did, staying right with him. Nobody was going to do any violent braking in that dirt. The curve was on top of us. I let up on the brakes and got onto the accelerator once more, judiciously, powering through the bend and taking the whole road to do it, sliding left and shutting the door on the little sedan.

I was too busy to see what happened to it.

The station wagon and trailer came around reluctantly. At the last moment the trailer swung out and hooked a wheel in the shallow outside ditch and I thought I'd lost it, but it came back again, slashing back and forth across the road behind us like the tail of a giant dog. Then it was rolling straight once more, and we had it made.

"Report," I said, letting the speed drop gradually to safer levels. I got no answer. "Damn it, Borden, report!" I snapped, still too busy to look around.

"You… you killed them!"

"Details, damn it!"

"They went off the road and hit a rock and flipped. The last I saw they were still rolling and bouncing. It was horrible!"

"Any fire?"

"I… I couldn't see any."

"Okay," I said. "I guess we can go back and take a look, as long as there isn't a lot of smoke and flame to bring spectators."

"But you *killed* them!" she breathed. "You just… just ran them off the road in cold blood and *killed* them!"

I glanced at her. Her face was white and her eyes were wide and accusing. I drew a long breath, and said, "I didn't ask them to come charging after me with waving pistols, did I, Borden? What was I supposed to do, just sit there and let them shoot me? And you, too, for that matter?"

"Don't try to justify it by claiming that you were protecting *me*, Mr. Helm!"

I was struggling to get turned around. At one time in the distant past, I'd got pretty handy with a horse trailer, but although those two-horse jobs are surprisingly heavy, particularly when loaded, they aren't very long, and I still had a little trouble backing a fifteen-foot boat on a seventeen-foot trailer.

"Justify, hell," I said, when we were headed back the way we'd come. "The world is a big and dangerous place, sweetheart. I can't make it any smaller, but I can make it slightly less dangerous, for me, by making damned certain that anybody who tries to kill me gets only one crack at it. Maybe whoever's behind this get-Helm routine will get tired of sending out a fresh murder crew every twenty-four hours… Here we are. If you're coming, you'd better put some shoes on. Arizona is a hell of a prickly place to go barefooted."

The little Ford was a total loss, lying upside down among the rocks. The driver seemed to be suspended inside by his seat belt; his gun-wielding companion wasn't visible. I found that one on the ground where he'd been thrown, off to one side. His neck was broken and his face was pretty badly cut up, but I could see that he was—

or had been—another young and eager character, clean-cut and square, like the handsome rifleman I'd drowned. It made me feel old and wicked, as if I were waging war against the Cub Scouts of America.

"Who is he? Is he dead?"

Crouching beside the body, I looked up at Martha Borden who, shod at last, had come up behind me.

"He's dead," I said. "As for who he is, I have a hunch I'm not going to like it when I learn the answer to that question."

I got the wallet out of the hip pocket and found that I was perfectly right. The first identification card I came to told me that I was looking at what remained of Mr. Joseph Armistead Tolley, age twenty-four, special agent of the Bureau of Internal Security of the Federal Information Center of the United States of America.

8

The man inside the Ford was also dead. I didn't haul him out to see exactly what had killed him. I just checked for a pulse in a dangling wrist and didn't find any. This one was older, his name was Howard March, and he was a senior special agent for the same bureau. Why the senior man had been doing the driving puzzled me briefly; but I reminded myself that I prefer to handle the wheel myself, no matter how many bright young people I have along to help me. Maybe Howard had felt the same way.

With some difficulty, I got the identification folder—unlike his assistant, he'd carried it separately—back into the inside coat pocket where I'd found it. I looked around. We'd left some footprints, and there would be tire tracks along the dirt road that a police technician could have lots of fun with, taking measurements and making casts to his heart's content. It didn't worry me greatly. If police intervention had been wanted, I'd have been stopped by an efficient Arizona state trooper hours ago. This was private business—well, private government business—and I had a hunch a lot of people would work very hard to keep it that way. They didn't need casts and measurements to learn whom they were after. They knew.

The girl beside me licked her lips. "Well!" she said. "I hope you're satisfied now! Now that you've killed two fellow-agents due to some kind of a crazy misunderstanding—"

"Three," I said. "Don't forget Mr. Joel Patterson and his crazy misunderstood little 7mm Magnum rifle. I'll lay you any odds you like that if we check him out carefully, we'll find that FINC paid his salary, too, not to mention supplying him with firearms and ammunition." I cut her off when, aghast and incredulous, she tried to speak. "Let's get out of here," I said. "It's not much of a road, but somebody must use it occasionally or they wouldn't have bothered to build it in the first place."

Martha Borden was silent during the ride back to Tucson, which was just as well. Spending three weeks' vacation with an incurable sentimentalist had been bad enough; dragging one along during working hours was getting to be a terrible strain on my tolerance. I pulled into the first filling station that had a public telephone and asked the man to fill the tank. We'd driven barely a hundred miles since Nogales, but the giant mill up front had an impressive thirst. Under the circumstances, I figured a full tank was a reasonable precaution.

"Come on," I said to the girl, and led her to the phone in a corner of the parking area. "I'm calling Washington," I said, fishing for a coin. "I want you to listen. It will save me a lot of explanations. Don't say anything. Just listen."

I dialed the number—the special number, this time—and got the connection after a lot of buzzing and clicking. Audibility wasn't even as good as the last time. When the familiar voice came on, I could barely hear it. We went through the same identification procedure as before.

"Where are you, Eric?"

I tilted the receiver so the girl could hear. "Tucson, Arizona, sir," I said. "I had the bright idea of spending the night at the ranch. That way I could start east with a good, safe night's sleep, I figured, but I was wrong."

"What's the matter?"

"Have you had any contact with the ranch recently, sir?"

"Not for a week or so. There's been no reason. Why?"

"Something is very haywire there," I said. "I ran into a deadfall, only it didn't fall quite hard enough. I need a cleanup squad. Tell the boys to take State Road…" I gave the coordinates. "Tell them to look for a white Falcon four-door and two bodies. One's in the car, the other was thrown out and wound up in a little wash about twenty yards east of the shortest line between the car and the road, about halfway out. A dreadful accident. You know how treacherous those desert roads can be. They were driving too fast and failed to make a curve. What did you say, sir?"

"Nothing." There was a little silence. "Did you determine the identities of these two men?"

"Yes, sir. What's the Bureau of Internal Security?"

There was another pause. "I'm afraid that's Herbert

Leonard's private police force, Eric."

"I see," I said slowly. "He's got a special bunch of snoops to snoop on us snoops—with the highest patriotic motives, of course. Well, he's got three less of them now, if yesterday's marksman was one, and I think he was." I waited, but Mac did not speak, so I said, "Even though the man has personal reasons not to like me, dating from the last time we met, I can't believe he's merely engaging in a private vendetta using government personnel. What's he actually doing, sir, making war on our whole outfit? Wiping us out wherever he finds us? Jesus! Either he's got delusions of grandeur, sicking one government agency on another like that, or—"

"Or what, Eric?"

"Or they're not delusions. He's got reason to think he'll have support higher up, even in murder. Of course, he wouldn't call it murder, would he? He'd figure out some good disciplinary reason. What excuse is he using in my case, sir?"

The voice on the phone sounded distant and very tired. "I don't know," it said softly. "I just don't know. Of course, we've never been a very popular agency. Probably he's afraid of us after the way we upset his plans a couple of years ago; he's making certain it doesn't happen again. We've already lost several good agents for bureaucratic or security reasons. He has scrutinized the files very carefully and taken advantage of every slight irregularity. I didn't realize what was happening in the field. I was aware that some of our people were failing to report on schedule, but this often happens. I didn't realize…" His voice trailed off.

I said, "Well, you'd better pass the word for the boys and girls to take cover until the storm blows over."

"I wish I could be optimistic enough to think it will," he said wearily. "But the political situation here in Washington is very tense. All kinds of people are recommending all kinds of violent and repressive measures to deal with people and movements they don't like. Leonard is apparently just taking advantage of the general climate of opinion to move himself into a position of real power. Since he sees us as an obstacle, I'm afraid his intention is to decimate us to the last man on one excuse or another. What the original reason was in your case, I have no idea, but now that three government employees have died at your hands…" He stopped and was silent for several seconds. I waited. At last he went on, rather uncertainly, "I—I just don't know, Eric. Maybe… I think you'd better come in and we'll see what can be done to clear up the situation. In fact, that's an order. I still have a few resources…"

I said, "The hell with that, sir. With all due respect, I doubt that I'd live ten minutes if these characters caught me inside four walls. But obviously Leonard doesn't want publicity for what he's doing. That gives me a slight edge. You go ahead and see what you can accomplish at your end, sir, but I'll keep on here as originally planned." I waited, but he didn't speak. I drew a long breath, and put some crude arrogance into my voice. "Oh, and tell our white-haired Herbie-boy that he'd better call up his first team if he's got one. The stuff he's been sending at me so far has been kind of pitiful, like swatting a bunch of sick flies."

Hanging up without waiting for a response, I expected the girl to jump me at once and tell me again what a horrible man I was, but she was silent all the way back to the car and until we got going on the highway once more. Even then, she wasn't her usual critical self at first.

What she said, as the car gathered speed, was, "He— he sounded so old. So old and tired, Mr. Helm."

"He's in a bad spot," I said.

With some of her former spirit, she said sharply, "And you didn't make it any better, demanding that he forward your crude message of defiance."

"Wake up, doll," I said. "Nobody needs to forward anything. Mac and I were both talking for public consumption. There's not a chance in the world that line wasn't bugged." I shook my head irritably. "I was just trying to take the heat off him, Borden. The tape will show that I was instructed to come in and refused, in my usual high-handed and arrogant manner. Mac can't be held responsible if an agent deliberately disobeys an order, can he? That's presumably why he gave it, and that's certainly why I said what I did. Okay?"

She glanced at me and looked away. "Maybe I was wrong. If so, I'm sorry. But if you knew you'd be overheard, why did you call at all?"

"So they'd know where their boys were and get out

there and rake them up before the police found them. One complication nobody wants is cops."

"I can't believe all this is really happening! The head of a government agency ordering men out to kill his own people!"

"It's not the first time," I said. "The spook shops have always been dangerous to cross. They've got a tremendous amount of power and, since their operations are secret, very few real restraints. But you're missing the point. The point is that we're *not* Herbert Leonard's people, and he knows we'll never be, from Mac right on down to the lowest filing clerk in the outer office. He can gain control of the big, sprawling organizations by the usual bureaucratic procedures, because there's seldom much personal loyalty involved there, but he knows he'll never really take over a small, specialized, one-man agency like ours. We'll always be Mac's people, not his; and apparently he doesn't trust Mac to go along with his grandiose political plans—I don't know what they are, yet, but if they're Leonard's they're bound to be grandiose."

"But," she protested, "but he's in charge! He could just—just fire you all, couldn't he? He doesn't have to *shoot* you!"

I grinned. "Sweetheart, you're forgetting a little thing called civil service. There's also the question of publicity; if he just up and cans us all, somebody may ask why. But you have spotted the really interesting angle: the fact that he feels he has to do it this way. I figure that means he's up to something pretty nefarious of which Mac would disapprove. He wants to make certain that, when the chips are down, Mac doesn't have the power—meaning the live, armed agents—to implement his disapproval in a practical way." I made a wry face. "Hell, the farther we go, the wilder it gets. Well, maybe Lorna has some answers we don't."

I sent the big station wagon through Tucson, easing westward cautiously, watching the mirrors. Nothing significant showed. I risked stopping at a drive-in for hamburgers, stalling, waiting for total darkness. Then I drove the rig out into the desert again, on the other side of town this time, gradually working my way on small back roads farther and farther out from civilization.

"Where are we going now?" Martha asked at last.

"To the ranch, of course," I said. "Hell, a lady's waiting for us there, isn't she?"

"But—"

I said, "Don't worry. We won't try the front door this time. Did you ever hear of a hideout that didn't have a secret escape hatch somewhere?... That's our turnoff, right there, but I'd better leave the boat around the bend, up the arroyo. As I remember, it gets rough from here. Be prepared to do some digging if we bog down."

We didn't. The sand of the arroyo was nice and firm, and I got the boat backed out of sight. I got out, unfastened the hitch, the safety chains, and the electrical connection, and cranked down the jack to take the weight of the trailer tongue. Then I gave the fiberglass flank of the boat an affectionate pat, to tell the little vessel that

I wasn't deserting it in this desolate spot: I'd be back. I mean, hell, I knew it was only metal and plastic, but did it know? Some day my life might again depend on an extra, willing, loyal knot or two of speed…

We got back into the car, found the side road I'd glimpsed in the headlights, and started down a track that had seen no traffic since the last rain, whenever that might have been. Presently I switched off the lights. It was a long, slow, rough ride in the dark, with brush squealing and scraping along the sides of the big station wagon in the tighter spots and the trailer hitch smacking bottom as we crossed the deeper gullies. I passed the right landmarks, but they seemed much farther apart than when I'd been shown this trail in daylight, years ago. At last the odometer showed the right mileage. I stopped, got the wagon turned around, and cut the engine. Getting out, I gave the oversized vehicle a reassuring slap on the hood, telling it not to get lonely.

"Come on, Borden," I whispered. "There's a flashlight in the glove compartment. Bring it along. Don't slam the door. Leave it open."

She came around the car to me. "You're weird," she whispered, as we moved off together. "You're really weird, Helm! You kill people, and then you pat a hunk of machinery on the nose as if… as if it was a horse or a dog or something. As if you really *liked* it!"

"Like it?" I said. "Hell, I think it's a miserable, sluggish, overstyled gas hog, but I wouldn't dream of hurting its feelings by telling it so. And I don't want it to worry while

I'm gone, either. I mean, it might get mad and refuse to start when we get back." I saw her glance at me sharply in the darkness, to see if I was serious. I grinned and stopped grinning. "That's enough talking. Watch where you're putting your feet. We're getting close."

Suddenly the fence was right in front of us. It was an impressive thing, all right, even in the dark, topped with barbed wire and equipped with enough warning devices—I knew, although they weren't readily visible—to protect those inside against anything but an open tank attack or inside treachery. But in our line of business we try to think of all contingencies, and no experienced agent is going to put himself into a place, even a forty-thousand-acre place, that he can't slip out of secretly if necessary.

I took the flashlight from the girl and, after some careful consideration, aimed it at a bush that was out of range of the TV monitor I'd seen on my long-ago tour of inspection. Hoping the installation hadn't been changed in the years that had passed—I should have been told, but that didn't necessarily mean I would have been—I pressed the button for three long flashes. I paused, gave two short squirts of light, and stuck the torch, as our British friends call it, into my pocket. Then I waited. I guess I was expecting something to go wrong: alarms to ring, searchlights to glare, savage hounds to come baying along the wire. Nothing of the sort happened. There was merely a soft rustle in the brush off to the right.

A woman's voice whispered, "Give me a word, whoever you are."

"Would Ragnarök do?" I asked.

"No, but you're close. Try some other Armageddon."

"How about Götterdämmerung?"

A slim figure in pants stood up, brushed the dust off her clothes, and came forward. "I hope you've got some water," the low voice said. "Or ice-cold beer for a preference. God, this is a miserable dry country to hide out in!"

9

There was a water jug in the car—in that part of the country, it's standard auto equipment, along with a shovel—but we had to wait until we got back to the boat and its built-in icebox, which I had replenished in San Carlos, before we could supply the beer. While the fugitive was quenching the remainder of her thirst with Carta Blanca, I hitched up the rig. Then I came forward once more, reached behind the front seat of the wagon, and produced a paper bag which I handed her.

"There's a hamburger," I said. "Cold, but better than nothing. I figured you might be hungry. But you'd better eat while we drive; I'd like to get as far from here as possible as fast as possible."

"Yes, of course. You didn't think to bring me any clothes?"

I'd thought it pretty damn considerate of me to buy an extra hamburger.

I said, "We've been a little too busy to go shopping,

lady. We practically had to fight our way in here tooth and nail. Two men died that you might live. I considered it a pretty good trade at the time, but I could change my mind."

The woman laughed softly in the darkness. "I'm very sorry; I apologize. It was sweet of you to think of the hamburger. I'll take the back seat; I'm too dirty to associate with civilized people. Before we start, is there any more of that wonderful Mexican beer?" As I was getting the station wagon rolling, starting up very cautiously so the rear wheels wouldn't dig down into the sand of the arroyo, her voice came from behind me: "Oh, I almost forgot. I know we should get out of here, but there's something… What are our chances of sneaking up to the front gate; and have you got any night glasses?"

"I've got a pretty good pair of seven-by-fifties," I said. "But as for the front gate, if the guards are doing any kind of a job, we haven't got a chance in the world of getting through—"

"I didn't say through, I said to. Just close enough for you to get a good look with your binoculars. There's been a sort of conference at the ranch. It should be breaking up about now, judging by what I overheard, and I think you might be interested in identifying one or two of the participants as they drive out."

I glanced at her over my shoulder. Even in the gloom of the car, she didn't look much like the well-groomed lady agent with whom I'd expected to make contact. She looked more like a great white huntress after a tough safari; the general impression was one of soiled khakis, sunburned skin, and stringy hair.

"How long have you been hiding out back there?" I asked.

"Two days. I didn't really expect you for another day or two; and I wouldn't have taken off so early with just a two-quart canteen and a couple of candy bars if I hadn't been warned... You remember Jake Lister?"

"The orthopedic man at the ranch?" The rig was picking up speed now on a solid gravel road. "Sure, I remember Dr. Jake. Always thinking up fancy new exercises to inflict on his victims—excuse me, patients. Aside from that, he's a good man. What about him?"

"Well," said Lorna dryly, "apparently Dr. Stern has been happily playing director in his usual trusting and democratic fashion, calling all the help by their first names and insisting they call him Tom. However, Dr. Jake's had a few reservations about some of the people hired lately, in spite of their glowing recommendations and iron-clad security clearances. Maybe being black tends to shake a man's innocent faith in all humanity. Anyway, Dr. Jake got word somehow that things were about to blow, and he tipped me off, since I was the only senior agent in residence at the moment. I just had time to change into something durable and grab a few basic supplies and get away. The enemy was closing in with inside help as I sneaked out. There was some shooting. I waited to see if Lister or Stern or somebody would make it clear, but nobody came."

There was a little silence. At last I asked, "What about this conference you mentioned?"

"That happened the next night, last night. Nobody seemed to be chasing me, or even to know I was missing, so I took a chance—I didn't figure you'd be that early, and if you were you could wait—and circled back after lying in the shade of a rock all day with a friendly Gila monster for company. I took up a position on the mesa south of the main ranch buildings and watched. Everything seemed quiet, but the guards weren't our guards any longer. Right after dark, a couple of cars came in. They got the VIP treatment from the help, so I figured it was worth risking a closer look. I made my way down there and crawled to where I could watch the long porch outside the living room, figuring somebody interesting might step out for a breath of fresh, unairconditioned oxygen—"

I said, "Around these parts, that porch is known as a portal, ma'am. Accent on the last syllable."

"All right, por*tal*. Anyway, pretty soon, out came guess who?"

There was only one logical answer, considering everything. I said, "A smart political operator who considers himself an intelligence expert, named Herbert Leonard."

"How did you know?" The woman in back sounded disappointed.

"I called Washington today," I said. "I've been kind of out of touch down in Mexico. I was told Herbie'd taken over practically, the whole intelligence community in some kind of a fancy power play backed by strong political influence, exact source unknown."

"Yes, of course. Well, Leonard must have learned of

the existence of the ranch somehow, and decided that a secret, well-protected installation like that was just the headquarters he needed for his political intrigues. But I bet you can't guess the name of the person to whom he was talking."

"Since you put it like that, I won't even try."

"If I said the lady was an elected representative of the US people, with strange political notions and strong presidential ambitions, would that help?"

I whistled softly. "You mean the senatress, herself?"

"I mean the lady senator from Wyoming, the first state to give women the vote." The voice from the back seat was dry. "I mean the gray-haired, motherly old bag who's been giving all women's rights movements a bad name, after they helped elect her, by associating herself with various sinister groups she apparently thinks will help her become the first lady president of the United States. Senator Ellen Love, in her standard costume of dowdy print dress and gold-rimmed glasses, and whether she's a naïve little old lady victimized by a lot of sharp operators, or a pious fraud, doesn't really matter. The final result is the same. I want you to see her for yourself, holding hands with Herbert Leonard, so that if anything happens to me you won't start wondering if maybe I wasn't having hallucinations in the heat."

I didn't try to bring the car near the vantage point I selected, from my memories of the terrain, as the most suitable observation post. For one thing, no road ran close to the spot and I didn't figure the big station wagon was up to any cross-country jeep antics. For another, even if we could have made it, here at the front of the ranch there were more guards, and probably more alert guards, than at the rear, and one of them might hear the sound of the engine. I settled for a two-mile midnight hike.

My two companions made no complaints as we picked our way across the desert, climbing gradually. I just heard an occasional stifled gasp as one of them encountered a cactus in the dark. I met a few sharp thorns myself. Then we were on the ridge overlooking the broad, shallow valley, rising and narrowing to the left. A dirt road ran up the valley and entered the ranch through a gate below us.

There was no guard house or sentry box. Here, it was just an ordinary-looking, padlocked ranch gate in a ranch fence that was just a little higher and sturdier than usual—the kind of fence a rich sportsman might put up who'd stocked his place with exotic game—but if you approached and tried to open it in the wrong manner, or if somebody had passed the wrong word about you or neglected to pass the right one, you'd find yourself subjected to an accurate crossfire from two neighboring elevations. At least that was the way it had been before Leonard took over, and while he'd undoubtedly changed the personnel, it seemed unlikely that he'd made much change in the security procedures on such short notice.

We lay there a while, watching the vacant, light streak of road in the empty, dark wasteland below. At last Martha Borden stirred and glanced my way.

"It doesn't look as if they're coming. Or maybe they've already gone."

I realized this was the first thing she'd said since we sneaked up to the fence together, a good many miles back. Apparently the presence of another woman had an inhibiting effect on her.

"We'll wait a little longer," I said.

"I don't want to seem inquisitive." This was Lorna's voice from the other side of me. "I don't want to pry, but just who is she?"

I said, "I'm sorry. I've been neglecting my social duties. Lorna, meet Nicki, and vice versa. I'm Eric, in case you didn't know."

"Even if I hadn't been told to expect you, there aren't all that many agents six-and-a-third feet tall. But what's she doing here, if I may ask?"

"She's a messenger girl," I said. "She carries the word from Washington, and doles out pieces of it as the spirit moves her."

"How far do you trust her?"

"Almost as far as I trust you," I told Lorna, "which isn't saying a great deal. But not quite as far. A little less."

I was aware of Martha giving me a quick, startled glance, but it was Lorna who spoke: "Why more doubts in her case?"

"Because I know you, by reputation at least. I don't know her, and she does some very peculiar things. For instance, this afternoon, two men came after us in a car. One had a gun. He'd have started shooting if I'd let him get into position. He'd have shot at me, to be sure, but he could easily have hit our girlfriend here. She was sitting right beside me. And if he had succeeded in hitting me, I'd undoubtedly have wrecked the station wagon, and she'd probably have been hurt or killed. However, I managed to run the would-be murderers off the road so they piled up fatally. What did our girl do? Did she throw her arms around me and kiss me for saving her life? No, she gave me hell for being a callous assassin. How far would you trust a girl with reactions like that, Lorna?"

"Not very far. Particularly not if she was supposed to have been selected and trained for our line of work." Lorna had got the point, all right. Her voice was cold. "But we'd better discuss it later. Get your binoculars ready. Here comes the caravan now."

We saw the loom of the lights back in the hills; then the cars appeared at the head of the open valley, raising clouds of dust that caught the headlight beams. There were two sedans, followed by a jeep.

"Check the lead car," Lorna's voice said. "The lady senator's homey image won't let her ride in a brand-new Cadillac, but she seems to figure she can get away with one five years old."

Watching the car through the seven-power glasses with the big lenses, I said, "You don't like her much, do you, Lorna?"

"I don't like suckers and I don't like phonies. She's either one or the other. Either she's putting one over on the American people or somebody's putting one over on her—somebody like, for instance, Herbert Leonard. Isn't that his slick white hair in the rear of the old Cadillac? Who's beside him?"

"I can't tell yet."

The first car stopped at the gate. A man opened the front door and hurried forward to deal with the padlock. Then the rear door of the big old sedan opened. Herbert Leonard stepped out. The headlights of the car behind him illuminated him clearly. He'd gained a little weight in the years since I'd seen him last, but he'd never been exactly slender: a chunky, solid man with a rather handsome red face and that dramatic, carefully combed white hair.

He turned to speak to someone remaining in the car, who leaned forward to answer. The interior lights showed me the face of a woman in her sixties, round and a little wrinkled like an autumn apple, framed by carefully waved blue-gray hair. I got an impression of sharp bright eyes behind the round, metal-rimmed glasses, but my binoculars weren't powerful enough to tell me the color. The body seemed plump and matronly, wrapped in a dark coat against the chill of the desert night.

"Do you see her, Eric? Do you recognize her?"

I said, "I recognize her."

"Then let's get the hell out of here. I need a bath and ten hours' sleep."

"Wait till they're gone."

Herbert Leonard bowed over the distant woman's outstretched hand. He turned away and walked to the next car, a newer Cadillac, and got in. The car began to turn around. Obviously, he was returning to the ranch, having done his duty as host by escorting his eminent female guest off the premises. The older sedan started up and drove through the gate and on down the valley out of sight. A lone man, after locking the gate, ran to the waiting jeep and was taken aboard. The two remaining vehicles headed back into the hills, and the valley was empty once more…

Some three hours later, towards dawn, we pulled into a motel with an all-night office, on the outskirts of Phoenix, a hundred and twenty-odd miles to the north. I registered as Mr. and Mrs. Matthew Helm and daughter, took the key, and drove to the unit that had been assigned to us.

"Go on in," I said, passing the key to Lorna. "I'll bring the luggage after I've parked the boat."

There was no space large enough for both car and trailer, so I backed the boat into a stall, disconnected it, and put the station wagon into the space beside it. Then I got my suitcase and Martha's rucksack and locked up. The door of the room had been left ajar for me. I nudged it open with my foot, since my hands were full, and stepped inside and stopped, looking at the tableau presented by the two women: the younger backed against one of the big beds, the older holding a short-barreled revolver.

"Take it easy, Lorna," I said.

"I had to make sure she wasn't armed. Anyway, I don't work with people I can't trust."

"You must lead a hell of a lonely life," I said. "Anyway, nobody's asking you to work with her. That's my chore.

Now put that damn gun away before it goes off and lands us all in trouble."

"My gun doesn't go off until I want it to go off. And nobody, particularly no man, tells me—"

"Oh, shut up and have a drink," I said, bending over my suitcase to open it. "Leave the kid alone. If you'd just use your eyes instead of waving that pistol around, all your questions would be answered." I straightened up with a bottle in my hand, and winked encouragingly at Martha, who'd sunk down onto the bed, sitting very still, watching the revolver. I set the bottle on the dresser, started stripping some glasses of their paper nighties, and said, "For Christ's sake, Lorna, take a *look* at the girl before you blow your stack. Obviously she's no trained agent, ours or anybody else's. I had to let you know that out there, in my oblique fashion, so you wouldn't be counting on her if we got into a bind."

"Then who is she and what's she doing here?"

I said, "She's playing with code names and passwords, but she can't control her high-principled indignation when reality doesn't match the pretty dream she's conned herself into believing: of a world in which everything lives and nothing dies. Yet, naïve though she is, the old gray fox in Washington trusts her enough to send her to me with vital information. Why? Can't you figure it out, Lorna? Where have you seen those bushy dark eyebrows before? Of course, they show up better against gray hair." I drew a long breath. "In case you need another clue, she says her real name is Martha Borden. Does that mean anything to you, or aren't you as nosy as I am?"

Lorna stared at me for a long moment, and threw a sharp glance towards the girl. Then the snub-nosed weapon disappeared inside the khaki shirt.

"Borden! You mean he sent his *daughter*?…"

10

At this hour of the morning, there wasn't much traffic to be heard outside, and no one inside the room broke the silence for several seconds. It was the first opportunity I'd had to examine in good light the female agent I'd just rescued. I was a little disappointed. Martha had described her as handsome, but while striking in an intense, hawklike way, she didn't attract me much: a lean and leathery lady with a rather thin and bony face turned reddish brown by recent sunburn. Her khaki pants were grimy and torn at one knee, and her khaki shirt was grimy and lacked a button—not the strategic top button that seductive movie females always manage to misplace in times of stress, but one lower down.

I reminded myself that after hiding out two days and nights on the Arizona desert, she could hardly be expected to be a flower of fashion, and in fairness I should reserve judgment. However, my initial reaction wasn't favorable. Of course, I may have been prejudiced by her domineering manner.

"Mr. Helm? Matt?" It was the girl sitting on the bed. Lorna and I turned to look at her sharply. She flushed, disconcerted by our sudden attention. "I... I don't understand."

"What don't you understand?"

"Daddy said that you didn't know... that nobody knew..."

It seemed odd to hear Mac referred to in that casually familiar way. I said, "Your dad isn't that stupid. What he probably told you was that nobody was *supposed* to know his real name. But I doubt that a man smart enough to manage a menagerie of snoops like us would ever kid himself that he could prevent them from doing a little snooping on their own time. As a matter of fact, I learned his name kind of by accident. One day, several years ago, I saw a car I had reason to believe was his personal transportation, parked in downtown Washington. He'd used it a few months earlier to send me help when I needed it in a hurry. It was a Jaguar sedan with a radiotelephone installation, a little too expensive and conspicuous a vehicle to be kept around for the use of ordinary agents, but fast, which I guess was why he'd risked lending it out in this particular emergency. Anyway, I couldn't resist waiting around to see if I'd guessed right. After a while, Mac walked up, got into the Jag, and drove off. I tailed him to a house in Chevy Chase. The rest was just a matter of basic research: Arthur M. Borden, respectable civil servant, exact field of employment unspecified, with a wife and one child, female."

There was a little silence, then Martha said, "My mother died two years ago."

"I'm sorry."

Lorna ended another awkward pause by saying briskly, "Well, I was checking old civil service records on another matter entirely when I came across a handwriting that looked familiar. The signature was A. McGillivray Borden, and there were papers on file—interoffice memoranda and such—signed McGillivray Borden, or simply Mac Borden. Apparently he disliked the name Arthur in his younger days. That was long before he got into this particular line of government work, before World War II."

Martha Borden licked her lips. "It would seem... it would seem that grown men and women would have better things to do than sneak around prying in matters that are none of their business!"

I said, "Hell, we work for the guy. We put our lives on the line when he says 'put.' Anything about him is our business. If he wants to be anonymous around the office, fine, none of us is going to blab what he's found out, but if a time ever comes when a little additional information is needed, we've got it. And I think he knows we've got it."

"Why would you expect to need information like that?"

I said, "I already have needed it, and so have you. If I hadn't recognized the name, and looked at you a little harder, and realized who you really were, you'd have been in a tough spot once I came to the conclusion that, with your attitude, you couldn't possibly be any kind of fledgling agent working for Mac in any capacity. And I'm willing to bet he was counting on that when he told you to use your real name."

After a moment, Lorna spoke abruptly. "That bottle does not have to be brought up to body temperature, Mr. Helm. It's not as if it were rare old brandy."

I'd forgotten the whiskey bottle I'd picked up once more but had not used. "Sorry," I said, pouring a drink and handing it to her.

She said, as if there had been no irrelevant interruption, "There is also the consideration that your father is not supernatural, Miss Borden. We respect him, but we do not attribute unearthly powers to him. Specifically, we do not consider him murder-proof or kidnap-proof."

"What do you mean?"

"There are people all over the world who have reason not to like him very much," Lorna said. "He could be shot down in the street today or turn up missing tomorrow. In either case, there would be decisions for us to make. If he were killed, we might want to avenge him. If he were to disappear, we'd certainly want to find him. In either eventuality, we'd need a better starting point than a three-letter nickname."

"Well, Daddy hasn't died or vanished yet, thank God," Martha said. "He was still answering his phone this afternoon—I guess that's yesterday afternoon now. Matt talked with him. But, as a matter of fact, he does seem to be expecting trouble, serious trouble."

"What kind of trouble?" Lorna asked.

"I don't really know. He didn't say. But if worse comes to worst, he's planning to do just as you say: disappear, for a while at least."

"That figures," I said. "He's a sitting duck as long as he stays in Washington. If Herbie Leonard feels secure enough to take over the ranch by force and send the extermination squads after individual agents like me, he's not going to hesitate to try for the head man when he figures the time is right. "Whiskey?"

Martha frowned. "What?"

"Do you want a drink?"

"Oh. Oh, no, thanks… Well, all right, just a little one. Matt, what's happening? What's it all about?"

I handed her a glass, lightly loaded. "I was hoping you could tell me."

She shook her head. "No, Daddy kept saying that the less I knew the better, except for the names I had to memorize for you. He said he was giving you enough information so you could figure it out, as long as I was sure to tell you the code was double negative."

I saw Lorna check a slight start and glance my way. I nodded minutely and spoke to the younger woman: "Okay, you've told me. Let's try to work it out from what we know. There's obviously a lot of political power involved. Somebody wants something big and is going to great lengths to get it. Well, we know what Senator Love wants: she wants her mail delivered to a certain address on Pennsylvania Avenue. In a Latin-American country, she'd be setting the stage for a coup d'état by making sure of the army. Here in the US where we don't change governments that way, she seems to be going about it a little differently. She's apparently making sure of the nation's intelligence services well before election time. How she plans to use Herbie Leonard and his newly conquered undercover empire remains to be seen, but obviously her first concern, and his, is to make certain he's actually in solid control. That means eliminating any oddball organizations that might not go along with the big takeover, like Mac's Murderous Mavericks and their notoriously independent chief."

Lorna frowned, sipping her drink. "I'm rather surprised they haven't struck at Mac already."

"Maybe they have," I said.

"That's silly!" Martha protested quickly. "He sounded perfectly all right when we… when you talked with him, Matt. A little tired, but otherwise all right."

"Maybe that's what got him tired, ducking knives and bombs and bullets," I said, and went on before the girl could speak again: "Look, Mac's been taking care of himself for a long time. I suppose he can be hit—anybody can—but it'll take more than a white-haired Washington glamour boy to do it. Leonard is ambitious and he may even be smart in his own way, but his genius, if any, is political, not homicidal. Hell, he's tried for me twice, or his boys have, and I'm still here. I suspect Mr. Leonard is discovering the hard way that good men in this particular line of endeavor are hard to find. Where's he going to recruit the necessary talent? He can't afford to deal with the syndicate, that would be political suicide, and there's only one government agency that really specializes in this type of work—and that's the one he's trying to eliminate."

Martha said sharply, "This type of dirty work, you mean!"

I grinned. "That's our girl. Keep after us. Maybe some day we'll straighten up and fly right."

"But it's… it's horrible! These times, when civilization has at last turned the corner away from war and violence, to think that a government organization run by my own father…" She ran out of breath and stopped.

I looked at Lorna. "What times do you think the kid is talking about? Have you seen us turning any corners lately, Miss Holt?" I used the cover name I'd been told about.

"Mrs. Holt, if you please, but you may call me Helen," Lorna said graciously. "Well, the body count in Vietnam was down just a little in the last newspaper I read at the ranch. And those people in the Middle East weren't killing each other much on that particular day. And the police hadn't shot or beat up any blacks or students within the previous few hours; and only one policeman had got killed that I noticed. Maybe things did seem just a little better, but I wouldn't say we'd actually turned a sharp and decisive corner, no."

Something she'd said screamed for attention. I frowned, realized what it was, and asked, "The cop you said got shot. Where did it happen?"

"He wasn't really a cop, just a sheriff's deputy. And I

didn't say he was shot. Actually, he was garotted, strangled to death. In Fort Adams, Oklahoma. That's where they had those student riots recently, I believe. Apparently somebody's been giving extracurricular courses in how to use the old piano-wire noose. Why?"

I hesitated, and shook my head. "Never mind."

Martha, who'd been trying to speak, broke in hotly: "You're so terribly, terribly amusing, both of you! It's very easy to make fun of the little girl, isn't it? The little girl who has the naïve and romantic notion that human life is something valuable and… and kind of sacred…"

I started to say something and checked myself. Lorna made an odd little sound in her throat and turned to the dresser and splashed more whiskey into her glass. She stood there for a moment regarding her sunburned features in the mirror, without affection. She spoke without turning her head.

"Do they all live in a dream world, Helm?" she asked softly. "Don't any of them ever wake up?"

I didn't say anything. Martha stirred angrily and blurted, "I don't want to wake up! Not if being awake will make me like you!"

Lorna, still without looking around, said, "Miss Borden, what is the one thing we have plenty of in this world? What is the single material that is not in short supply these days?"

"I don't know what you mean!"

The older woman said quietly, "We're running out of clean air and water, are we not? And not only clean water. I read in the same newspaper that in the capital city of New Mexico, practically right next door, they are not watering their lawns or washing their cars this summer because they have hardly any water, clean or dirty. We are running out of important metals and minerals. Some areas of the world cannot produce enough food to support their populations adequately. Fuels of all kinds are becoming scarce. In fact we are running out of just about everything, Miss Borden, with one spectacular exception. What is the one resource that's practically unlimited?" The girl licked her lips and didn't answer. Lorna said, "The one thing we have plenty of, my dear, is people."

Martha licked her lips once more. "Assuming that what you say is true, Mrs. Holt or whatever I'm supposed to call you, what's your point?"

Lorna sipped her drink, still studying the tanned, aquiline face in the mirror. Her voice remained very soft. "We are going to have to take a long hard look at the so-called sacredness of human life in the very near future, if the race is to survive. We are going to have to apply a little logic to the problem, instead of continuing to wallow in the sentimental humanitarianism currently fashionable. And the simple fact is, Miss Borden, that on strictly logical grounds we should consider war a tremendous, if rather inefficient, blessing. We should look at the yearly traffic toll as a great, beneficial contribution to population control. We should applaud every suicide as a public benefactor voluntarily yielding up his place on this crowded planet and making it available to somebody else."

I didn't like it. When they start thinking deep thoughts, and particularly when they start talking about them, they're apt to get kind of unreliable in action.

I said, "Hooray for cancer and emphysema. Bring on your drugs and cigarettes. Cut it out, Lorna. You can solve the problems of humanity some other night. Right now let's tackle something important, like who's going to sleep where."

She paid me no attention, and neither did Martha. The younger girl said, "You must be crazy, Mrs. Holt! That's a terrible way to think!"

Lorna shrugged. "I'm not crazy, just realistic. The basic trouble with your generation, Miss Borden, is that you will not face the facts. Subconsciously you realize that you're mostly superfluous—that the world would be much better off if only a fraction of you had been born—but you can't bring yourself to admit it and face the logical consequences: that your lousy little lives are not particularly valuable, let alone sacred. There are too many of you. Anything that plentiful can't be worth much, can it?"

I said, "Damn it, Lorna, shut up! It's too late at night—"

"No," said the woman at the dresser, gulping down the last of her drink and reaching for the bottle again, "no, it's not too late at night, and no, I will not shut up! I am fed up to here with children who consider themselves something special simply because they happened to be born. And I am particularly tired of the hypocritical attitude towards death they all display. They live on death.

Every antibiotic they take—and they gobble penicillin like candy—kills millions of living organisms. The slaughterhouses of the nation run knee-deep in blood to supply them with hamburgers and hotdogs. Even if they're vegetarians, they're eating bread and cereal and salads from fields protected by lethal farm chemicals that murdered countless innocent insects that had a perfect right to exist—and after all, a stalk of wheat or a head of lettuce is a living thing, too, something they carefully ignore. This girl is right now sitting in a motel room which was undoubtedly constructed on the graves of hundreds of small living creatures, slaughtered and dispossessed by the cruel bulldozers…"

"You're here, too!" the girl protested.

"My dear, *I'm* not carrying on a crusade against death. You are. It's the great fashionable cause of modern times. The Victorians thought sex was horrible, but they accepted death. You accept sex, but you think death is perfectly dreadful. That makes both of you hypocrites. No life is any more sacred than any other. Why should you be more important than a streptococcus or a mosquito, just because you happen to be a little more highly developed from one point of view—your own? Either all life is sacred, which is ridiculous, since most life forms, men included, have to live by preying on other life forms; or no life is sacred, not mine, not Helm's, not yours. Of course, his and mine are a little more sacred than yours—"

"Why?" Martha demanded. "Because you're older? That's just silly!"

Lorna started to drink from her replenished glass, but frowned and set it aside carefully. She gripped the edge of the dresser, staring at her image in the mirror. She spoke, still without turning her head.

"Not because we're older," she said slowly and deliberately, "but because we make our lives more valuable by making it damned tough for anyone who tries to take them away from us. But they could have your life just by reaching out for it, couldn't they, Miss Borden? You wouldn't defend it. You've backed yourself into a philosophical corner from which you can't strike back; and even if you could bring yourself to do it, you wouldn't know how. Which, my dear, makes your life about as valuable as that of a sick mouse, worth only the slight effort required, by anyone who doesn't mind messing up his boot heel, to stamp down hard. And in the truly overcrowded world that's coming, those who aren't prepared to fight will get stamped on, girl, and that goes for nations as well as individuals. We haven't turned any peaceful corners and I can see none ahead. I see just a very tough battle for room enough to live in halfway decent fashion…"

Her voice stopped abruptly. Her fingers released the edge of the dresser; and she slid to the floor in a dead faint.

11

Kneeling beside the woman on the floor, I was aware of Martha Borden rising from the bed and coming to stand over us.

"Is she… is she drunk? She certainly talked as if she were drunk."

I said, "Help me get her on the bed. Now, unlace those clodhopper boots and get them off her, will you?" I arranged the pillows under Lorna's head and went into the bathroom for a towel, which I moistened under the tap and brought back to wipe off her face, oddly pale now under the recent sunburn. I said, "Call it what you want. She's just spent two days on the desert living on a couple of candy bars and half a gallon of water. Maybe the alcohol hit her, maybe just reaction… Hi, there," I said to Lorna as she opened her eyes. "Come back and join the party."

She made a wry face, lying there. "What happened?"

"You gave us a lecture on the desperate state of this overcrowded world, and passed out."

"Oh, God," she said. "I ought to know better than to drink on an empty stomach. It always makes me gloomy as hell. Call me Cassandra for short."

She started to sit up. I pushed her back down. "Stay put. Martha, pop out to the candy machine by the office and get a fistful of Hersheys or something to fill the aching void until the restaurant opens. Here's some change."

When the girl had left, Lorna sighed and patted her hair back from her face with both hands.

"Sorry, Helm."

"Think nothing of it."

"I don't particularly want candy. I'd rather wait for bacon and eggs, if you don't mind. That one little hamburger just reminded me of how many meals I'd missed, I guess."

"You don't have to eat the stuff. I just wanted her out of the way for a moment. Remember, Mac said double negative. Even her daddy realizes the kid presents something of a problem. You did frisk her, didn't you?"

Lorna was watching me carefully. "Yes. She's clean."

"Where's your gun?"

"Right here."

"Keep it handy. I want you feeble and helpless, understand, but armed and ready. Okay?"

She frowned quickly. "Are you giving me orders?"

In the armed forces, they've got discipline. It must be nice. All we've got is temperament. I said, "I sure as hell am, Mrs. Holt. Mac sent the girl to me, not to you. Take it up with him when you see him next. In the meantime, keep that gun handy, please."

She hesitated; then she smiled faintly. "Very well. As long as you say please. I hope you know what you're doing."

"That makes two of us. Shhh, here she comes now."

In the early morning stillness, the approaching footsteps sounded very loud outside. Martha entered with half-a-dozen candy bars, which she dropped on the bed. Then she turned to me.

"Who's Cassandra?" she asked.

"What?"

"Mrs. Holt said to call her Cassandra for short. What did she mean?"

The woman on the bed laughed quickly. "Cassandra was a Greek girl who could foretell the future, Miss Borden. The only trouble was, nobody'd believe her."

Martha looked back to me. "And what's Ragnaroak or however you pronounced it? Back when you were giving her the password, you asked, 'Will Ragnaroak do?'"

I said, "Ragnarök is the Scandinavian equivalent of Götterdämmerung, which is the German equivalent of Armageddon. The end of the world in Technicolor."

"Thanks, I just like to get these things straight. I hope you're feeling better, Mrs. Holt."

"I… I feel fine as long as I don't try to stand up," Lorna said bravely. "I'll be all right in a minute."

I said, "Well, you just lie there while Martha gives us the word from Washington." The girl glanced at me quickly. I went on. "All the words from Washington, doll. Names, addresses, and telephone numbers. The whole list you're carrying. All ten names. Well, nine, since we've already made contact with number one." When Martha hesitated, I asked, "What's the trouble now?"

She glanced towards the bed, and back to me. "I was supposed to tell it only to you, Matt."

I shrugged. "The minute you tell me, I'll tell her, so what's the difference?"

"Do you trust her that much?" The younger woman's voice was sharp.

"I have to trust her that much," I said. "In this business there are two kinds of damn fools. There are the damn fools who trust everybody, and then there are the damn fools who trust nobody. I try not to be either kind."

"All right," Martha said reluctantly. "All right, but it's your responsibility."

She had a good memory. She stood there with her eyes partly closed and rattled off, without any hesitation, the code names of nine agents, their current cover names, where they were to be found, and how they could be reached by telephone. Some of the names were familiar to me: men and women with whom I'd worked in the past. Others I'd never heard of. Well, they'd probably never heard of me, so we were even. I made the girl go over the list once more; then I repeated it back to make certain I had everything straight. I knew Lorna was assimilating the material right along with me.

"That's it?" I asked when we were finished. "That's everything you were supposed to tell me?"

Martha's eyes wavered slightly. "Yes, that's it. Daddy

said you'd know what to do without having it spelled out for you."

I regarded her for a moment, rather grimly, trying to figure the whole thing out: why Mac had used his daughter on this critical mission—even with a built-in warning code—instead of sending a trained agent, and what additional information he'd given her that she was now holding back for some screwball reason of her own. Looking at her I realized, with some surprise, that properly cleaned up she could be beautiful. Even in her dirty pseudo-pirate outfit she was an attractive kid, not that it mattered. What was important was that she was an infuriating nut, if not worse.

"There's another list, there's got to be," I said slowly. Her face told me I'd guessed right, so I went on: "It's got ten names on it, too, or maybe eleven. Give."

"I… I can't!" She frowned suspiciously. "How did you know there was another list?"

"I told you. There had to be. Mac said I'd know what to do. Sure, I know. But I don't know who to do it to. Tell me."

"I can't!" she protested. "If I do—"

"What?"

"If I do, I'll be responsible for what happens to them."

"That's right," I said. "And if you don't, you'll be responsible for what happens to us, your dad included. Not to mention a couple of hundred million fellow citizens who may be adversely affected by your decision." I grimaced, and went on flamboyantly, "The fate of your country is in your hands, Borden. George Washington and Abraham Lincoln are counting on you."

She said angrily, "Stop it! You're not funny!" She was probably right at that. After a moment, she went on: "You can't really believe that just you and she and Daddy and a few others are going to… to *change* anything? And even if you can make a difference by using violence, how do you know you're *right*?"

I said, "Go to hell, doll. How do *you* know we're wrong? Can you take the responsibility of assuming that your father is just a bloodthirsty nincompoop who doesn't know what the hell he's doing?"

She stared at me for a long moment. Her gray eyes were wide and shiny; I thought she was going to burst into tears. Abruptly, she drew a long, shaky breath and said, "Bainbridge, Joseph W., office 2243 Federal Annex A, home 77 Archuleta Circle, Phoenix, Arizona; Dunn, Homer P., office…"

There were ten names again, in alphabetical order. Again I went over them with her until I had them and got a nod from Lorna saying she had them, too.

"Fine," I said to Martha. "And now the date. There's got to be a date."

She drew a long breath, shaky with anger this time. "Damn you, if you can read minds, why do you bother to ask questions?" When I didn't say anything, she said, "June 17."

"Just June 17. No hour or minute?"

"No. The date was all he gave me."

I regarded her bleakly. "Why are you so reluctant to

cooperate, Borden? You took the job, didn't you? Why—"

"Yes, and I wish to heaven I hadn't!" she gasped. "After watching you kill three men just like snapping your fingers… Anyway, I don't trust you and I don't trust your Mrs. Holt with her dreadful ideas, and I'm sure if Daddy really knew what kind of people he'd hired… Now that you have all the information, what are you going to do with it?"

I said irritably, "Oh, stop trying to kid your lousy little conscience. You knew what we were going to do with it before you gave it to me, so don't ask stupid questions you don't want to hear the answers of." I turned to Lorna. "He's got them pretty well divided," I said, "east and west of the Mississippi, five and five. You take the Western division of both lists. Get in touch with the other four agents out here. He's got each of them located pretty close to a target address, you'll notice. I guess the one in Phoenix was meant for you. Of course, if one of your people gets into trouble, or you can't make contact with him, you'll have to arrange for his touch to be made by somebody else, or make it yourself. Oh, and tell your people it had better look as accidental as they can make it look."

"Yes," she said, "but you've forgotten something, haven't you, Helm?"

I looked down at her. She waited, smiling faintly. I grinned and said, "Goddamn a world full of temperamental females. Please?"

"That's better."

I looked at Martha. "Okay, is that it? Is there anything else you were supposed to tell me?"

"No," she said, "no, that's all. Just the two lists of names, and the date, and that you'd know what to do."

I studied her grimly. She never gave up. She was still holding out something. After a moment I realized what it had to be.

"You're forgetting one item, aren't you, Borden?" I said wearily. "One more thing he told you. An address, a place on the water, but where?" She faced me and didn't speak, but the resentful gray eyes told me I was right. I said, "Eleven hot-shot agents, the best he's got, specially selected, carefully hidden out of harm's way. Eleven agents but only ten targets. That's one left over: me. Me, and a boat he was very eager for me to have. Tell me where I'm supposed to go boating, Borden, and when."

She started to blurt out something frustrated and furious but held it back. "He… he wants you to report to him the night before."

"The night of June 16th. Where?"

She glanced towards Lorna, and back to me. "*That* I'm not going to tell you in front of her! If you want to risk having her know Daddy's hiding place, you'll have to tell her yourself."

Lorna swung her feet off the bed and stood up. "It's something I'm better off not knowing, anyway," she said. "If I don't know, it wasn't I who spilled it. Excuse me, folks, while I go wash my face."

The younger woman watched her go, waiting until the bathroom door had closed fully. Then she looked at me once more. "If you betray him, I'll kill you!"

I said wearily, "Oh, shut up, doll. Don't make loud noises about things you're not going to do. You're the little girl who doesn't believe in killing anything, remember?"

She glared at me. "Damn you! Why do you have to be so—" She stopped and drew a long, ragged breath. "It's in Florida," she said, "but I don't know the exact... There's a man Daddy goes fishing with, a friend, Hank Priest, Congressman Henry Priest, who's got a waterfront place near a little town called Robalo, on Robalo Island. That's on the west coast. You're supposed to get in touch with him. He'll tell you where to go and get you a reliable guide. Give yourself time enough so you can pick the right tide. It's somewhere out in that maze of mangrove islands off the edge of the Everglades, I think, but you'll never find anything in there without a guide—anything, that is, except snakes, alligators, and mosquitoes."

"It sounds real inviting," I said wryly.

"Of course you're supposed to make sure nobody follows you."

"Of course," I said. "Naturally. A station wagon the size of a Greyhound bus towing a great big white boat, and I'm supposed to drive it invisibly across two-thirds of the continent—"

"It's spring. The roads are full of cars towing boats. Anyway, Daddy's got confidence in you for some reason. He knows, with the information I've given you, you'll make it good."

I nodded slowly. "All right, I'll try to live up to his goddamned confidence in me." I regarded her deliberately, until she shifted position and licked her lips as if to protest. Then I said, "Now tell me how much of all this is the truth, if any, and who *really* told you what to say. *Lorna*!"

The bathroom door opened, and Lorna stood there in her stocking feet, with her little revolver steady in her hand.

12

Martha Borden stared incredulously at the armed woman in the bathroom doorway. "*Now* what do you think you're doing with that silly little pistol?" she demanded.

Lorna shrugged. "Ask Helm. It's his play."

"Matt, have you gone absolutely crazy—"

"Over here," I said. "Hands against the wall. That's right. Hold the pose." Moving in to make the frisk, I apologized to Lorna over my shoulder: "Not that I think you'd miss anything that was there at the time, but she was outside for several minutes getting the candy just now. She could have picked up some kind of a weapon." I went over the girl carefully, finding nothing. "Okay, you can lower your arms and turn around."

Martha's eyes were hot and angry as she swung to face me once more. "Well, that's one way of getting a cheap thrill!"

"Relax, little girl," I said. "I hate to disillusion you, but your body isn't all that stimulating. I've frisked lots more irresistible ladies without blowing a fuse." I studied her for a moment longer, frowning. I wasn't sure, of course. Either she was a hell of a good actress—better than she had any right to be—or I was making an embarrassing mistake; but it had to be checked out. I felt around the edge of the bed where she'd been sitting earlier, and found nothing there, either. "Sit down," I said. "Keep your hands where I can see them."

"Watch it!" Lorna said quickly. We both looked at her, startled. She said, "Don't sit on the candy bars. I guess I will have one, after all."

I raked them all up and handed them to her. She put her gun away and moved to a nearby chair and sat down, carefully peeling a Hershey's with almonds.

Martha asked, "Well, should I sit or shouldn't I?"

"Sit," I said.

Lorna munched chocolate and nuts and asked, "What's the problem, anyway?"

"There are two problems," I said. "The first is that she knows too much. The second is that she's probably a lousy little traitor."

I made it rough deliberately, so that I could study the reaction. Martha made a shocked sound of protest, but whether or not it was genuine was hard to tell.

Lorna asked, "How do you figure that, Helm?"

I said, "I've been playing along with her to find out what she was going to say. Now we've got to figure out how much of what she's told us was the truth, if any of it was. If it wasn't, we've got to figure out who got her to lie, and what the real truth is."

"Everything I told you was the truth!" Martha blurted indignantly. "You have absolutely no reason to call me a—"

"Every reason in the world, doll," I said. "We'll come to the evidence in a minute."

Lorna swallowed another bite of chocolate and said calmly, "I gather you're not contending that she isn't Martha Borden. You're saying that Martha Borden is a traitor—a traitress, to be precise."

"That's right. The resemblance is too damned close. She's got to be the right girl. Only she's gone wrong. Well, she's not the first kid who's turned against her parents these days."

"What makes you think she has?"

"Like I said, she knows too much. A lot of the names she used were those of genuine agents; maybe all of them were. But the really interesting thing is what she doesn't know, or says she doesn't know. She can't tell an impostor from her own father. At least she pretends she can't."

"What do you mean?" That was Martha, jumping to her feet. "What do you mean, an impostor?"

"Sit down!" I waited until she'd obeyed. Now that I was marshalling the evidence, it looked fairly convincing. I spoke to Lorna. "Suppose you were to dial the special number, Mrs. Holt. And suppose the voice at the other end, a fairly familiar voice, told you he was afraid a gent named Leonard intended to decimate our organization to the last man, what would you think?"

Lorna's eyes widened. "Mac never said that!"

"You're damn right Mac never said that," I said. "But the man at the other end of the line—a line carefully rigged to be nice and weak and noisy—said just that. And the dutiful daughter here listened to him saying it and made no comment. In fact, she's gone out of her way this evening to point out how I'd talked to *her father* so he must be alive and doing well. Hell, anybody who knows him, knows Mac couldn't have said a fool thing like that in a million years!"

Martha licked her lips, looking lost and bewildered. "But I… I don't understand! What's the matter with—"

"Oh, cut it out, Borden!" I snapped. "That poor-little-stupid-me line is getting pretty damn stale."

"Just a minute, Eric." Lorna peeled the paper off a second candy bar and spoke patiently: "My dear girl, your father speaks English, not gobbledygook. The word 'decimate' comes from the Latin word for ten. In the old days, if a conquered village misbehaved, the Romans were much nicer about it than we are nowadays. They didn't wipe it out with bombs and napalm. They simply marched a legion into the place and lined up all the male inhabitants. Then they yanked every tenth man out of line and stuck a spear or sword into him. That's decimate, to kill one-tenth of. The word has also been used loosely to mean inflict large losses upon, but it does not and cannot possibly mean to massacre or annihilate. It's logically impossible to decimate to the last man. You'll always have nine men left."

Martha looked indignant. "You can't accuse me of treachery because of a silly old definition that nobody pays any attention to—"

I said, "In my previous conversation with Washington, when I called from Nogales, the same gent told me he was disinterested in a certain murderer. He also said that a certain agent was presently in a certain town in Oklahoma and that I was supposed to contact him there. Obviously, they've got a mimic sitting at that phone who's got a pretty good ear but no brains. He's got the voice down pat, but he's been talking Washington gibberish and hearing others talk it for so long, that it simply doesn't occur to him that some people do prefer the English language. And I gave you the direct quotes, Borden, and you didn't even raise an eyebrow. That's when I first began to suspect that everything wasn't as it should be between you and your pa."

The girl's face was pale. "I really don't understand. Please, I'm not trying to act dumb or anything, but—"

Lorna spoke in the same calm and patient voice: "Miss Borden, disinterested does not mean the same thing as uninterested, which is presumably the word for which the man on the phone was fumbling."

"A judge is supposed to be disinterested," I said. "That means he's got no obligations or commitments to the parties appearing before him: he's quite objective about the case. But he's not supposed to be uninterested. That means he's just bored with the whole proceeding, and that is the meaning the man in Washington really wanted to convey."

Lorna said, "And presently does not mean the same thing as at present, Miss Borden; and your father is very sensitive about this distinction."

"But *everybody* says—"

"Not everybody," I corrected her. "Not Mac. The office girls would catch hell if he heard them telling somebody that he was presently in conference, meaning right now. Presently, to him, means in a little while, as it meant to everybody until a relatively few years ago, when ignorant people started fancying up the language regardless of meaning. The correct, old-fashioned usage is, 'At present, Mr. Mac is in conference, but he will see you presently.' That's what Mac learned in school and what I learned a generation later. The fact that some permissive dictionaries may already have adopted the recent bastard usage doesn't make it sound any less affected and pretentious to his ears or mine." I drew a long breath. "And, honey, contact is not and will never be a verb in your father's vocabulary. Anybody who orders me to contact somebody just damn well isn't Mac, and you know that as well as I do."

"But I don't!" the girl protested desperately. "I mean, all these ridiculous little grammatical distinctions, who cares? Who pays any attention to that stuff these days? I mean, *really* Mr. Helm, with all the big, *relevant* issues…" She stopped, breathless, looking from me to Lorna and back again.

I stared at her. The idea that our language had suddenly become irrelevant while my back was turned was difficult for me to grasp. I turned towards Lorna, who seemed to have become the acting referee.

"Is the kid serious," I asked, "or is she putting me on?"

"I don't know. I really don't know." Lorna frowned at the seated girl. "Remember, she'd apparently never heard of Cassandra or Ragnarök. We have to face the possibility that the young lady is practically illiterate."

Martha jumped to her feet. "I don't have to take a lot of insults—"

"Sit down," I said. "Goddamn it, sit down!"

"But she said—"

"Don't worry about what she said. Worry about the fact that if you can't come up with something that makes a little sense, I'm going to have to take you out somewhere and shoot you."

"*Shoot* me!" Martha sank onto the bed. "Why... why, you're *mad*!"

"What the hell do you think happens to double agents who get caught? And don't think being Mac's daughter will save you, sweetheart. If you've sold us out, well, he knows the rules, and he knows they go for everybody. After all, he made them."

She licked her lips. "But I'm not a... I haven't..."

Lorna interrupted. "Just how clear was the voice on the phone, Helm?"

"Not very clear. And, as I say, the guy was a good mimic. On that bad connection, I'd have accepted him as Mac if he'd said the right things." I shook my head. "But, hell, we all know Mac's little language hangups.

You can't tell me his own kid—"

"You're behind the times, Eric. Nobody listens to language any more. It's no longer a means of precise communication, it's a club to hit people over the head with; and the exact meanings of words no longer count. I think the girl is quite serious. I think she never in her life stopped to listen to how her father talks. Besides, he's been a very busy man as long as we've known him. The chances are, she hasn't had even as much communication as we have."

"You're so right about that!" Martha's voice was stiff. "He's been practically a stranger around the house as long as I can remember. I... I was all shook up, a few weeks ago, when he asked me into the study to have a serious talk. I thought he was going to tell me about the birds and the bees, or something, at *my* age! Instead of which... instead of which he asked me to undertake this melodramatic..."

She stopped. There was a little silence. At last Lorna said, "You're forgetting something, Eric. You're forgetting that I was on the list."

"So?"

"So if she'd sold us out, if she'd passed that list of names on to Leonard, or got it from him, he'd have known I was at the ranch. His men would have come looking for me when they seized the place, if only to prevent me from getting away to spread the news of the raid. But nobody came."

I regarded the girl for a moment longer. Instinct told me that she was dangerous and not to be trusted.

Depending on anybody with her attitudes was simple suicide. However, I could be wrong in this particular instance. That she'd betray us, and me in particular, if she got the chance, I had no real doubt. She'd think it was her duty to humanity and society. However, her chance might not have shown itself yet. In any case, she wasn't going anywhere I couldn't keep an eye on her, so I might as well pretend to be convinced of her innocence.

"Okay," I said. "My mistake. My apologies, Miss Borden."

"Your apologies are *not* accepted!"

Lorna said, "When you're quite through snapping at each other, we ought to take another look at the situation. If Leonard has a substitute holding down the office phone, it seems likely that Mac is no longer in Washington. We can hope that he got away safely and is sitting out the storm in his secret hideout, the one you were just told, about, Eric. But that means we're pretty well on our own."

I said, "We'll wait until the stores and restaurants open. We'll need some food, and a car for Lorna, and clothes for both of you—"

"I have my own clothes, thanks!" Martha snapped.

"We're going to try a dramatic disguise, Miss Borden," I said mildly. "We're going to bathe you and put you into a nice clean dress so nobody'll recognize you. Okay?"

She started to protest and stopped, but her gray eyes hated me.

Lorna said, "I suppose we'll be splitting up here, as

soon as we're all well fed and respectably clothed. In the meantime, does anybody mind if I try sleeping in a bed, just to see what it's like?"

13

In spite of the late morning start, Martha and I managed to cross half of Arizona and most of New Mexico before pulling into a large motel in the town of Tucumcari, near the Texas border, around nine o'clock that evening. Parking in front of the office, I started to get out, but remembered something and reached into my pocket.

"Here," I said. "You'd better put this on, for appearances' sake."

Martha glanced at the inexpensive wedding ring I'd picked up while she was shopping with Lorna in another department of the Phoenix store we'd patronized. She didn't move to take it.

"Don't be silly," I said impatiently. "For your own protection, you're going to have to share a room with me. Would you rather be my sister, or my daughter, or just a very good friend? I like you better as my child bride. Take it."

Reluctantly she took it and put it on. "How many

'brides' have you had in the line of business, Matt?" she asked tartly, and answered her own question. "Obviously, enough that you can pick the right ring size at a glance. But speaking of protection, who's going to protect me from you?"

I sighed. She was really a pretty corny young lady. I said, "You certainly do have a high opinion of your sex appeal! Frisking you is supposed to turn me on like a rampant stallion; and sharing a room with you is supposed to start me pawing the wall-to-wall carpet like a prize bull. Relax, Borden. You're a pretty husky girl, and I'm tired. I think you'll be able to fight me off if you try real hard."

There were three vending machines by the office doorway, displaying newspapers from near and far—well, as far as El Paso, Texas. I bought one of each and went inside to register us as man and wife. Then I drove around the landscaped motel maze until I located the second-floor room with the correct number, facing an asphalt parking area, a chain-link fence, and weedy vacant lot. It made for a longer walk with the luggage, but I parked over by the fence where there was plenty of room, so I wouldn't have to unhitch the trailer.

Locking up the station wagon, I wondered where Lorna was sleeping tonight, if she was sleeping at all. Well, she had her mission, and I had mine. I hoped she'd lay off the drinking and thinking. It wasn't her job to solve all the problems of humanity, just the one Mac had sent us...

"Are you all right?" Martha asked behind me.

"What?" I realized I'd been standing there longer than

necessary. "Sorry. Just a little groggy from all the driving, I guess. That, and keeping track of all the cars behind us."

"Do you think we're being followed again?"

I started across the parking lot. "Actually, I've seen no indication of it," I said. "Of course, it doesn't really matter. They don't have to follow us, remember? They know where we're going. They can figure out the roads we'll most likely use. They can pick us up anywhere. After all, it was your phony daddy in Washington who ordered me to Fort Adams, Oklahoma, after Carl."

"You mean it's a trap. Then why—"

"Why are we driving into it? Because we need Carl. Mac didn't put him number six on the list for nothing. He's presumably supposed to organize the last five agents, as Lorna's handling the first five, leaving me free to join your dad in Florida according to instructions. Of course, I could do without Carl if I had to, as far as the primary mission is concerned, but there's also the fact that I've got to get him the hell out of that town. That's a little problem Mac apparently didn't know about when he briefed you, that I'm going to have to solve on my own, with Leonard and his agents breathing down my neck, not to mention the local *polizei*."

"I don't understand. What's going on in Fort Adams, anyway?"

I stopped at the foot of the stairs to rearrange my burdens so I could slip her one of the newspapers I'd bought.

"Front page, lower right," I said.

When I heard her gasp, I knew she'd found the right

item. I headed up the stairs, aware of her coming slowly along behind me, trying to read as she climbed. I found the right door off the long balcony above, unlocked it, turned on the lights, went in, and dumped the luggage on the nearer of the two beds. Martha moved past me and sank down on the other bed, still reading.

Standing there, I regarded the seated girl thoughtfully. It was the best opportunity I'd had to view the effect since she'd made herself over with Lorna's help. The grubby, barefoot, girl pirate was gone, replaced by a civilized young lady. The costume Lorna had selected for her consisted of white sandals and a sleeveless light blue summer dress that hung straight from her shoulders to a waistline—if you want to call it that—located well down on her hips. There was a brief, pleated skirt below.

With its pale color and tricky pleats, I wouldn't have picked it as a sensible travel garment, but apparently, in clothes as in language, I was way behind the times. Lorna had explained to me that this type of double-knit cloth, whatever that might be, in addition to being wrinkleproof, was practically dirtproof. If it did get soiled, a quick rinse and a few shakes would have it clean and dry and crisp-looking once more. These new synthetic knits, Lorna had said, were the answer to a female undercover operative's prayer. I noticed that she'd bought herself a tailored pantsuit of the same material...

"But this is horrible!" Martha gasped, looking up from the paper. "If it's your friend Carl who's doing it, he must be mad!"

"So the local sheriff seems to think," I said. "Let me read it again. I just gave it a quick glance. Here, you can get some more background information from these other papers."

I handed them to her, and sat down on the big motel bed beside her. For a while there was no sound but the rustling of newsprint. I frowned at the article in the El Paso paper, trying to get at not only what the reporter had written, but what he'd known but hadn't felt free to write.

COP-STRANGLER STRIKES AGAIN

Fort Adams, Okla.: Two bizarre murders, following on the heels of a violent student riot that claimed three lives, have brought renewed tension to this college town.

This morning, Patrolman Harold Grumman, 23, of the Fort Adams Police Force, was discovered strangled to death in his parked patrol car. The murder weapon, found at the scene, was a length of fine music wire equipped with two short handles apparently sawed from a broomstick.

Local authorities consider the weapon a significant clue, since an identical garotte figured in the violent death of Deputy Sheriff Marcus Wills, 47, whose body was found in the bushes beside the garage of his home in a Fort Adams suburb, just a few days ago. More force appeared to have been used in this earlier case, as the body had been almost decapitated by the thin wire.

In addition to the weapon used, the two crimes also have in common the fact that both officers were involved in the recent disturbance on the campus of the Fort Adams State College, when all local law-enforcement agencies were called upon to help deal with a riot in which three students died as a result of police gunfire. However, the county sheriff in charge of the murder investigation, Thomas M. Rullington, discounted this as a possible motive.

"Those college kids are kind of wild, sure, but they aren't cold-blooded assassins," Rullington told the press. "We are proceeding on the theory that this is the work of a homicidal maniac, probably hopped up on drugs…"

There was more on an inside page, giving further details about the riot, about the two slain officers, and about Sheriff Rullington, who'd apparently been in command of the forces of law and order at the time of the campus confrontation. There was also a brief rundown on the three dead students: Charles Dubuque, Mark Hollingshead, and Emily Janssen. Only Dubuque, it appeared, had been taking active part in the disturbance when shot. The other two students had fallen some distance from the scene, victims of stray bullets.

A local jury had exonerated all other law-enforcement personnel involved, the sheriff specifically calling the death of Hollingshead self-defense in the line of duty—

apparently the youth had been found with a brick in his hand—and the other two deaths regrettable accidents. I got the impression that the jury's regrets had not been very deep or very sincere.

I lowered the paper and found Martha looking at me. "What are you going to do now?" she asked. "You can't possibly—"

"I told you what I was going to do," I said. "I'm going to get him out of there if I can. I've got to try. For one thing, Herbert Leonard is just yearning to have one of our men get caught strangling a few cops. You'll note that although he knew where Carl was heading and why, he apparently never bothered to warn the authorities around Fort Adams. There's no indication that they were expecting trouble or know who's causing it. Herbie *wanted* Carl to get in good and deep. Then, when I called and seemed to accept his mimic as the genuine Mac, he saw how he could improve on the picture by using me instead of killing me. He had me sent after Carl to make it look as if our whole organization was involved instead of just one grief-crazed agent. Obviously, he's gambling that we'll both be caught. The publicity will give him the excuse he wants to lower the boom on us officially, something he's apparently been afraid to do so far."

Martha frowned. "But those men outside Tucson tried to kill you *after* you'd got the orders to head for Oklahoma."

I reminded myself not to forget that she wasn't dumb. "I think we can blame that on a communications lag," I said. "It took us less than an hour to get from Nogales to

Tucson. Even if the word was passed immediately to let us through, it just didn't have time to get out to the units already in the field with orders to stop us, dead. That little Ford had no telephone or two-way radio, remember?"

"So… so those two men just died for nothing."

"Would you rather it had been you?" She didn't speak. I said, "The other reason I'm going to get Carl out of there, as I've already said, is that I need him."

"But you can't make use of a crazy *murderer*—"

"Little girl," I said, regarding her grimly, "you have a serious identity problem, don't you? What are you and who are you for, anyway? I thought you'd be weeping for those college kids brutally shot down by the lousy pigs. I thought in your circles anything that happened to a cop was just great. So what's a little dead fuzz among friends, anyway?"

"But the horrible way your friend did it! You can't possibly sympathize—"

"What's sympathy got to do with anything?" I demanded. "Your dad didn't put me here to dish out sympathy to anybody, certainly not to a guy who's supposed to be sitting quietly in New Orleans awaiting instructions, instead of stalking around Oklahoma with a lousy wire noose. Anyway, a man in our line of work isn't supposed to indulge in personal vengeance. That's kind of like the character responsible for a nuclear weapon pushing the red button because his wife burned the toast that morning." I shook my head. "The fact is, I need the guy. I've got work for him to do. Sympathy is

not the problem. Understanding is. We know why he's
doing this, but we've got to figure out what he's doing—
exactly what he's doing."

"Isn't it obvious?"

"Not if you know Mr. Anders Janssen," I said. "He has
certain berserker tendencies to go with his Scandinavian
name and blood. In case you're not up on your Viking
history: the Berserkers were the forerunners of the Japanese
kamikazes. And any time things get tough, Carl's instinct
is to take a big swig of mead—well, beer will serve—and
grab his big two-handed sword and charge in there to get
as many of the dirty bastards as he can before they chop
him down. When we were working together, I had to sit on
him a couple of times to keep him from turning a simple
job into a goddamned suicide mission."

"I don't see what you're driving at," Martha protested.
"What has this to do with our... with your problem?"

I said, "Well, if he's in his kamikaze mood right now,
we're in real trouble. In that case, he's ready to die, and
his only plan is to keep on killing cops until they get him.
But in that case, I don't think he'd be using a silly weapon
like a garotte. He'd be sniping at them from the rooftops
with a long-range rifle and laying for them in the alleys
with a sawed-off shotgun. He'd be working towards
the big, final, glorious shoot-out when, surrounded at
last, he'd teach those trigger-happy uniformed clowns
the difference between knocking off a helpless young
girl and an experienced gent who knows how to handle
firearms. But I don't feel that's the big scene that's

shaping up here." I hesitated and went on: "I think he's got something altogether different in mind. Three dead kids; three dead cops—"

"But there have been only two so far."

"So far," I said. "So there's one left to go, if he isn't just waging a general war against uniforms and badges. And if I'm right, there's not much doubt who he's saving for the big third spot. The question is how we can reach him without pulling Leonard's gang down on top of him, and us… Get up."

Martha looked startled. "What for?"

"Get up. Walk around the room. Let me look at you in that rig." I watched her as, rather self-consciously, she rose and walked to the door and back to me. "Did you think of getting stockings along with all the rest of the flossy paraphernalia?"

"We bought some pantyhose. Lorna thought I might want to look super-civilized some time."

"Put them on."

"Why… Oh, all right, but turn your back."

Covering her long legs with nylon didn't accomplish a great deal. She still looked like a tanned tomboy—a tanned tomboy on her best behavior. Anybody who'd seen her in Guaymas, as some of Leonard's men undoubtedly had, would recognize her instantly, despite the ladylike dress and hose.

"What's the matter, Matt?" she asked.

I said, "You look too damned much like Martha Borden, that's what's the matter."

"Maybe this is what you're after," she said, turning to the brand-new suitcase on the bed. She got something out, hiding it with her body, and bent far over to put it on. Then she faced me abruptly, straightening up and tossing back the long hair of a shining wig that covered her own cropped hairdo completely. After a moment to let me appreciate the view, she walked to the mirror and touched some vagrant gold strands into place. The change was almost shocking. Instead of a boyish brunette, I suddenly had for a roommate a glamorous and feminine-looking blonde.

"Lorna thought I might need a real disguise," she said calmly.

"That Lorna," I said. "I don't know what we'd do without her."

"I feel just like Mata Hari," Martha said, regarding her blonde and beautiful image in the mirror. "And what I can't help remembering is that girl was shot."

14

After a long time, I felt the car stop. The door opened and footsteps came around to the rear. Then the trunk lid above me was lifted, daylight came in, and Martha stood there looking down at me, her tanned face in shadow, her blonde wig very bright in the sunshine.

"Are you all right?" she asked.

I sat up painfully and said, "It won't kill me, I guess. But keep that air-conditioner blasting unless you want roast Helm for dinner."

I got out of the trunk and stretched, looking around. We were parked by a small dirt road or lane, under some cottonwoods that apparently got their water from the underground seepage of a muddy stock pond nearby. Some bored-looking Herefords stood around the pond, watching us suspiciously. The lane ran on up across the open range to a house over a mile away, sheltered by more trees, the only other trees in sight.

In the opposite direction, the ground sloped down

gently to the distant horizon. The highway was out there, a straight streak across the plain, infested with cars and trucks looking like ants crawling both ways along an endless twig. It was wide-open county, but it didn't have the spectacular, desolate vistas you find farther west, and there were no faraway, wind-eroded buttes and mesas to add interest to the flat landscape.

"Where are we?" I asked.

"We're still in Texas. I thought there might be a roadblock at the Oklahoma border, and I'd better check on you before we hit it."

I said, "I doubt very much the police will be stopping cars on the highway, particularly cars heading *into* Oklahoma. Hell, they can't go searching every car in the state for old banjo strings, or a saw and what's left of a broomstick. It's not the cops I'm worrying about; it's Leonard's people, some of whom probably know us by sight from Mexico and Arizona, or think they do. Let's hope they're all looking for a couple in a dark green station wagon with a boat towing along behind, so hard they'll pay no attention to a lone blonde in an unencumbered white sedan."

I glanced at the big car, another Chevy that Martha had rented that morning in Amarillo, Texas. It didn't have as much power as the wagon we'd left behind temporarily at a motel, but then it didn't have as much to pull, either. Actually, she'd picked it, on my instructions, not for speed, but for its heat-reflecting color or lack of color, for its large trunk, and for its efficient cooling system that included some ventilating louvres in the trunk lid that might help a man survive back there on a bright summer day. I stretched once more, trying to untie the knots in my back and neck. While the car trunk was about as big as they come, it hadn't really been designed for comfortable occupancy by gents six-feet-four.

Martha was checking her reflection in the car window, touching her bright new hair into place.

I said, "Stop fussing with it, Goldilocks. It's all right. You're beautiful."

"Am I?" She turned to look at me. There was quick mischief in her eyes. "You didn't act as if I were last night. All you did was snore."

"Make up your mind," I said. "Yesterday evening you were mad because you thought I was going to rape hell out of you. This morning you're mad because I didn't."

She smiled. "I'm not mad. But you didn't have to sleep *quite* so soundly. A little insomnia would have been more… well, diplomatic." Embarrassed, she stopped smiling abruptly and said, "Well, if you're all right, we'd better hit the road again."

An endless time later I realized that we'd left the interstate freeway for a secondary road: the pavement was rougher, the speed was less, and there was a lot of the braking and accelerating that goes with driving a two-lane highway. Now and then there'd be a series of stops and starts indicating that we were passing through a town. Once I picked up some bruises when she took a set of bumps too fast, presumably a railroad crossing. Then there was a final town, more country roads, and a stop. The trunk opened.

"I hope you survived all that," Martha said.

"Everything except that damned railroad track you hit at ninety miles per hour," I said, crawling out of my metal womb. I looked around. The country had changed. The view was not as big as it had been. This was more rolling farmland with a stream running through it. "Did you find the sheriff's house?" I asked.

"Back down the road three point seven miles," she said precisely. "I thought of stopping near a kind of knoll nearby from which you could have seen the layout for yourself, if you didn't mind climbing a little, but then I thought somebody else might have the same idea."

"Smart girl." I reached into the back seat to get a beer out of the cheap plastic-foam icebox we'd picked up in Amarillo, along with the rental car and the address of Sheriff Thomas M. Rullington, obtained from a friendly telephone operator. "Beer or coke for you... Okay, let's go sit on the riverbank while you tell me what it looks like."

Martha laughed. "In these ladylike clothes you've put me into? My nylons wouldn't last two steps in that brush. Maybe I can make it to that log over there without casualties." She made it to the log, and I opened the coke she'd indicated and handed it to her. She said, "Thanks. Actually, it's a small farm just outside the town, with a shiny new Cadillac in the yard. You go through some brand new ticky-tacky suburbs, real crackerbox stuff, and just as you reach open country, there it is, with a mailbox out front that says 'Rullington, Route #3' and a number I didn't have time to read as I drove by. The house is white clapboard that could use another coat of paint. In front, a kind of sad-looking, fenced-in flower garden and mangy-looking lawn with a tricycle and a set of swings. At the side, as I said, a big Caddy sedan. In back, a barn and corral with a couple of horses in the corral. Farther back, some fields with cattle in them. That's about all I could see going by, except that there was a man sitting on the corral fence looking at the horses as if he didn't like horses much. And fifty yards down the road was a parked pickup truck—blue, if it matters—-with a man in the cab smoking a cigarette as if he'd had so many they were beginning to taste awful."

"Good enough," I said. "We'll make a secret agent of you yet."

"I certainly hope not." Martha's tone was dry. After a moment, she went on. "What are you going to do, Matt?"

I said, "The real question is what Carl's going to do, and what Sheriff Rullington's going to do—or hopes he's going to do—about what Carl's going to do."

"You're certain the sheriff is next on the list."

"It figures that way," I said. "Apparently nobody knows just whose bullet hit Emily Janssen in all that shooting, but it's well established who gave the order to fire. But just how Carl plans to reach him… Wait a minute! You said there were some kids' playthings in the Rullington yard?"

"Yes. Why?"

"Because, damn it, Carl is a pro. He can figure the

opposition as well as we can. The first killing was easy. Nobody was expecting it. The second was probably almost as simple; nobody was really looking for an encore. But now the whole state's alert, knowing there's a systematic cop-killer loose who's more than likely to strike again. Carl can't help but know he hasn't got a chance of sneaking up on another policeman, let alone the sheriff himself. What will he do? Hell, it's obvious. He'll make the sheriff come to him, assuming he can get his hands on the proper bait. Let's find out just how many kids the Rullingtons have and where..." I stopped, seeing that she was about to go into one of her righteous seizures. I said, "Shut up, Borden! Just keep your Goddamned high-minded disapproval to yourself, so I can get on with my work."

"But kidnaping children—"

"We don't know that's how he'll work it. Anyway, don't forget, Carl is short one child. Maybe he figures he's got one coming. If Rullington can shoot them, why can't he kidnap them?"

"You can't be serious!"

"I'm not talking about me. I'm talking about the way Carl's mind is working. The more I think of it, the more I'm convinced that's the way he'll do it: poetic justice or something... You said there was a natural vantage point from which we could have studied the sheriff's farm, only you were afraid somebody might have beat us to it. Well, suppose you're right. Suppose Carl's keeping the place under observation while he learns the Rullington family's daily routine. It's a long shot, but it's worth trying. Let's go."

They don't have mountains in Oklahoma to amount to anything, at least not in that part of Oklahoma. They don't even have anything you'd call a real hill, if you were brought up in a more rugged landscape as I was, but there was a kind of undernourished brushy ridge across the highway from the sheriff's farm—or where my scout informed me the sheriff's farm was located. I still hadn't seen it for myself.

"That little twisted oak or whatever it is," Martha said as she drove. "Up on the ridge right next to that bare-looking knob. I think the house is just opposite that, although it's hard to tell from this, side."

We were cruising slowly down a narrow dirt road that left the highway a mile or so outside Fort Adams and kind of wandered behind the ridge in question. I was in the back seat, ready to hit the floor at the sight of another person or car. If anybody remembered the white Texas Chevy, I wanted him to remember it with only one occupant, female.

"If there's any kind of a road leading into that clump of trees to the left, take it," I said. "Right there... What's the matter?"

She had slammed on the brakes an instant after turning into the trees, throwing me off balance. "There's a car hidden in there already! What do I do, Matt?"

"Sit tight. I'll go take a look."

I was dropping out of the sedan on the off side as I

spoke. I slipped around, the rear with my revolver ready, and made my approach cautiously, working from tree to tree. The vehicle had been backed into a clump of brush to hide it. To call it a car was an exaggeration. It was a Ford panel delivery truck, and not much of a truck at that.

It was well over ten years old, and it had led a hard life. Black paint had been sloshed over it when the original pigment expired. The battered Kentucky license plate was held in place with rusty baling wire. However, the headlights were clean and intact and the tires were new. There was nobody inside.

I made sure of this, and frowned at the interior. The upholstery of the front seat had worn out and the owner had arranged a folded blanket to sit on, driving. There were other blankets, and some pots and pans, in the rear. Apparently he'd been sleeping in the truck and doing his own cooking. The doors were locked and I let them stay that way. I opened the hood instead, and looked at the large and fairly new V8 motor inside. The original mill had probably been a six and considerably less powerful.

I stood there for a moment, considering. Maybe my gamble was paying off. An automotive relic with new tires, good lights, and a muscular replacement power plant in good condition could easily be Carl's idea of camouflage. With that license, the vehicle certainly didn't belong to a local squirrel hunter, even if the Oklahoma squirrel season was open this time of year, which I doubted. I waved to Martha to drive up.

"What is it?" she asked through the open window of

the sedan. "I mean, whose is it? Carl's?"

"Maybe," I said. "I certainly hope so. It would save us a lot of time and cleverness—assuming I can sneak up on him up there on the ridge without getting shot. You stay here. If somebody comes, particularly somebody with a uniform, you're sound asleep. When they wake you, you say you got tired of driving and turned off the highway to find a quiet place to take a nap. You don't know anything about the truck. It was here when you got here. You thought it was just an abandoned wreck. While you're resting, you can figure out a plausible story to explain why you rented a car in Texas and drove it into Oklahoma. Good luck."

As I started to turn away, she said, "Matt."

"Yes?" I said over my shoulder.

"No, come back here a minute. This is important."

I turned back. "Shoot. But make it snappy, please."

Her face was very serious, looking up at me from the car window. The heavy, dark eyebrows made a startling, but somehow not unbelievable, contrast with the long shining hair.

"I've helped you," she said. "Haven't I? I put on this masquerade for you, and drove the car for you. Didn't I?"

"You helped," I said.

"Then you've got to tell me something."

"What?"

She licked her lips. "You've got to tell me that you're going to stop it. You're not going to let him kill him. Otherwise… Otherwise I'm going to have to go to him and warn him."

There were some confused pronouns in that, but the meaning was clear enough. I studied her face for a moment longer. "Just what is this thing you have for cops, anyway, Borden?" I asked.

"I don't have a thing for cops! I just have a thing for… for human beings!"

"Only sheriff-type human beings. Not Carl-type human beings."

She said sharply, "That's just the point! Your friend Carl is not a human being any longer. He's a machine, a ruthless vengeance-machine. You've got to promise to stop him."

I drew a long breath. "Sure. I'll do my best to stop him. Hell, that's what I'm here for. Keep your fingers crossed."

I turned away, wishing I was leaving behind me a good, reliable agent like Lorna—if I had to have somebody along. At the moment, operating alone, with nobody's temperament to consider but my own, seemed very desirable. Maybe I could talk Mac into giving me an assignment all by myself next time out, if there was a next time out.

It wasn't bad stalking country. The brush was pretty thick, but it wasn't dry and crackly; and the ground was reasonably soft. There was plenty of cover. Moving quietly and staying out of sight was no problem at all. Picking the easiest and most silent route, I kept finding tracks in the ground ahead of me: heavy work shoes, considerably worn. Well, Carl was pretty good about detail. Footgear like that would match the truck below.

He'd been brought up on a farm, I remembered, and was pretty good outdoors, unlike some of our city-bred agents who are hell in streets and alleys but tend to get lost in a forty-acre pasture.

The thought made me careful. I remembered the ultimatum Carl was supposed to have delivered, to the effect that anybody Mac sent after him wouldn't come back. It sounded like Carl. He hadn't actually been speaking to Mac when he said it, of course, but he didn't know that. He did know me, however. If his mood was still the same, he'd undoubtedly jump to the wrong conclusion and try to blow my head off the instant he saw me, unless I arranged to prevent it somehow.

I made the last hundred yards on my belly, an inch at a time, and there he was. At least there was somebody in the brush to my left. I could make out the vague shape of a man. He was holding a pair of binoculars to his eyes; it was the slight movement he'd made to focus that had drawn my attention. Lying beside him was some kind of a rifle I couldn't make out clearly.

Very cautiously, I worked my way up to where I could see the blacktop highway half a mile away, and the ticky-tacky urban blight off to the left, and the farm dead ahead just as Martha had described it except that a blue Volkswagen and a white official sedan with a buggy-whip antenna were standing in the yard along with the Cadillac sedan she'd mentioned. A short, heavy man was just getting out of the radio-equipped car. He wore a big white hat and an ivory-handled revolver—well, at that distance, it could have been white plastic or adhesive tape. A thin, tall woman in jeans and a short-sleeved white blouse was speaking to him as he got out.

I lost the rest of the scene. The man just down the ridge had caught my attention once more, raising his head from the glasses, perhaps to rest his eyes. He wasn't Carl.

15

He was, it turned out, a slight and skinny older man, somewhere in his sixties, with a gaunt country face—a mountain face, rather—stubbled with gray beard. His hair was also gray, rather thin and wispy beneath the ancient felt hat that fell off when I jumped him from behind. He was stronger than I'd expected, all wire and whipcord, and it was a good thing I hadn't missed my grip or he'd have given me real trouble despite the difference in our ages. As it was, he managed to get me once on the shin with the heel of his heavy shoe, before I could apply pressure properly and put him out.

I laid him down, rubbed my shin, and took inventory. First I checked that the brief flurry, of action on the ridge had attracted no attention at the house half a mile away. Then I massaged my shin some more, and looked down at the man who had kicked it. In addition to the lethal, high-laced shoes and the now-misplaced hat, he was dressed in overall pants, a gray work shirt, and the dark coat of an old suit, frayed at wrists and elbows. The rifle beside him was a .300 Savage Model 99, perhaps the best of the old lever actions, although the Winchester was the one that got all the glory. This specimen was so old that the bluing had worn off all the metal parts, leaving them silvery, and no finish remained on the stock, but the bore was clean and seemed to be in good condition. His optical equipment was an ancient pair of fieldglasses that could have gone to war with Robert E. Lee or maybe Ulysses S. Grant.

I found some keys on him, a pair of rimless glasses in a hard case, a small plastic container of unidentified pills, a blue bandana handkerchief, some loose change, and a two-bladed pocket knife with the stag handle worn quite smooth. There was also a wallet containing a driver's license made out to Harvey Bascomb Hollingshead, 72, of Bascomb, Kentucky. I sighed, looking down at the thin, stubborn old face. I'd missed the age by a few years. I nibbed my shin once more. For a septuagenarian, he kicked hard.

I tied his wrists with his belt and his ankles with mine, used his handkerchief to gag him, and slung him over my back. Well, I'd like to be able to say it was as easy as that. Actually, slight as he was, he made a heavy and unwieldy load, and I was out of practice and maybe a little out of condition. Swimming and fishing in Mexico with attractive blonde company isn't the best preparation for heavy backpacking.

It took me three tries to get him up; and then I thought I'd end up in the coronary ward before I managed to transport him through the brush to the grove of trees in which Martha was waiting. I didn't take him all the way to the car, however. I didn't dare leave him alone with the girl. Her unpredictable humanitarian impulses might well cause her to revive him and turn him loose. Having labored hard over this warm body, I had no intention of losing it.

I hid the old man in a ditch, therefore, and went back up the hill for the rifle and glasses I hadn't been able to manage on my first trip. I also remembered to pick up the fallen hat. Martha wasn't very good about obeying orders. When she heard me coming, instead of playing possum as instructed, she jumped out of the rental car and ran to meet me.

"Matt, what have you been doing all this time? I've been going out of my mind worrying… What's that?"

"Spoils of war," I said, moving past her to lay the stuff on the hood of the car.

"So you got him." Her voice was suddenly flat. "Did you… did you have to hurt him?"

I glanced at her sharply, but she was quite sincere, and quite oblivious to the fact that the man whose health she was now worrying about was a man whom she'd recently been denouncing as totally nonhuman.

"I got something," I said. I fished out the ring of keys I'd confiscated and handed them to her. "Find the right one and open up the back door of this ancient hearse, will you, while I bring it in."

She had the doors open by the time I came staggering up with my bound prisoner. I dumped him into the rear of his vehicle, not too gently. I was getting tired of lugging him around, and my shin still hurt. Martha stared at him.

"But that old man isn't… That can't be the Carl you've been telling me about!"

"You're so right," I said. "He can't be. Get that gear from the hood and toss it in here, will you? Don't be scared of the gun. I've got the cartridges in my pocket." While she was gone, I checked the bandana gag to make sure it wasn't too tight. To hell with his wrists and ankles. I didn't want to strangle him, but gangrene didn't worry me. He could do a lot of talking before he died of gangrene. As I've said, I was a little tired of the old gent, and he was a complication I didn't appreciate. "Okay, you drive the Chevy; I'll handle this wreck," I said as Martha put the rifle, hat, and glasses beside the old man. "Follow me, but stay well back so it won't look too much as if we're together. Hold it!"

We stood motionless, listening, as a car drove by on the dirt road, but it went on without slowing or stopping. Martha was looking down at the unconscious captive.

"But… but who is he?"

"Miss Borden," I said, "allow me to present Mr. Hollingshead, of Bascomb, Kentucky."

"Hollingshead?" She frowned briefly. "Hollingshead! That was the name of one of the students who… Dubuque, Hollingshead, and Janssen."

"Right," I said. "Apparently, Mr. Hollingshead is another of those perverted oddball characters you object to so strongly, who resent having their kids shot. At least I can't think of any other motive that would bring him clear from Kentucky and put him on the ridge above the sheriff's house with a loaded rifle."

She didn't respond to my sarcasm. She just said: "But haven't you got him tied awfully tightly, Matt? Those straps look as if they're cutting off the circulation."

I stared at her, a little awed. She was so consistently inconsistent it approached true genius.

I said, "Sweetheart, what in the world, are you worrying about? By your own definition, that's not a human being lying there. That's just another vengeance-machine. Who cares about its lousy circulation?"

"Damn you, Matthew Helm…"

She glared at me, swung away, and marched over to the white sedan, her long, phony hair and the brief, crisp pleats of her skirt bouncing indignantly in unison. The car door slammed, and the engine started with a roar. I got the old truck going without any trouble. Half an hour later we were a safe distance, I hoped, from Fort Adams and its burly sheriff. We were parked beside a dim wheel-track across the open prairie, in a kind of fold of land that hid us from the highway a few hundred yards away. I went back, opened the rear of the truck, and saw that my passenger's eyes were open. I turned to Martha, who'd come over, and drew her aside to where the old man couldn't see or hear us.

"There are two ways of doing this," I said. "I can trick him into talking, maybe, or I can try to force him to talk. It's up to you."

"What do you mean?"

I said, "If you don't play along with the lies I'm going to tell, I'll have to get rough. The choice is yours. Cooperate, or watch me go into my Inquisition routine. I'm real good at twisting arms and pulling fingernails, if I do say so myself."

She hesitated. "All right," she said reluctantly, after a moment. "All right, Matt. I'll play along as well as I can."

I went to the truck and untied and ungagged Mr. Hollingshead. I put my belt back where it belonged, and moved my short-barreled revolver from a pocket to its home in front of my left hip, now that there was something to hold it there once more. It took a little while for speech and circulation to return to the old gent, but it took him no time at all, after he'd managed to sit up, to spot the location of his lever-action rifle.

I saw his eyes flick that way and back to me. I reached into my pocket and brought out a handful of .300 Savage cartridges and showed them to him. He nodded slightly and paid no more attention to the rifle. I saw perspiration appear on his forehead as the blood started working its way back into the constricted areas. At last he licked his lips and spoke.

"Help me stand up, Sonny." A look of faint amusement came into his faded blue eyes as I hesitated. "What's the matter, you afraid of a feeble old man teetering on the edge of the eternal grave?"

"Feeble old man, hell," I said. "You forget, Gramps, we wrestled a little. I've got a big bruise to show for it. I don't want any more."

"You slipped up on me real nice there," Hollingshead said. "And that was some kind of a fancy wrestling lock you put on me. What's your name, Sonny?"

"Janssen," I said. "Anders Janssen."

Martha did fine. Maybe she gave a slight start, but I didn't think it was enough for the old man to notice, particularly since his attention was all on me.

"Janssen, eh?" Hollingshead worked his dry lips together and spat. "Well, that figures, I guess. You live in Washington, don't you? I was thinking of getting in touch with you, but Indiana was more on my way, heading west. Indiana, and a man named Roger Dubuque, if you want to call that a man."

"What's wrong with Roger Dubuque?" I asked.

"What's wrong with a white-faced city feller that's real embarrassed—Shamed and embarrassed—because his boy's been killed by the police? Not heartbroken, mind you, not angry, just embarrassed and afraid of what all his city neighbors might be thinking. He had no idea of taking any action, not he. I told him that down our way, if the constable can't handle a kid with a rock without shooting him to death, we kick him the hell out and get a new constable who knows his business. It made no difference to that city man. He had half a mind to curry favor with the police by giving them my name, he did, but I talked him out of that."

I grinned. "Just how did you talk him out of it, Mr. Hollingshead?"

The old gent smiled thinly. It wasn't a very nice smile.

"Why, I told him that no matter how long they put me in prison for, I'd manage to live long enough to come back and shoot hell out of him. He scared easy."

"I'll bet," I said.

"It made me leery of you, Sonny, being as you lived in the city, too. Maybe I misjudged you. When I got here, I soon found somebody else was working along the lines I had in mind. That you?"

"That's me," I lied.

Hollingshead nodded slowly. "Well, I can't say I hold with them foreign methods using slip-nooses and all. A gun's always been good enough for us Hollingsheads and Bascombs, but maybe I'm being finicky. Anyway, it seems to me you've had your fun, Sonny. Why not go home now and leave that child-murdering bastard of a sheriff to me? I'll take care of him for both of us."

"How?" I said. "You're not going to make a .300 Savage shoot half a mile no matter how hot you load it; and that old gun of yours hasn't even got a scope on it."

"The day I clutter up a good rifle with a lot of glass will be the day they bury me. Give me a hand, will you? The old legs aren't what they used to be, and you didn't do them a damn bit of good... Ahhh." He stood for a moment, stamping his feet cautiously. Then he spoke as if there had been no interruption: "Wasn't going to take him from that ridge, Sonny. There's other places... The boy didn't come home from school. You know anything about that?"

"I might," I said, and it wasn't entirely a lie, this time.

"The older girl's married and moved away. The younger one drives that little blue foreign car to her high school. Sheriff, he made some money selling land to that development next door, and seems like first thing he did with it was buy new cars for everybody. The boy's about ten. He rides the school bus. Generally he's home by four o'clock. Today he didn't get off with the other youngsters, at the corner. The woman, she flagged the bus down and talked to the driver. Then she ran into the house. Ten minutes later, sheriff comes driving up with his tires on fire, and that's when you jumped me. I don't know as I care for the idea of using a man's younguns against him, Janssen, if that's what's in your mind." I didn't say anything. After a moment, Hollingshead shrugged his thin shoulders, dismissing the subject. He looked towards Martha. "Who's she?"

"Never mind," I said. "You don't need to know who she is. And don't lecture me, old man. My daughter's dead, and your son—"

"Grandson. Last Hollingshead male, if that means anything to you. Sometimes I get to thinking nobody knows what family feeling is these days."

"I know," I said.

I felt shabby and fraudulent as I said it. The more I talked with him, the less I liked lying to him, but likes and dislikes—those of any agent—are totally irrelevant, as Mac would be the first to point out.

"Reckon you do," Hollingshead said. "My son, now, he don't. Just like that Dubuque, but my son was brought up right. He ought to know that if you let them get away with it… The old man drew a long breath. "You can't let them get away with it. Not ever. There's things no man's obliged to take, like having his kin shot down for nothing. When they step over that line, they've got to die, no matter if they're wearing pretty blue uniforms or big white hats and fancy badges. But my son, he's got a good job in the city pumping gas, and a little mouse-faced wife, and he wasn't going to do anything. Just like that Dubuque, he was thinking of his neighbors, not of his boy dead. So I came instead. Somebody's got to die, Janssen, for spilling the last of the Hollingshead blood, and rightfully it ought to be a Hollingshead that kills him."

I said, "If you feel like that, Mr. Hollingshead, why did you approach Dubuque at all? If you're set on doing the job yourself?"

The old man hesitated. "Well, Sonny," he said, "I'll tell you, I was kind of bluffing when I told that man how long I was going to live if he went to the police about me. Chances are, he'd have been safe doing all the talking he wanted. Fact is, I haven't got one whole hell of a lot of time left, according to the doctor, and I'll thank you to give me back those little pills you took out of my shirt pocket. Can't tell when I might need them in a hurry."

"You'll get them back. They're in the truck," I said. Neither of us moved at once. "You don't fight like a man with a bad heart." I said.

He smiled wryly. "Wasn't thinking of my heart when you jumped me. Anyway, I wasn't real sure I'd last the trip out, let alone be fit enough to do the work when I got here. That's why I wanted somebody else along, to take over if it turned out that way. But now I'm here, I feel I'm going to make it, Janssen, and I'd be much obliged if you'd leave me to it." He regarded me for a moment. "I tell you, I'll make a deal with you. You let me have that sheriff and I'll… You got one of those wire nooses with you? And the wire and stuff you made it out of?"

"I might have," I said, weaseling out of the direct lie.

"Well, you just toss it into my truck there. When they catch me—with my heart, I'm not about to run very fast—I'll say I took care of all three of them, leaving you free and clear. That's fair enough, isn't it?"

I hesitated. "I'll have to think about it. First, I'll get you those pills."

I walked to the truck and made as if to reach inside, although the little plastic container was actually in my pocket. There was something else I had to get out, and I had to turn my back on him to do it inconspicuously. Then I returned, holding out the pill bottle, and managed to let it drop before he could grasp it. When he reached down for it, I slipped the hypodermic needle into his neck, and caught him so he wouldn't hurt himself as he fell.

"Pick up that pillbox and put it into his shirt pocket so he's got it handy." I said, supporting the dead weight once more. There was no movement. I saw Martha standing there, staring at me with big, accusing eyes. "Oh, for Christ's sake, it's, only a sedative!" I snapped. "He'll wake up nice and rested in four hours. Now pick up the pills, please."

16

I didn't like returning to the same grove of trees. It was poor technique to use the same hideout twice. However, Oklahoma isn't exactly jungle country, and I knew of no other place in the area with cover enough to hide two vehicles.

After parking, I left Martha to babysit the sleeping prisoner, and slipped up on the ridge with my binoculars. There was time for some apprehension before I reached the crest. I could have blown the job—the Carl-phase of it, anyway—by leaving the house unwatched. If my vengeful colleague was working fast, he could have set up a rendezvous already, and the sheriff could be heading for it right now. If so, there'd be no way in the world for me to catch up, not knowing where he was going.

However, Rullington's official car was still parked in the yard, along with the shiny new Volkswagen and Cadillac. There was also a blue pickup truck, presumably the one belonging to the cigarette-weary sentry Martha had described. In addition, there was a second official vehicle complete with buggy-whip and cherry-top. Two men lounged on the shadowy front porch of the house. I caught a glimpse of at least one wandering around back, near the barn. The lights were on in the house, behind drawn windowshades.

As I watched through my big old seven-by-fifty night glasses, liberated on another continent in another war—if what I was currently engaged in qualified as a war—the sheriff came out of the house with two men, both with big hats, revolvers, and badges. He accompanied them to the second cop-type car, held them for some last-minute instructions, and sent them away. I had a good look at him in the dusk through the powerful lenses, as he stood there alone for a moment, bareheaded: a chunky, balding man with things on his mind. Then he turned and disappeared into the house after speaking briefly to the two men on the porch.

Anyway, he was still there. Well, I hadn't really expected Carl to get on the phone so quickly. He'd want to let them worry a while. He'd want to let them check out all the unlikely angles: that the boy had picked this day to run away from home, or had become the victim of a hit-run driver or a homosexual child molester, or had tried to crawl through a drainpipe after a rabbit and got stuck halfway. He'd want to let them use their imaginations, dreaming up the very worst that could have happened, so that the phone call would actually come as a relief.

I made a little scouting expedition off to the east about

half a mile along the ridge, and found a better vantage point—better in that it was closer to the road. From it, I couldn't get a good view of the house and yard any longer, but I could still spot anybody driving into the place or out of it; and if a car emerged and turned my way, I'd have a little warning before it reached me.

If it went the other way, I'd lose it from sight almost immediately, but in that direction was Fort Adams. I had a hunch Carl would want to keep things out in the open. From the Rullington house, the country opened up much faster to the east than to the west. It was, I figured, considerably better than a fifty-fifty chance that when the sheriff came, he'd come my way.

I didn't like leaving my post, now that I'd found it, but there were a few more things to be done, and I slipped out of the brush and hurried back to the cars. Martha was nervous and irritable when I got there, demanding to know what had kept me so long, and insisting that I examine the old man to make sure he was really all right. His breathing, she said, sounded kind of funny. It sounded to me just like the breathing of an old man under sedation, and I said so, but she wasn't reassured. She obviously suspected me of having something sinister and ruthless in mind, and of course she was perfectly right, but her attitude helped me to the decision I'd been trying to arrive at ever since I'd seen how the situation was shaping up.

"Goodbye, Borden," I said.

Her head came up sharply. "What?"

"So long," I said. "It's a one-man operation from here.

Take the Chevy, drive it back to Amarillo, and turn it in at the rental agency. Wait for me at the motel where we left the station wagon and boat. If I'm not there by checkout time tomorrow, you're on your own, but if I were you I'd try to make it to Florida and get in touch with that gent who was supposed to put me in touch with your dad. Priest, Congressman Henry Priest, Robalo Island, remember? Here are the keys to the wagon, and to the boat in case you need it."

She took the keys reluctantly. "But I don't understand. What are you going to do? Can't I help?"

She sounded reasonably sincere and naturally I'd considered using her. It was still a tempting idea. Attractive as she was, she'd make a good decoy. Even a dedicated officer of the law with grave personal problems would stop for her, if I set it up right. However, with her built-in prejudices and inhibitions, I didn't think there was a chance she could pull it off successfully: flagging down Rullington's car, say, and holding his attention while I got the drop on him.

"Help?" I said scornfully. "How the hell could you help? We have very little use for gutless wonders in this business, Borden... No, let me get something out of my bag, please, before you rush off mad."

A minute or two later, I watched the tail lights of the rented car disappear down the little back road at a reckless rate of speed. I hoped she'd slow down a bit before she cracked up or got herself arrested; otherwise, the longer she stayed angry the better I liked it. She wasn't as likely to think up bright, perverse ways of interfering as long as she was mad.

I looked down at the object in my hand and stuck it into my pocket as I headed back up the ridge. We don't usually pack badges or ID cards, but there are times when some kind of official documentation can be useful. For those rare emergencies, Mac had supplied us with some very impressive leather-cased identification folders as classy as anything carried by the FBI or Treasury boys. There was a special compartment in my suitcase in which I kept mine hidden, just in case somebody came snooping who wasn't supposed to know I was respectable.

When I got back up on top, I checked first to make sure nothing had changed at the farm. Nothing had. In that respect, at least, luck was still running strongly my way. Since Carl had been nice enough to give me all the time I needed to get set, I didn't feel entitled to resent the lengthy wait that followed. Anyway, the night was warm and pleasant, there were no biting bugs to harass me, and I could use the interval trying to think my way into his mind.

Crouching in my brushy hideout, handy to the road, I decided that he would, of course, demand money. You don't ask a man to drive out to meet his death, not right out like that, not even for his child's sake. You give him some hope to cling to. You tell him, sure, you killed a couple of cops to show you meant business, but you're through with that. Now you want reparations, ten thousand dollars, say, delivered personally, safety guaranteed if all instructions are followed to the letter.

Rullington, unless he was a fool, wouldn't believe it. As an experienced police officer, he'd know deep down that the killer stalking him wasn't after money. However, the businesslike demand for ransom would give him something reasonable to tell his wife, and himself. It's hard to march out to be a suicidal hero in cold blood, if only because it makes you feel a little like a damn fool. I suppose I should have sympathized with the poor man whose son was in danger, and the poor woman, too, sweating it out in that shabby clapboard house with the shiny new cars in the yard, but sympathy is an emotion you learn to control in this business, right along with your likes and dislikes…

It was just another set of headlights at first, one pair of the dozen or so that had come into sight from the direction of town and passed below me—only these lights didn't pass. I saw them dip as the driver put on the brakes approaching the Rullington driveway. They came to a complete halt, which puzzled me briefly; then another pair of headlights emerged from the sheriff's place and turned away towards town.

Through the night glasses, I recognized the blue pickup truck. It seemed to be full of men. There were at least three crowded together on the cab's single seat, and there could have been four. I wondered where the sheriff was sending them all; and then I realized that he'd received his instructions at last: *Step Number One, get rid of all guards and deputies as a gesture of good faith.*

With the entrance clear, the strange car swung into the

driveway, a big, dark, dignified sedan such as a banker might drive. *Step Number Two, obtain the money in used bills of small denomination.* The question now was, would there be a second call to check that the money had actually arrived, or would the sheriff already have his orders for *Step Number Three, proceed unarmed and alone to...*

He came so fast that he almost got by me. If his car had been facing out instead of in I'd never have made it. As it was, I started scrambling down the slope the instant I saw the white car with the flasher on the roof lurch out of the driveway in reverse. By the time he'd got it going in the right direction—towards me, as I'd gambled—and covered the stretch of highway between us, I'd made it down the hill, under the fence, and over the ditch. I jumped out into the glare of the headlights, first waving my arms to flag him down, then jumping back to safety as, brakes locked, he screeched to a halt where I'd been standing. The near window was open, and I could hear him swear.

"Who the hell..."

I shoved my classy ID folder at him through the window. "Federal Government," I said. It didn't mean much, but I hoped it sounded important.

He pushed the leather case away. "To hell with you!" he snapped. "I'm busy! Come to the office in the morning, G-man." Then, starting to drive off, he had an afterthought as I'd hoped he would, and hit the brakes once more. "Well, maybe... Okay, get in but make it fast!"

17

Neither of us spoke for a minute or two. As I caught my breath, I was glad I'd decided to use the direct approach instead of playing devious games with beautiful female decoys. Fast as it had happened, the girl would have loused it up for certain; besides, this way I got to talk to him more or less as one public servant to another.

I noted that he had his big hat on once more, but that his revolver and cartridge belt were missing. As far as I could make out in the dark, even the car had been disarmed. There were brackets that might have held a rifle and a riot gun, but they were empty.

"What's your name, Mr. Federal Government?"

His voice carried less of a cornpone accent than I'd expected of an Oklahoma lawman. It reminded me that it's always a mistake to classify people into types before you know something about them.

I said, "Well, it isn't Janssen, if that's what you're thinking."

That could be a mistake, giving him information he didn't have, but I was gambling that he'd done his homework and already determined the names of his most probable suspects. Apparently he had. Carl's name seemed to cause him no surprise. He just laughed shortly.

"It did cross my mind just now that the murdering bastard could have told me to meet him in Budville just to see if I was playing it straight, while all the time he was planning to pick me up right across the road where I wouldn't be expecting him."

"Budville," I said, keeping the elation out of my voice. My gamble had paid off handsomely. The information I'd ventured had brought back information I needed, for which I would have paid much more. "Budville? Where's that?"

He looked as if he regretted letting the name slip. Then he shrugged. "Hell, it's on any road map," he said. "Thirty miles east. Just a store and a gas pump by the side of the road. And I didn't say where in Budville, G-man."

"By your description, there's not much choice."

"There's a way it's to be done. No other way will work, the voice said on the phone."

"Sure."

"And if your name isn't Janssen, you're no use to me. If you know so much, you know he's got my boy, Ricky. There isn't a damn thing you can do to help and I don't want you even trying."

"Ricky?" I said. "Eric?"

"That's right. Why?"

"Never mind," I said. I was neither superstitious nor

sentimental, and the fact that the missing boy's name was the same as my code name had nothing to do with anything, I told myself. "Talking about names, how did you learn Janssen's?" I asked.

"There were three obvious candidates. Two could be checked on by their local authorities. They'd been right where they were supposed to be, all the time a couple of good men were dying with wires around their necks. The third was a mysterious Washington character with a government job that seemed to involve a lot of traveling. Nobody could find out just what it was. They hit an official security wall when they tried. This man was missing. Anders Janssen." Rullington glanced my way. "One of yours?"

I nodded. "One of ours. And we want him back."

"To hell with you, Mister. He's a murderer, a kidnaper, and probably a maniac. The law has first crack at him now."

I said, "You're heading out to make a deal with this murderer and maniac, aren't you?"

"He didn't leave me much choice. If I didn't come, he said, fingers and toes and ears and... and things would start arriving in the mail. But once I get Ricky back... He gripped his steering wheel hard. "If I ever get my hands on that sadistic sonofabitch..."

I laughed. He turned to look at me, startled and angry. I said, in a superior and condescending way, "Cut out the melodrama, Sheriff. Settle down. As far as Janssen is concerned, we're not really too much concerned about his ultimate fate—agents are expendable—but we don't want you to make a public spectacle of him. We can't afford that."

He drew a long, ragged breath. "If the bastard is yours, you ought to keep him in a cage."

"Shit," I said. "Don't tell us what we ought or oughtn't, or we'll just tell you that you oughtn't to go around shooting people's kids, Sheriff. Sometimes it makes them real mad."

He glanced at me once more and started to speak hotly but checked himself. That told me something. He wasn't really happy about that campus affair, professionally speaking, which meant that, as an undercover big shot from Washington, I could lean on him a bit and get away with it.

After a pause, he said without expression, "The Janssen girl was an accident."

"Sure," I said. "An accident. You and your boys fired a couple of dozen rounds at a mob less than fifty yards away, if the newspaper reports are correct. Out of that whole barrage, you got one solid bulls-eye on a legitimate target—the Dubuque kid with a brick in his hand—you got a few scratch hits, and you sent so many wild bullets flying around that you killed two innocent bystanders seventy-five and a hundred yards behind the line of scrimmage. Now, really, Sheriff, what the hell kind of marksmanship do you call that? That's not an accident, that's just plain incompetence!" I grimaced. "Janssen's a pro. He knows that things happen and people get killed. What he can't face, what's sent him off his rocker a little, is having his daughter shot that way, quite unnecessarily, by a bunch of panicky uniformed jerks who were then patted on the back by a local jury instead of having their guns and badges taken away from them and shoved up their stupid incompetent asses."

He was close to exploding, but he still managed to control himself. He said sharply, "I suppose it would have been better if we'd got two dozen dead college kids to go with those two dozen bullets!"

I sighed. "If that's supposed to be sarcasm, Sheriff, you're not reading me at all. I'm trying to give you the professional viewpoint, Janssen's viewpoint, the viewpoint of a man who knows guns. Sure it would have been better."

"You and your friend have a damn funny way of looking at things!"

I said patiently, "If you'd had a dead body to show for every bullet fired, it would have proved, at least, that you and your people knew what you were doing, whether or not it was the right thing to do. It would have demonstrated that you didn't shoot until you knew where your shots were going; that you weren't all just banging way blindly without knowing or caring whom you might kill. And if you'd been picking your targets the way you should, Emily Janssen wouldn't have died, or the Hollingshead boy, either." I shook my head. "Well, if your boy dies tonight, you'll have one consolation, Rullington. You'll have the satisfaction of knowing he was killed because somebody had a reason for wanting him dead, not just because some trigger-happy cop or deputy couldn't be bothered to aim his pistol properly."

There was a little silence. The car kept rolling along the dark road at a reasonable speed.

"You push hard, Mister," the sheriff murmured at last.

"You started it," I said. "You wanted us to keep our wild animals in cages. My point is, you haven't done so well with yours. Now, shall we stop making faces at each other and see what we can do to get this particular maneater back into the zoo? How much did he ask for?"

There was another silence; then the answer came reluctantly. "Fifty grand." I didn't say anything. Rullington felt obliged to explain the size of the figure: "I sold off a big piece of my land last year. Janssen must have learned about it."

I said, "He doesn't give a damn about your, money. One grand or a hundred, it means the same to him: nothing. You know that."

The chunky man's shoulders moved almost imperceptibly under the khaki shirt. When he spoke, there was resignation in his voice. "What the hell can I do but play along with the gag?"

"Janssen will kill you," I said. "That's all he wants from you, your life."

"It's been tried before."

"If you've got a derringer up your sleeve or a knife under your shirt collar, forget it. Try to remember that you're dealing with a pro, not some lad who went joyriding in a stolen car." He said nothing, and gave nothing away.

He was something of a pro himself. I said, "Suppose I could save you your money, your life, and your son's life; and give you an answer to your cop-killings…"

He threw me a sharp glance. "I thought you wanted Janssen for yourself."

"I didn't say I'd give you the *right* answer, Sheriff."

There was another pause. I hoped I'd given it the right buildup: the arrogant, ruthless, unscrupulous government emissary prepared to stop at nothing to protect the reputation of his agency. Come to think of it, that wasn't so far offbase.

Sheriff Rullington said, in a faintly wondering voice, "So you're going to frame some poor bastard—"

"This poor bastard I found on the ridge overlooking your house, with a loaded .300 Savage beside him. He's got motive and opportunity, what more do you want? His name's Hollingshead."

I didn't owe the old man anything. The fact that I'd kind of liked him meant nothing at all. I hadn't promised the colorful old character anything, not a thing.

"You're a liar," said Rullington.

I drew a long breath. I wanted to hit him. Well, I wanted to hit somebody, and the trouble was, the only really logical target was me.

"Oink, oink," I said.

Strangely, after all the heavy stuff I'd fired at him without effect, this childishness got to him. The car bucked as he hit the brakes hard.

"Now, listen, you federal sonofabitch—"

I grinned. "You cops!" I said. "You can call anybody anything you want, but if somebody badmouths you it's a criminal offense. What the hell do you expect when you call a man a liar, kisses and flowers?"

After a moment, the car picked up speed once more. "Nevertheless, you're lying, Mister," Rullington said at last in more reasonable tones. "Or mistaken. I told you, I checked on all of them. Arnold Hollingshead works at a filling station in Sedgeville, Kentucky. He hasn't missed a day in the last three weeks. He's still there. My office would have been notified if he'd disappeared."

"Arnold. That must be the papa of the boy who got shot," I said. "Good enough as far as it goes, but you didn't go far enough, Sheriff. You didn't check on Grandpa, an old feuding type from the hills. Harvey Bascomb Hollingshead, 72, of Bascomb, Kentucky."

That shocked him more than anything I'd said. I saw his jaw tighten as if at a blow. "Jesus!" he breathed. "Christ, has the whole world gone crazy? Does every one of the goddamn brats have homicidal relatives? I suppose that brick-throwing Dubuque punk's got an uncle or a cousin sneaking around with a blowgun or tommyhawk or other crazy weapon!" He shook his head angrily. "If they'd just bring their kids up right, to respect law and order—"

"You tell them, Sheriff," I said. "You tell them. I don't know about Dubuque, but I do have Hollingshead. He'll make you a fine scapegoat. And once he's in jail, I guarantee, the mad strangler of Fort Adams will never strike again. You'll be a hero."

"Where are you holding the old coot?" When I grinned and didn't speak, Rullington said, "Damn it, I'm the law around here, Mister! I don't care how many federal badges you have, you can't come into my county and…" He was just making noise and he knew it. His voice trailed off. Presently he said, "Come to think of it, I didn't get a real good look at that badge. And you didn't tell me what your name was, just what it wasn't."

I passed him the fancy ID case. He switched on the dome light and examined it, slowing the car. Then he gave it back and switched off the light.

"Matthew L. Helm," he said. "What does the 'L' stand for? Never mind. I've seen better-looking credentials passed out free with breakfast cereal."

He could have been right about that. I said, "You're wasting time, Sheriff. You said thirty miles and we've come nineteen. Do you want the deal or don't you? If you do, you'd better get on your squawker and send somebody where I tell you—only first I want your word that you're going to cooperate."

He hesitated. "How are you going to pull it? How do you figure on catching Janssen without risking Ricky's life?"

I said, "Either you let me do it my way or you do it yours, which will certainly get you killed, and maybe your boy as well."

"Why should I trust you?"

"Because I want Janssen even worse than you do, and without any more dead bodies cluttering up his back trail."

He frowned thoughtfully. After a moment, he shrugged

his shoulders and reached for the microphone. "Okay, it's a deal. Where do I send them?" When I told him, he made a face as if it was a joke on him that Hollingshead was hidden so close to his house, and maybe it was, but he got the message through to the other car, and hung up the mike. "Okay, now what…" His voice died. He was watching the rear view mirror.

"What's the matter?"

"We're being tailed. If it's Janssen, he's seen us together and we're in trouble. Ricky's in trouble."

"What kind of a car?"

"I can't… Wait a minute." We swung through a series of curves, and he said, "I can't make out for sure in the dark, but it looks like a white Chevy sedan with a woman driver."

I tried not to react, and I think I was successful, but I thought: *The stupid, perverse, interfering little bitch…*

"It's all right," I said easily. "She's one of ours. You didn't think I was handling this all by myself, did you?"

"Well, you'd better get rid of her before Janssen spots her. He said I was to come alone."

"Sure," I said. "Pull up and I'll go back and give her some instructions. Where the hell did those Detroit geniuses hide the door handle on this one?"

He made an impatient sound, and reached over to work the camouflaged handle that looked like an ashtray. The needle slipped through his khaki sleeve and into his forearm. I pushed the plunger home.

18

As I dragged the stocky, unconscious body from under the wheel and propped it up more or less securely in the front passenger seat, headlights pulled up behind us, a car door opened, and footsteps hurried towards me. I didn't bother to turn my head. I knew who it was even before I heard the indignant feminine gasp.

"You promised!" Martha Borden's voice said accusingly. "You gave me your word you'd do your best to save his life!"

I said, "He's alive. Put a stethoscope on him if you like. You'll find his heart beating like a metronome." I got him where I wanted him and closed the door, straightening up outside the car and turning to look at her. "You're a funny girl, Borden," I said. "You weep for the whole human race, but you seem to be just yearning to spend the rest of your days with the death of a ten-year-old boy on your conscience."

"What do you mean?"

"Carl has undoubtedly sworn to wipe his hostage off

the face of the earth if his instructions aren't followed," I said, "meaning, among other things, if the sheriff doesn't proceed to, and arrive at, the rendezvous alone."

"Then what are *you* doing—"

"I don't count," I said. "He knows me. He knows I don't take orders from hick sheriffs. If he sees me, he'll know it's no plan of Rullington's. He'll know I'm there strictly on my own. He may talk to me or he may just shoot me, but he won't take it out on the kid because what would be the point? What happens to Ricky Rullington means very little to me; he's not my kid; and I don't weep for the whole human race."

"You don't have to tell me, that!" she said sharply.

"I don't have to tell Carl that, either," I said. "I'm just pointing out the reasons I can move in without endangering the boy's life. But if strange cars are lurking in the shadows with strange people in them—he doesn't know you—he'll think Rullington is pulling a fast one. He'll use his wire noose on sonny, figuring he can't get at daddy safely, and he'll fade out and never set foot in Oklahoma again."

Martha shivered. Then she looked up sharply. "How do you always know exactly what Carl is going to do and feel?"

I said, "It's simple. I just figure out what I'd do and feel in his place, that's all."

She licked her lips. "But that makes you as crazy as he is!"

"Let's hope so," I said. "If I'm far off, some people are going to die tonight, maybe even us." I regarded her bleakly in the glare of the Chevy's headlights. "I can't trust you, can I? Nothing I say gets through. You still think this is amateur night on the prairie, don't you?"

She said stiffly, "The trouble is, Mr. Helm, that I can't trust you! You've used me to get you here. I'm involved. I rented the car. I did the driving. I've got to see that I haven't been made accessory to a murder, don't I?"

I said, "Of course, I've got just about one full dose left for my little needle. I could put you to sleep." I grinned as she took a step backwards. "Relax," I said. "I can't leave you here by the side of the road; I don't know who might find you. And I haven't got time to waste hiding you properly, so... okay."

"Okay, what?"

"We'll play it straight, and I mean *straight*. Don't try to be clever. Don't even think. Just get back in that heap and come along with me, but this time make no effort to be invisible. In fact, I want you riding my rear bumper all the way. Don't get more than a couple of car-lengths back under any circumstances. Headlights on at all times. When I stop, pull up alongside as if you had an engraved invitation to the party. Everything straightforward and out in the open, nothing sneaky or devious. Do you read me, I hope?"

"I... I don't understand, Matt. How are you going to catch him like that?"

"You don't catch a guy like Carl, doll. You don't even try, unless you like to see a lot of blood spilled in a hurry, maybe even your own. You either kill him, if you can, or you..."

"Or you what?"

"Or you let him catch you. Let's go."

Budville was a larger town than the sheriff had indicated by about fifty percent. There were not only the filling station and the two-story general store—both dark at this hour—but there was also a big barn or shed off the road a little ways, a quarter-mile to the east. There was a gate in the barbed wire fence open. Whether or not it was the place specified for the rendezvous, it was the only place I could see that was suitable for the act I had to put on, so I turned in.

The sheriff had indicated that the approach had to be made in a certain manner, but I didn't worry about that. The whole performance was going to come off a little differently from the way Carl had planned it. I was counting on the fact that he wasn't an amateur who'd go off half-cocked. Of course, there was always the possibility that he'd really flipped his wig brooding about his dead daughter, which could make things awkward. He'd never been a particularly well-balanced character— as if any of us are in this business.

I drove the cop car, which worked like any other car, along the rutted track to the barn which was decorated with a tremendous faded advertisement for some kind of chewing tobacco. The other car followed me closely. I swung around behind the big building and parked among the weeds, headlights aimed at the weathered door. Martha pulled up beside me according to instructions. She got out, and I heard her draw an annoyed breath.

"Damn!"

"What's the matter?"

"I just ruined a perfectly good pair of pantyhose in these damned weeds."

"Jeez," I said, "that's terrible! A whole two dollars and ninety-nine cents or whatever it is, shot plumb to hell! Maybe we'd better just go home and let the boy die rather than make such dreadful sacrifices."

"You're not very funny," she said stiffly. "Where do you suppose he is?"

"Carl? Don't worry about Carl. He's around. Give me a hand here." I was dragging Rullington out of his car. "Grab the feet," I said as Martha came up.

"Where…"

"Over against the barn door there, right in the limelight, so Carl can see what kind of a present we've brought him… That's fine. Let him down easy, and watch out for that cow turd unless you like wiping it off your shoes."

She sidestepped and glared at me accusingly. "You're going to let Carl have him! But you promised—"

"Sweetie," I said wearily, "I don't know why I bother to talk to you. You simply never listen. Sure I'm going to let Carl have him. I'm going to let Carl have all of us, just like I said… What's that? No, over there by the cars!"

She posed prettily, staring in the direction I'd indicated, and I clipped her neatly on the chin. It's not a procedure I recommend, except for the movies. It can lead to broken jaws and teeth, not to mention busted knuckles for the one who does the clipping. In this case, however, it worked fine. I didn't hurt my hand too much, and she wasn't seriously damaged, either, I determined after catching her and easing her down against the door beside the unconscious sheriff.

Then I pulled her dress down modestly, shook my head over the run in her stocking, and straightened up in the glare of the two sets of headlights. Deliberately, I took out my .38 Special, held it up, and placed it carefully on the sheriff's chest. I took out the folding knife I carry—Carl would remember that—displayed it the same way to whomever was lurking in the outside darkness, and laid it beside the gun. I sat down against the barn door on the far side of Martha, safely distant from the sheriff and the weapons, facing the painfully brilliant lights with my hands in plain sight on my knees. I waited. After a while he came.

"Can you hear me, Eric?" The origin of the whisper was the corner of the barn to my right.

"I hear you, Carl," I said.

"Why shouldn't I shoot you now? I warned Mac, when I resigned, what would happen if he sent anybody after me."

"No, you didn't."

"Listen, I told him plainly—"

"You told somebody plainly," I said. "You didn't tell Mac. You talked to a mimic, a fink working for a guy named Leonard, who's taken over the whole damned undercover works for sinister reasons still to be determined. The country's going to hell, the outfit you've spent most of your working life with is being blasted out of existence, the head man is in hiding if he isn't dead, and Super

Secret Agent Carl is sneaking around Oklahoma with a silly wire noose playing The Mad Avenger! Nuts! Why don't you grow up and be a big boy for a change instead of moping around crying because somebody broke your pretty dolly."

There was a long, tight silence. "You take some awful, chances, Eric."

"I have to deal with some awful people."

"Do you really think I'm going to believe that the guy I talked with wasn't Mac?"

"Did he say for you to 'contact' him if you changed your mind? Did he tell you things were 'presently' in a very critical state and he wished you'd reconsider? Hell, did you listen to him at all, or did you just listen to the bleeding of your lousy broken heart?"

"Damn you, Eric—"

"I've been telling people you're a pro," I sneered. "You're no goddamn pro, Carl. You're just a mushy sentimental slob who'll let your job and your country go to the dogs—well, to a bitch named Love—while you sacrifice a bunch of poor dumb country cops to the memory of your sainted offspring. Tell me just how many dead men do you think Emily would **want** you to pile on her grave?"

There was another long silence. "Love?" he said. It was a weight lifting, a shadow lightening. I knew I had him. "Love? Ellen Love, the she-senator from Wyoming? What's she got to do with—"

"What the hell do you care?" I was being real offensive

tonight, to just about everybody. Well, it was working, wasn't it? I said harshly: "What do you care? You're Retribution, Inc. You're Vengeance, Ltd. You're the sword of destruction, the noose of Nemesis. Come on, come on. Here's victim number three, all set up and waiting for you. Break out your goddamned piano wire and do your stuff. I hear you're pretty good. You almost yanked one guy's head clean off. Give us a demonstration, Carl. I always wanted to see a top garotte-man in action..."

Martha Borden stirred beside me and started to speak. I grabbed her wrist and dug my fingernails into the flesh to keep her quiet. I heard him coming. His body blocked the glare of the lights. There was something in his hands. He walked past us and stood over the unconscious form of Rullington.

"What did you give him?"

"You know what I gave him," I said. "He'll be out for four hours—well, say three and a half, now. You've got nothing to worry about. You've got all the time in the world."

"Shut up!"

There was still another long silence. I heard a funny little choked sound like a gasp or a sob, and a whispering metallic noise. He'd dropped the garotte into the lap of the seated sheriff, among the other weapons.

He stood there a moment longer, looking down. Then he turned without a word and strode away. Martha started to move, but I clamped down on her wrist once more, and we sat there waiting. He came back, carrying something bulky and, from the way he walked, fairly heavy. It was

a child, tied and gagged. He set it down beside its father,
studied the picture they made together and leaned down
and removed the gag.

"Okay, boy?"

"I… I think so."

"You'll have a bit of a wait. Your daddy's asleep.
When he wakes up, he'll turn you loose and you can both
go home. Don't try to get free by yourself. You can't do
it, and you'll just lose a lot of skin… Eric."

"Right here."

"Grab your toys if you want them. Let's go somewhere
and talk."

19

Carl joined us at the motel back in Amarillo, Texas, after stalling long enough on the road somewhere to start me worrying that, perhaps, he'd changed his mind about coming at all. That was undoubtedly just what he'd intended.

He arrived at last, however, bland and unapologetic, and we had a briefing session that lasted well past dawn. By that time, the girl was curled up asleep on the bed nearest the wall, and the motel room was saturated with Carl's cigar smoke and littered with his discarded beer bottles—he'd cleaned up the supply of Carta Blanca I brought from Mexico in the boat's ice chest. That didn't worry me. I knew that his capacity for beer was practically limitless, which was more than I could say for my own.

"Anything else you need to know?" I asked as we broke it up at last and moved towards the door.

"Are you kidding? There's everything else I need to know. Only you can't tell me." He grimaced, looked down at the soggy stump of his latest stogie, and mashed it out in the ashtray on the little table by the door. "But I've got the names memorized, both lists, and the date. And the fact that it's supposed to look nice and accidental. Did you notice something about those lists, Eric?"

I threw a glance over my shoulder at the sleeping girl, in a supposedly meaningful way, and said, "Stop blocking the doorway and let me get some fresh air, will you?" I moved past him, out of the air-conditioning into the warm new daylight. As he joined me, pulling the door closed behind him, I said softly, "I'm paid to notice things about lists and so are you. But we're not paid to talk about what we notice in front of Tom, Dick, Harry, or Martha. If you know what I mean."

"She's sound asleep. Anyway, I thought you said she was his daughter." Carl studied me narrowly. "Maybe there is something else I ought to know, after all."

I regarded him for a moment, a tall man, a big man, in jeans and a thin, gaudy sports shirt that was unbuttoned far enough to display a fairly hairy chest. It's getting so the men are going in for these pectoral peepshows just like the women—unisex, I suppose. He was a couple of inches short of my own height of six-four, but constructed along considerably huskier lines. He had a long, square-chinned face that showed a good growth of blond stubble in the early-morning light. His hair was yellow and wavy, and his eyes were so blue it almost hurt to look at them—so intensely blue they seemed unnatural. Maybe they were.

I moved my shoulders casually. "Security clearance isn't hereditary, you know," I said. "Even Mac is quite aware of that. He's passed the word that all numerical information transmitted through the girl should be factored minus twice, just in case. Code double negative. Got it?"

The blue eyes watched me steadily. "Got it. Throw away two. Does Lorna know?"

Normally, I wouldn't have told him about a part of the operation that was somebody else's responsibility, but I've seen too many complicated jobs loused up because some security-happy would-be leader of men didn't trust his subordinates with facts that later turned out to be vital. I once killed a woman because nobody'd trusted me enough to tell me she was on my side, even though I'd asked. As it turned out, she'd been on both sides, but that didn't make me feel any better at the time.

Anyway, it seemed to me that under these special circumstances, everybody who was stuck with this last-ditch assignment was entitled to just about all the facts I had, which didn't really overburden them with information.

"Lorna knows," I said, and went on lying a little, "it's not that Mac doesn't trust his kid, or that I don't. It's just that, well, she *isn't* cleared and we can't take chances. As for what you noticed about those lists of names, tell me your idea and I'll tell you if it agrees with mine."

He nodded. "Five pairs of names in my bunch." he said. "Five cities. New Orleans, where I was supposed to be. Chicago. Bangor, Maine. Knoxville, Tennessee. Miami. And that's all, east of the Big Miss. Funny, isn't it?"

"It seemed that way to me," I said. "Not one name from Boston, New York, Philadelphia, or Baltimore, where you'd expect a kind of concentration."

"And not one solitary name from Washington, D.C., where you'd expect business to be really booming. Well, I suppose if it were our business, we'd have been told. The one good thing about him is, he generally knows what he's doing. At least I try to cling to that thought. Well, I'd better be on my way."

"Two questions first," I said. "Satisfy my curiosity. I gave him to you. Rullington. Why didn't you take him?"

The unnaturally blue eyes hit me with a cold blue gaze. "You know damned well why I didn't—when you gave him to me unconscious, with hours to go before he came around. Any pigs I kill, I want them to know it. And you were counting on it, don't pretend you weren't. Next question."

"Why the wire?"

He grinned abruptly, showing big, white, even teeth. "Hell, man, I *like* guns. I wouldn't want to give them a bad name by shooting some slimy cops with them, when there are so many other interesting weapons around." His grin faded as abruptly as it had come. "Those big-bellied bastards! They dish out gallons of self-serving propaganda about how the world is going to hell because more and more people are killing more and more crummy policemen. Doesn't it ever occur to them that it just might be because more and more crummy, policemen are killing more and more people? Ah, hell!

You shouldn't have got me started on that. Do you want to know something funny, Eric? I used to think the police were on our side. That's what I tried to teach my kid, anyway, after her mother died and I had to make like both parents. So the cops she'd been taught to trust went and shot her in the back while she was trying to get to safety inside the girls' dormitory!"

"It was an accident, Carl!" I said. It sounded just as ineffectual as when Rullington had said it to me.

"Accident, hell!" he snorted. "Cops aren't supposed to have accidents like that! If there's a choice between risking the life of an innocent citizen and getting killed, a cop is supposed to stand right there and die, goddamn it! Hell, you and I, Eric, we've both had the cyanide capsule between our back teeth, ready to take a bite of death just to save our native land a little embarrassment. Show me the place in the Constitution that says we're supposed to give up our lives for our jobs and our country but a lousy policeman is supposed to live forever!"

As he said, I shouldn't have started him on that. I was getting pretty tired of temperamental agents: Lorna with her morbid philosophy, and Carl with his vengeful prejudice. I studied the big blond man grimly, hoping that no unfortunate highway patrolman had occasion to stop him for speeding during the next day or two. He was a bomb set to go off at the sight of a badge.

"Eric," he said.

"Yes?"

The brilliant blue eyes stared at me hard out of the

unshaved face. "You were pretty rough back there. You know that."

"Hell, I was sticking my neck way out, *amigo*. I had to jolt you before you lopped it off."

"You jolted me," he said coldly. "Maybe I'll forget it, and then again, maybe I won't."

The whole damned outfit was crawling with prima donnas, male and female, each one considering himself or herself the toughest, smartest thing to inhabit the continent since the sabertooth tiger became extinct. There was only one way to handle that.

"Sure," I said. "Any time we've got nothing better to do, I'll be happy to discuss it with you again."

His grin flashed on once more, like a nervous neon sign. "That's safe enough to say. When does he give us that much time? Tell me something: why do we do it for him? I quit, even if I quit to the wrong man. Why don't I just tell you to tell him to go to hell?" He didn't wait for a reply, which was just as well since I didn't have any. He glanced towards the motel room. "Tell the Borden kid goodbye for me. I won't wake her. Ask her to give my regards to her parent, when she rejoins him wherever it is you're taking her." It was the one thing I'd held out on him, as on Lorna; it was a responsibility they didn't need. Carl grimaced. "That cold-blooded human spider spinning his lousy webs of intrigue!" he said. "And you're pretty damned spidery yourself, come to think of it. *Auf wiedersehen*, Eric. Maybe."

I didn't like that. I didn't like anything about him, the

way he was. It was like dealing with nitroglycerine, ready to explode at a touch. But I particularly didn't like that qualified *auf wiedersehen*—which means, in case you're not up on your German, 'until we see each other again.' If he wasn't really expecting to see me again, I hoped he'd get his job done before he went and got himself killed in some berserk damn fool way.

I watched him drive off. Then I turned, and went back into the room, woke up Martha, and told her she could finish sleeping in the station wagon. By nightfall, we were well into Louisiana, on our way to Florida, and the car radio had informed us that the vicious strangler of Fort Adams, Oklahoma, an elderly gent named Harvey Hollingshead, captured by diligent police work on the part of the local sheriff's office, had wound up the case very neatly by dying of a heart attack in his cell after confessing to his crimes.

20

They have a funny law in Texas. Apparently they don't like to see all vehicles on the highway rolling along safely at the same speed. I guess it's dull around those parts with the Kiowas and Comanches no longer on the warpath, so they try to make life a bit more interesting by slowing down the cars with trailers so the cars without can get a good crack at them. At least that was my theory until I got into Louisiana and found the same crazy speed restrictions in force, only worse.

What with the ridiculous, discriminatory speed limits and the atrocious, crowded roads—I guess we Southwestern desert dwellers get kind of spoiled by our lonely, high-speed highways—I found myself straining hard to make time, which is no way to drive. There wasn't all that need for haste, anyway. It was only the eleventh of the month. I wasn't due in Florida for several days yet.

I pulled into the motel in Shreveport, therefore, a little after dark. Martha remained in the car while I checked us in as Mr. and Mrs. once more. Again, I found a spot at the rear of the parking area where I could leave the long rig without unhitching. I grabbed the luggage and headed for the room assigned to us—on the ground floor, this time—aware of her following along in silence. I didn't waste any effort on conversation, or attempts at conversation. I mean, I was truly and legally married once, and I know when I'm in the doghouse. I'd been there ever since we'd heard the radio report informing us of old Mr. Hollingshead's fate.

Inside the room, which looked like any two-bed motel unit, I placed one suitcase on the luggage rack at the foot of each bed, opened mine, got out the whiskey, poured myself a drink, and went into the bathroom to dilute it. Martha was still standing just inside the door when I came out. She regarded me coldly.

"Yes," she said, "I should think you would need some alcohol about now! Quite a bit, in fact. How much does it take, Mr. Helm?"

I grinned at her. "To drown my conscience, you mean? Sweetheart, you flatter me. The feeble little thing expired years ago."

"You left him there unconscious for the police to find! That poor old man!"

I sighed. "Won't you even *try* to be consistent, Borden? Just make a slight effort, please, for my sake. That poor old man was stalking a human being with a rifle, remember? As far as I'm concerned, it's nothing against him, but you're supposed to disapprove of that kind of behavior. Well, if that's your attitude, for Christ's sake stick to it! Don't act as if his dying has suddenly made him a martyred saint." She didn't speak. I hesitated, but there wasn't any sense in pussyfooting around. There were enough secrets between us already without my leaving more lying around for us to trip over. I said, "Anyway, you're overestimating Rullington and his deputies. Find, hell! They're not that smart or that thorough. I told them where to look."

Her eyes widened. "You *told* them? But that… that's *sick*!"

"Is it? Was I supposed to let him loose to murder that nice sheriff whose life I'd promised you I'd save? I'm a man of my word, Borden. Why are you raising hell with me for doing what you asked me to? Rullington's alive and safe, isn't he? I never promised you a damn thing about Hollingshead."

She gasped, "If you think you can blame *me* for your—"

"All right, all right, simmer down," I said. "I was kidding a little, maybe. The fact is, I'd like things to settle down around Fort Adams, and people to stop asking questions and making investigations. I don't want Rullington on Carl's trail, maybe lousing up Carl's job. The sheriff's got his life, his money, and his son back, but he's a cop, and he'd never have been satisfied as long as he was stuck with two unsolved cop-killings on his books. I knew that, so I made a deal with him. He gave me Carl, whom I needed, and I gave him an answer he needed. It wasn't quite the right answer, but very few people know that, and he was willing to settle for it, under the circumstances. It got him off the hook, and it got him out of my hair."

"And Mr. Hollingshead went to jail for something he didn't do, and died there, but that doesn't matter!"

I said wearily, "Why don't you wake up, little girl? It's like Lorna said, you've got a thing about death. Nobody's supposed to die, ever, in your pretty little dream world. Well, fine, but in the real world, everybody dies sooner or later. And sometimes somebody's got to do some picking and choosing. It becomes a question of who dies now, and who gets to live a little longer because of it."

"And *you're* the one who decides?" Her voice was sharp with scorn. "Really, Matt, you are sick, with delusions of grandeur. What makes *you* think you have the right to—"

"The fact that my stalking was better than the old man's hearing gave me the right," I said bluntly. "If he'd heard me sneaking up on him, and got the drop on me, the choice would have been his." I drew a long breath. "Just tell me, Borden, what would you have done with the old gent? What would you have had me do? He could stay free and kill, or he could go to jail and die. I didn't know he'd have a fatal attack behind bars, of course, but okay, say I'm responsible. If I'd left him free, he'd probably have managed to shoot Rullington. He was willing to sacrifice his life to do it, and a man like that is hard to stop. So tell me, what would you have done about him, in my place?"

"Well, I certainly wouldn't have betrayed him to—"

"Cut it out!" I said sharply. "Betray means a breach of faith. How could I betray Hollingshead when I didn't owe him anything and hadn't promised him anything?" I grimaced. "And why *wouldn't* you have tipped off the police, for God's sake? You're a good citizen who disapproves of homicide, aren't you? Your duty and your conscience should have sent you racing to warn them about a potential murderer sneaking around with a loaded firearm and a king-sized grudge. Why not?"

She said sulkily, "You're just twisting things around!"

"Before you start slinging around loaded words like betray," I said, "before you start lining me up alongside Judas and Benedict Arnold, why don't you give a little consideration to the victim himself and what he thought about it. It doesn't look very much as if Mr. Hollingshead felt seriously betrayed, does it?"

"What do you mean?" Martha demanded. "How can you tell what the old man felt before he died?"

"Hell, he told us," I said. "You heard the radio report. He said it loud and clear. He deliberately confessed to two murders he hadn't committed. That was his little trick on the cops, and his message to me."

"Don't be silly! They must have given him the third degree—"

"Oh, Jesus Christ!" I said disgustedly.

"What's the matter now?" she demanded.

"Nothing," I said. "Nothing at all, just the way you keep switching the cast of characters to suit your mood.

Now that worthy, abused, law-enforcement officer whose life you were so desperate to save a few hours back turns out to be a sadistic bully who beats confessions out of his prisoners. And that brave and noble old gent for whom you've just been weeping large tears has suddenly become a cowardly, chicken-livered old creep who'll cravenly sign his name to anything after a couple of minutes' interrogation. Hell, they only had him for part of a night, Borden. I don't put a little rough stuff past our sheriff friend, but do you really believe that any bunch of cops, singly or in relays, could have made that tough old rawhide character out of the Kentucky hills confess to anything he didn't want to confess to? Well, okay, anybody can be broken in time, but if Rullington can crack a man like that in just a couple of hours, he's got techniques that Hitler's Gestapo never learned."

Martha shook her head in a baffled way. "Then it doesn't make sense! If they didn't force him to confess, why—"

"I told you why!" I snapped. "You just won't listen. I told you, he was putting one over on them. And he was sending me a message. He was telling me, wherever I was, that the joke was on him and there were no hard feelings. To prove it, he was taking the heat off me by claiming official credit for my two killings—he thought I was Carl, remember—just the way he'd offered to do when we talked earlier. He was heaping coals of fire on my head, so to speak. He was putting me under an obligation. In return, he hoped I'd do a little something for him."

Martha licked her lips. "What… what did he want you to do for him?"

"You know what," I said shortly.

"You mean… you mean you think he expected you to kill the sheriff for him? But that's insane?"

"Nothing insane about it. He thought I was Carl. By confessing, he was just getting the cops out of my way so I could do more easily what he thought I was planning to do anyway. It was his contribution to the cause of revenge. It seems a pity to let it go to waste." I grinned abruptly. "Don't jump down my throat, Borden. I was just kidding, in my crude way. I can't go around shooting officers of the law to oblige a bloodthirsty old feudist, even a bloodthirsty old feudist who did me a favor by taking the heat off Carl."

"I'm glad you told me," she said tartly. "Otherwise I'd certainly have wondered, considering the creepy way your mind works… Damn you!"

"What have I done now?" I asked.

"Ever since I've been with you, everything's been backwards. You just turn everything around. I think you do it on purpose!" She drew a long breath. "I think you're the most thoroughly ruthless and amoral man I ever met!"

"Don't kid yourself," I said. "You've got one in the family who's got me beat in spades."

Martha said, "My father, you mean?" After a while, when I didn't say anything, she went on: "That's not fair, using him against me. But then, you aren't fair, are you, Matt?"

"Fairness is for Boy Scouts," I said. "Now, if you don't

mind, all this weighty conversation has made me hungry as hell—"

She touched my arm as I started to turn away. "Matt?"

"What?"

There was an odd, strained note to her voice. "You think I'm just… just a backward child, don't you?"

Something changed in the room. It always does when they start telling you what they think you think of them. I stopped, and looked down at her carefully. Her gray eyes had changed, and her mouth, bare of lipstick, had changed. Well, I should have known it was coming when she called me amoral and ruthless. That's generally the first step. The second is when she says you think she's a child. The third, and final, step is when you tell her that you don't.

"You may be backward, Borden," I said, "but you're certainly not a child."

She wasn't.

21

After a long time, she stirred in my arms. We were lying on top of the bedspread, on the big bed nearer the door. As it had worked out, we hadn't managed to get between the covers, or even undress, or turn out the light.

"My God, talk about instant passion!" Martha breathed. "Do you realize I never even got my shoes off?"

She began to wiggle beside me. I heard one sandal hit the rug and then the other. She continued to squirm. An elbow hit me on the nose.

"What the hell are you doing?" I asked, trying to avoid opening my eyes and coming to grips with reality once more.

"Getting rid of this cockeyed wig… There! If you were a gentleman, you'd get up and turn out the light."

"If I were a gentleman, would I be here?" I asked. "*Now* what's the matter?"

"This damn dress is cutting me in two." Comfortable at last, she was silent for a little. Then she spoke again: "Why do you suppose… It doesn't make sense! Like that, wham! With the lights on, yet. No ladylike restraint, no discreet disrobing, just flopping on the bed with the guy fully clothed and… and frantically helping him yank up my skirt and… and rip hell out of my… Oh, well, they had a big run in them, anyway. But with a man I don't even like!"

I said, "Borden, you talk too much. And at the wrong time, too."

"But I *don't* like you," she protested. "I mean, I hope you're not kidding yourself that this… this wanton, nymphomaniac display means I've fallen madly in love with you, or something."

"Relax," I said. "I know you hate my guts. You still think I'm a cruel, cold-blooded, calculating homicidal type who should be shot on sight, except that you don't believe in shooting anything. And I still think you're a sentimental female dope who lets her mushy emotions get the better of what little immature intelligence she's got. That's the way it is, and nothing's changed. Okay? Satisfied?"

She didn't reply at once. Maybe she thought I'd put it just a little too strongly. But when she spoke again there was no resentment in her voice.

"It must have been the way we've been fighting ever since we met. We simply transferred the… the conflict to a different battleground, don't you think?"

"Sure," I said. "And since it's agreed that we don't love each other, quite the contrary, I don't suppose you'll be hurt if I zip up my pants and go get something to eat. Intercourse just seems to have made me hungrier than ever."

She made a small, giggly sound. "Okay, if you'll bring me a coke and hamburger when you come back. I don't feel up to facing my public at the moment. Matt."

"What?" I asked, standing up.

Her voice was mischievous: "I could tell Dad."

"I don't think you will," I said. "Not that it matters. I'll tell him myself, if he asks. I doubt he'll be very surprised. He's too smart to set up a situation like this and expect us to keep it pure. If that was what he'd wanted, he'd have wished you off on Lorna or some other female agent, not on me."

She laughed softly. "I love the flattering way you put it, as if I were an incubus or something. Ha. There's a fancy word for a girl who's supposed to be practically illiterate. Why don't you think I'll tell, Matt?"

I grinned. "Because, smart as he is, your dad's got some old-fashioned notions that pop up now and then, and they don't all concern the English language. He might just take it into his head that we ought to get married."

Martha laughed again. "Ouch! That *would* be a fate worse than death, wouldn't it? You can count on my silence, sir. Just don't forget the hamburger, medium rare, with everything. And the coke with ice, please…"

In the morning I caught up with my shaving in a bathroom that had a freshly washed blue dress drying on a hanger suspended from the shower rod. Some torn nylon stuff had been tossed casually into the wastebasket. When I emerged, Martha was still in bed, awaiting her turn. I told her it was all hers, and I'd see her in the coffee shop. I took my suitcase out to the car, threw it inside, and inspected all the tires on the rig, the trailer bearings, the hitch, the boat tie-downs, and the brace that supported the massive outboard motor at an angle while trailering, holding the lower unit clear of the road.

Finished, I went over to the motel office and checked us out. I picked up a newspaper on my way into the restaurant and had time to glance through it over a preliminary cup of coffee. There was a short front page recapitulation of the case of the Fort Adams Strangler that held my interest briefly, until I'd determined that nobody seemed to have the slightest intention of questioning the official verdict. Sheriff Rullington had his man, and the situation was under control. The story was all wrapped up, ready to take its place among the classic murders of history.

The second item that caught my attention was a syndicated piece on the editorial page by a Washington political commentator, remarking on the surprising momentum gained in recent days by the candidacy of Mrs. Ellen Love. Her campaign had started slowly, said the expert, in fact many people had scoffed at it as just another token Women's Lib gesture, but now, with the party's convention just around the corner, well-known political figures were beginning to jump onto the accelerating bandwagon.

It was currently conceded, I read, that the lady senator would have a real chance at the nomination, although many students of Washington affairs remained puzzled by the motives of hard-bitten professional politicians in rejecting regular party candidates they would normally have supported in order to follow such a risky and unconventional standard-bearer. Of course, said the columnist, it was possible that they all had the same basic arithmetic in mind: the fact that half the nation's votes were cast by women…

I refolded the paper and laid it on the table. To hell with politics; I had my own problems. I took out of my shirt pocket the motel bill I'd just paid and frowned at an item: L DIST—$4.37. Then I tore the bill across and stepped over to drop it into the wastebasket by the cash register. The damned little amateur Mata Hari, I thought grimly as I sat down to my coffee once more; the clumsy little fool, charging her secret long-distance call to the room, for Christ's sake!

To hell with all amateurs, I reflected, particularly young amateur female conspirators and their notion— they all have it—that the way to render any man, even an experienced agent, totally deaf, blind, and stupid, is to drag him into the nearest bed. After a while in the business you get so that, the minute the lady starts unbuttoning her blouse, you start looking for the hidden double-cross. The trouble is, you generally find it. I'd found it.

She'd made the call last night, right after I'd gone out to eat, leaving her alone. According to the desk clerk, she'd asked for a number in Washington, D.C., that I knew by heart; a number that, as she was well aware, was currently being monitored by a mimic in Herbert Leonard's employ. There could hardly be an innocent explanation for her calling that number or, for that matter, for her sudden, passionate assault upon my feeble virtue. I dismissed the idea that she'd belatedly come to realize, although she still wasn't quite ready to admit it, what an attractive person I really was. Kidding yourself like that is lots of fun, but in my line of work it can be fatal.

I didn't suppose she'd had much trouble getting the man imitating her father to put her in touch with Leonard. All she'd had to do was give her name and hint that she was willing to make a deal of some kind, any kind, and the man would have strained his circuits to get her the connection. An underling who flubbed a break like that—a promising contact with a trusted member of the opposing team—wouldn't last long in any undercover organization.

Well, it wasn't a totally unexpected development. Mac, the real Mac, wouldn't have used the warning code if he hadn't thought there was a possibility that she'd turn against us. He might even have been counting on her doing just that. The more I thought about it, the more likely it seemed. It would explain why he'd used her for a messenger, instead of a trained agent he could trust.

The outlines of his strategy were beginning to take shape: put a sentimental girl into the company of a ruthless agent under circumstances in which the man's actions were bound to offend her idealistic, non-violent principles, and the results should be fairly predictable. The final straw, from Martha's standpoint, had obviously been my turning old Hollingshead, with his bad heart, over to the authorities and thus, indirectly, causing his death. However, if that hadn't happened to show how evil and depraved I was—we all were, her dad included—something else undoubtedly would have. It had been almost inevitable that sooner or later she'd come to the conclusion that, as a concerned young member of society, she was required by her conscience to take positive action against us, and to hell with filial devotion, if any.

So now we had her in contact with Leonard, as Mac seemed to have planned from the start. You had to hand it to the guy, I reflected. He was consistent; you might even say he was fair. Like his daughter, he wasn't allowing himself to be influenced by any tender feelings for a member of his own family. He was using her weaknesses—she'd probably call them strengths—just as he'd have used those of any agent in his employ. If it seemed a little cold-blooded, well, I reminded myself, nobody'd forced the girl to pick up the phone and make the Judas call. Mac had merely foreseen that such a thing might happen and set up a situation to take advantage of it some way. I thought I could see roughly what he had in his intricate, scheming, unsentimental mind...

Something touched me lightly on top of the head, and I realized that I'd been kissed. "I didn't mean to keep you waiting, darling," Martha said.

"You're just one cup of coffee behind," I said, rising to help her with her chair.

Today she was wearing her own short brown hair, and a simple, tan, short-sleeved pantsuit. Seated, she smiled up at me, looking so young and tomboyishly innocent that I was almost ashamed of my dark suspicions, but her smile was too good to be true. It was a confident Mata Hari smile, not the shy and uncertain expression suitable for a relatively inexperienced girl who'd found herself in bed with a man she didn't really like without knowing just how it had happened.

"Welcome back, Miss Borden," I said, sitting down to face her.

She frowned, puzzled. "What do you mean?"

"Well, there's been a glamorous blonde imposter—"

She laughed quickly. "Oh, *that* tramp! I really don't understand what men see in her, Mr. Helm. So *obvious*, don't you think?"

She was too feverish and intense and gay; she'd forgotten that Martha Borden was basically a relaxed, barefoot, nature-girl type. She was seeing herself, instead, as an irresistible *femme fatale* who could wind even a dangerous character like me around her tanned little finger. That evening, several hundred miles to the east in Montgomery, Alabama—having requested a little shopping time along the way—she treated me to her version of the sheer-black-nightie routine. It wasn't embarrassingly bad, but I'd seen it done better.

The following evening we reached Robalo Island, Florida, well after dark, too tired to play any phony, sexy games. In the morning, we went to see Hank Priest.

22

We got the boat into the water at a small marina next door
to the picturesque and rambling old waterfront lodge at
which we'd spent the night. The launching ramp was
coated with a mat of the slickest green weeds I've ever
encountered. The weather was clear and beautiful. The
marina was located on a wide waterway—actually part of
the Intracoastal Waterway that follows this western coast
of Florida—but there seemed to be estuaries heading off
in just about every direction. To the west, through a gap
between Robalo Island and the next island north, I could
see the open ocean—or, to be strictly accurate—the Gulf
of Mexico. Frankly, I'm enough of a landlubber that any
piece of water I can't see across is an ocean to me.

The big motor started at the turn of the key. I left it
idling, warming up, while I ran the car and trailer back
up into the parking lot. When I returned to the dock on
foot, Martha had removed her modest pantsuit, revealing
herself in an immodest bikini, striped blue and white

wherever there was material enough to hold a stripe. Well, she was gaining on it, I reflected sourly. She'd started by seducing me fully clothed, progressed to a semitransparent nightie, and from there to a couple of inadequate strips of striped cloth. Total nudity was just around the corner. I could hardly wait.

"Which way do we go?" I asked. "You did say his place was on the water, didn't you?"

"Yes, of course. It's back down the Waterway a mile or two. You remember, I showed you the gate when we passed it on the road last night." She hesitated. "But maybe it would look less obvious if we took a trip around the island and came at it from the other direction. Besides, it's pretty early. Uncle Hank probably isn't awake yet. If we wait a little, he'll probably be down at his dock working on his boat; that's how he spends most of his time when he isn't making like a politician."

"Uncle Hank," I said. "You didn't tell me he was your uncle."

"He isn't. And Aunt Frances isn't my aunt, either. I just call them that. They're old friends of Daddy's, and we've visited them a lot, particularly since Mommy died."

"Fishing, you said."

"Yes," she said, "Uncle Hank put a special radiotelephone gadget on his boat so Daddy could keep in touch with his office even when he was out on the water."

I'd never thought of Mac as a sportsman, or even, really, as a man with friends outside the office. I discovered that I was jealous in an odd sort of way. It was a disconcerting idea that the cold gray man whose orders I'd been taking for the best part of my adult life had been in the habit of slipping away from Washington to go fishing with an old friend. Come to that, I'd never thought of Mac as a parent, either, even though I'd known he'd managed to produce, or assist in the production of, a female child. He'd always been a voice on the phone or a face in front of a bright window. I wasn't sure I wouldn't rather he'd stayed that way.

"Give me the guided tour around the island," I said. "Robalo. What kind of a name is that?"

"It means snook, a kind of game fish. There are lots of them around, but Daddy prefers tarpon because they're bigger."

I said, "Well, I might as well make sure this little put-put is running right, after dragging it all this way…"

It was a pleasant boat ride, but it was a hell of a shallow coast. Bucking a strong flood tide, we ran out through the gap between the islands—she called it a pass, apparently a local term for inlet or channel—and headed straight out for a while. After the Gulf of California, where you can be in a hundred feet of water within spitting distance of the shore, it seemed unnatural to have the land a couple of miles astern and only six or eight feet down, easily visible through the clear, blue-green water. A bunch of playful porpoises escorted us on our way.

Turning south at the buoy Martha indicated, I kept the little boat skipping along at conservative planing speed; there was no need to advertise its hidden virtues. The opening from which we'd come soon merged into the low, green, featureless shoreline; and it occurred to me that finding my way around these waters might present problems, particularly at night. I'm not the world's best pilot and navigator, and here there were no spectacular shoreline cliffs or peaks to head for; no distinctive landmarks such as I'd used in Mexico. Well, Martha had said that when the time came, I'd have a guide. I hoped he knew his business.

"Where is it you figure your dad's hiding out?" I asked the girl presently, raising my voice above the roar of the motor.

She pointed straight ahead. "Farther south a ways. It looks like a solid coastline from out here, but it's actually all broken up into mangrove islands and swamps and channels running every which way. You could hide a battleship in there, if you had a battleship that drew only a couple of feet of water... You can swing back inshore now. That point over there's the one you want. Cut it close; the deep water's right next to shore."

The tidal currents grabbed us, sweeping us inland with a rush as we neared the entrance. We crossed a wide estuary and headed into a twisting channel that was well marked with tall posts that had small wooden arrows, red or green, indicating the safe place for passing. The tangled vegetation grew right down to the water that in here looked like strong and murky tea. Martha indicated that wasn't such a farfetched simile: the coloration was largely due to tannic acid from the mangrove roots. She said the dead fish floating in the channel were due to a visitation of the lethal organism known as Red Tide that had recently afflicted this part of the coast.

"Of course, many of the locals don't really believe in the Red Tide," she said. "They think it's all the government's fault for dumping a lot of poison gas put in the Gulf some years ago. No, you'd better cut inside that little island up ahead. There's a good channel this side of it; you'll see the markers in a minute. Is this as fast as this thing will go?"

"Not really," I said, "but it's as fast as I'll go in water this shallow. I do have a spare propeller somewhere on board, but I don't feel like changing props today."

"I won't put us aground," she said confidently.

I shrugged, and ran the revs up until the nautical speedometer read thirty miles per hour—although why a boat speedometer should read in miles per hour instead of knots still baffled me. The little vessel was by no means fully extended, but the increase of speed seemed to satisfy the girl up forward; and in those narrow, shallow waters thirty was plenty fast enough for me. I was throwing us around the channel markers slalom-fashion as it was, glancing back occasionally to see our big white wake breaking on invisible shoals that we'd missed by only a few yards.

We slowed down a few times for other boats and once for a small village. At last, having come clear around the island, we passed under a high, new bridge I recognized as the one we'd driven over the night before, leaving the mainland. We were back in civilization. You could tell by the private docks and by the neat seawalls protecting the pretty little houses on the pretty little lawns, and by the earth-moving machinery tearing up the mangroves and the marl underneath, to prepare the way for more pretty little houses on more neat little lawns. Beyond this raw, new construction were some larger and older waterfront residences.

"Uncle Hank sold off part of his land to the developers. I'm not sure he doesn't regret it now," Martha said, looking that way. "There he is! The thirty-footer with the outriggers and the tuna tower. The gray-haired man in the cockpit… Can we just stop, or do you have to make like a secret agent and sneak through the bushes or something?"

I grinned. "Sometimes the bold move is the best. Uncle Hank, here we come."

23

He was a big, weathered man with stiff gray hair that, cut quite short, made a kind of wiry brush on top of his head. His face was square and seamy, with a big mouth and a blunt nose. He had bright blue eyes, rather like Carl's, but somewhat paler and lacking the crazy intensity. He was wearing only a pair of faded khaki shorts. His deeply tanned body was in good shape for his age, which I placed somewhere in the early sixties. He leaned against a mop handle as he looked down at us from the cockpit of the big sportfisherman—at least it looked big from where I was sitting, at the wheel of my open, fifteen-foot job.

"Marty, girl," he said, "aren't you ever going to stop growing? Damned if those aren't just about the longest legs I've seen all week. And you're Helm? Well, you can make fast to the dock back there, astern of the Whaler, while I finish swabbing down this cockpit. Better give her a bit of slack. The way the kids from that new development go racing past, she'll yank those tin cleats right out of that plastic gunwale if you snub her too tight."

"Yes, sir," I said.

I guessed at least four stripes of gold braid and a silver bird on the collar, at one time or another. It's a principle of the profession that it never hurts to be respectful to the brass, ex- or otherwise. It makes the relationship a lot smoother in the beginning, and it doesn't make them a bit more bulletproof in the end, if it should come to that.

I backed us past a small, shovel-nosed, open boat with a large outboard motor on the stern, and did a reasonably good job, if I do say so myself, of maneuvering into the indicated opening. Martha jumped ashore with the bow line while I secured the stern. On foot, we approached the big boat once more.

She was a real fishing machine, with the tall, thin outriggers pointing skywards on either side of the tapering, spidery framework of the lookout tower surmounting the cabin and the flying bridge. I could see how a Tinkertoy skyscraper like that might come in handy on occasion, but it wasn't really a structure I longed to be on top of, particularly if the boat was rolling in a heavy sea. There, were two husky fishing chairs bolted to the deck aft. The name on the stern was *Frances II*.

It was an impressive hunk of seagoing machinery. They come much larger, of course, but at a grand or more a foot, she was a lot of boat and a lot of money. Well, Sheriff Rullington had sold some land and put a Cadillac into his back yard. We all have our dreams.

Uncle Hank Priest emptied a bucket over the side as

we came up, and put the mop to dry in one of the fishing-rod holders set into the cockpit gunwale.

"Marty, why don't you run up to the house and say hello to Frances?" he said.

The girl laughed. "Somehow, I get the strange feeling I'm not wanted," she said, and ran off towards the big house on shore.

The gray-haired man watched her thoughtfully. "I've known that young lady a long time," he said without looking at me. "I'd have bet my life she'd never…"

"You'd have lost," I said, when he stopped.

"You're sure?"

"Sure enough. Does it matter? I figure we're supposed to go through the same motions in any case. Am I wrong?"

He shook his head, and turned to look at me. "So you're the man he calls Eric. He has a lot of faith in you. I hope it's justified, but I'm beginning to wonder, when you come charging up to my dock in broad daylight."

I said, "Why play games, sir? You're known, and your association with him is known. Anybody who sees Martha and me here will know we're here to make contact with you."

"Yes," Priest said, "yes, of course. But I must say, this complicated kind of intrigue isn't really in my line."

"No, sir," I said. "If it were, you'd be in the Pentagon with the rest of the conniving brass, wouldn't you?"

He looked a little startled; then he grinned. "Come aboard and have a beer," he said. "Keep your damn feet off the brightwork—varnish to you." As I stepped down into the cockpit, avoiding the varnished rail, he glanced astern automatically; the admiral checking the disposition of the fleet before leaving the bridge. "Do you know why they call them Boston Whalers, son?"

He wasn't that old, and I wasn't that young, but I saw no reason to take offense. "No, sir."

"Because they aren't made in Boston and were never used for whaling." He laughed at his own joke, if it was his, and as senior officer preceded me into the deckhouse without apologies. "Get a couple of beers out of the refrigerator, will you, son, while I find my shirt and dig out the chart."

He disappeared into the dark cabin forward that seemed to consist mainly of two berths meeting in a V towards the boat's bow. l looked around for something that might hold beer and keep it cold. The deckhouse had plenty of glass and daylight. It seemed to be half dinette and half kitchenette—excuse me, galley. One corner was reserved for the seagoing john—excuse me, head. I found the refrigerator under the counter to starboard and extracted two bottles as Priest emerged from the cabin buttoning a khaki shirt, with a folded chart clamped under his arm. He spoke as if there had been no pause in the conversation.

"You found the little flares on board your boat?"

"Yes, sir. In the battery compartment under the helmsman's seat."

"Never mind the red ones. They're standard emergency equipment and came with the kit. The white ones are what you want. They're in a separate tube."

"I saw them," I said. I hesitated. "It's a neat little gadget, but I shouldn't think it would have much range."

"We figured concealment might be more important to you than range, son," Priest said. "Keep it with you at all times, loaded, with as many extra flares as you can hide out. Arthur said you people were pretty good at hiding things. When the time comes, I'll be standing by, as far in among the islands down there as I can get the Frances without putting her on the mud. I'll have the Whaler in tow, ready to go. There'll be a man up in the tuna tower. From up there, he'll be able to see quite a ways over the mangroves. A white flare will bring the Whaler in looking for you with plenty of firepower. That's not saying they'll find you, of course. Those are tricky waters. But it's the best support we can offer you."

"Yes, sir."

"Of course, it's expected that you'll have your job done before you signal for help."

"Of course."

"And you know what the job is."

"Yes, sir," I said.

His eyes narrowed sharply, as if he'd set a trap and caught me. "How do you know? It was, er, left out of the instructions we passed you through Marty."

I said, "Admiral, when you've worked for a man as long as I have, you don't need much in the way of instructions. Don't worry, sir. I know what he wants—I guess I should say I know who he wants. And I know, roughly, how he expects the job to be done; all I need is the final details from you. If the target is there, I'll make the touch for him." There was a little silence. I broke it by saying, "I've been with him for… Well, never mind exactly how many years, but I never knew he was a fisherman."

"He isn't, son. He's a tarpon fighter."

"I don't talk the language, sir. You'll have to translate."

Priest grinned. "The habits of fish are pretty much a mystery to Arthur. He trusts me to take him to the right places at the right times. He can barely rig a bait properly, he's just average at casting, and he doesn't really want to learn more about it. What he comes down here for is simply to get one of those big, mean, silvery, high-leaping battlers on the line somehow and slug it out until the fish says uncle. Oh, he'll oblige me by fishing for other species occasionally, but he loves tarpon because, he says, they've got the right spirit and they're the right size."

"The right size for what?" I asked.

"For fighting, son," said the gray-haired man. "Smaller fish, you've got to give them a break with light tackle to get a real battle; you've got to be gentle and careful; you can't just sock it to them with everything you've got. Bigger fish, well, it becomes a grim endurance contest with a lot of heavy equipment between you and the fish. You've got to use a fighting chair, a harness, and a great big derrick of a rod and reel; and you don't really fight alone, you're a team with the man handling the boat. But a tarpon is just right. You can battle him from a motionless boat if you like; and you can use tackle heavy enough to lean on hard, but still light enough to let you fight standing up in the cockpit like a man, just you against the fish—at least that's the way Arthur feels about it. I don't suppose you're fisherman enough to understand."

"No, sir," I said.'

"He also likes tarpon because they're not much good to eat, so he's free to turn them loose when he's beat them. He'll reach down and pat the big fish on the head and clip the leader, saying 'Goodbye, Eric, see you next time around.' He calls it occupational therapy. He says it keeps him from committing murder back in Washington when some goddamn prima donna agent gives him a lot of lip… How about opening those beers before they get warm, son? The opener's right there at the corner of the sink."

I pried the caps off and held out a bottle to him. His face was expressionless. I decided I was going to like him.

"Yes, sir," I said. "I suppose I should be flattered. I mean, he might have gone in for carp or suckers."

Priest grinned his old-salt grin, the one that crinkled the weathered skin about his eyes. "Incidentally, it isn't admiral, just captain," he said. "They wanted to pin some stars on me before I retired but I wouldn't let them. Four stripes are hard enough to live down these days. Politically speaking, I mean."

"You seem to have managed it, sir."

"Temporarily, but there's another tough election coming up, and us old warmongers are in a bad spot." He shook his head quickly. "Do you ever feel you're not living in the same world as other people, son? I mean, God Almighty, who *doesn't* want peace? But how the hell can anybody think the way to get it is to drop your trousers and bend over, inviting everybody to kick your bare ass? But that's what everybody seems to want these days. We're supposed to take off our national shirt, pants, and skivvies, and stand there buck-naked in the cold, cold international breeze; and all those nice people across the water are supposed to feel so sorry for us they'll leave us alone."

"Yes, sir," I said.

It was a safe thing to say, I hoped. I wondered how many more deep-thinking characters would unload their political and social philosophies on me before this job was finished. There seemed to be one behind every bush.

Priest said, "Well, that's why I went into politics. This jackass war has given soldiering and sailoring a bad name, but the fact is we're going to need our shirt and pants for some time to come. International nudism isn't in style quite yet. Somebody's got to see to it that we keep a few rags of protection for another few years, until the light of universal peace glows brightly all over the world… Ah, hell. You don't vote here. Why the hell am I wasting all this rhetoric on you?"

I said, "With all due respect, I was wondering the same thing myself, sir."

He blinked. I'd got back at him, a little, for the tarpon and the prima donna agents, and he wasn't used to being got back at. Then he grinned and saluted me with the bottle in his hand.

"To fair winds and gentle seas."

"*Salud*."

"Talking about votes, there's a little political meeting scheduled here for this evening. You might be interested in listening. Eight o'clock sharp."

I looked at him for a moment. He wasn't going to order me to come, I saw, or tell me what I'd learn if I did come. I was supposed to be bright enough to come of my own accord.

"If you say so, sir," I said. "Eight o'clock. Front door or back?"

"Use the boat if you like. It's just a short run down from the lodge. Go in the kitchen door, over there, and turn right. You'll find a good place to listen right off the pantry. Don't cough or sneeze and nobody'll bother you. I'll have your guide waiting in the kitchen afterwards. I'll have some equipment for you, too."

"I'll be there." Looking through the wide, deckhouse windows, I saw the slim, brown, bikinied shape of Martha Borden emerge from the kitchen door just mentioned. The girl paused to say goodbye to a thin, white-haired woman in slacks. "Is there anything else I ought to know, sir?" I asked.

"A shoal-draft houseboat, around thirty feet long, powered by twin outdrives, came by the day before yesterday and disappeared among the islands. Judging by the whiskers, she had some pretty good communications gear on board. We can't positively connect her with anything or anybody, but she's still in there somewhere. I'd say it was a hopeful sign, wouldn't you?" He was watching the girl come running down towards the dock, and took my nod for granted, not looking aside. He went on, "Well, I'd better get you oriented. Let's have a look at the chart." He spread it on the dinette table; and raised his voice slightly. "The place you want is Cutlass Key. Here. Don't forget the name. The south end of Cutlass Key. That's where the cabin is. You'll see the old dock on the point."

"Yes, sir," I said, as Martha dropped into the cockpit, causing the *Frances II* to rock slightly. "I won't forget, sir. Cutlass Key…"

24

The lodge was a pleasant, rambling hostelry overlooking the marina and the Waterway. Our ground-floor room was in one of the outlying buildings, white clapboard like the main structure which, I'd been told, had once been a rich gentlemen's fishing club. Entering, I went over to my suitcase to unpack some clean clothes. I was aware of Martha examining her tanned reflection in the big mirror on the bathroom door.

"You'd better cover up if you go out again," I said. "You're pretty well cooked already."

"It doesn't hurt," she said. "I don't burn very easily. Did Uncle Hank tell you where Daddy's hiding?"

It was still a little difficult for me to think of Mac as anybody's daddy. "He told me," I said.

She glanced at me quickly. "But you're not telling me?"

"That's right," I said.

After a moment, she laughed. "Don't you trust me,

Matt? Not even where my own parent is concerned?"

"Trust?" I said. "What's that? You're speaking to a pro, sweetheart. And as Lorna said, if you didn't know, it wasn't you who told, not even under torture or scopolamine. If anybody asks, refer them to me." I rearranged the remaining clothes in the suitcase a certain way, and closed the bag, making a mental note of its position on the luggage rack. "How about lunch? Are you hungry?"

"No, darling," she said. "I'm not *hungry*."

Her voice came from directly behind me. I turned, and there she was, smiling a little, all pinky-brown and shiny from the sun. She'd made it at last. The blue-striped bikini, discarded while my attention was elsewhere, lay in a little heap on the rug where she'd been standing.

I made a little whistling sound to indicate my appreciation of the view that was being offered me. "Why is it," I asked, "that every time I start talking about food, the girl gets one of her nymphomaniac spells..."

Much later, lying on the bed beside me, she said softly, "Matt. Are you awake?"

"Uh-uh. Now I am."

"You've been asleep for hours."

"Must be all that sun," I said. "Or something."

"*Now* I'm getting hungry," she said. "It must be almost dinnertime. Matt."

"Yes?"

"If anything should happen—"

"Call him Matthew after his daddy," I said. "Or Matilda. I'll even make an honest woman of you if you insist."

She giggled. "That's not what I meant!"

"There's no indication that anybody knows where we are or gives a damn," I said. "All we have to do now is stall for a couple of days—your dad is a punctuality fiend, meaning people don't keep appointments with him either late or early. On the night of the sixteenth of the month we take a little boat ride with a guide the admiral has lined up for us. Then I looked discreetly away so as not to intrude on the happy family reunion. Okay?"

"I suppose so." She drew a long breath. "That means if nothing happens… well, it's almost over, isn't it?"

"Yes," I said. "One way or another, it's almost over."

"It's been kind of nice," she said slowly. "Actually. It started out so awfully, but it ended up being… well, kind of nice. I want you to remember that, no matter what happens."

First the standard striptease, I thought, and now the ancient no-matter-what-happens-it-was-nice speech. Every cliché in the book. Amateurs!

"I'll remember," I said. "Shall we flip for who gets the first shower?"

"Matt."

I looked at her. "What?"

"Take me seriously. Please."

"I've never taken you any other way, Borden," I said. "You can remember that, no matter what happens."

When I came out of the shower, she was still lying naked on the bed approximately where I'd left her, but my suitcase had been disturbed. I suppose I should have been happy. Things were working out very well, just the way Mac had planned them, if I was reading his mind correctly. The funny thing was, I didn't feel nearly as triumphant as I should have. I guess the trouble was that it didn't seem quite fair, two old experts at intrigue like Mac and me ganging up on a young beginner. Of course fairness was, as always, totally irrelevant.

I watched her get dressed in the blue sleeveless dress we'd bought her in Phoenix, Arizona, the one with the pleated skirt. It was rather intriguing to watch the amateur mind at work. Obviously, if I had any suspicions of her at all, after the last amorous interlude, her choice of costume would lull them now. I was supposed to figure that, if she was expecting a hectic night full of action, she'd have put on slacks, not the only pretty dress she owned here in Florida. Finished, she smiled her confident Mata Hari smile and presented herself for inspection and approval.

"Nice," I said. "The admiral will like it, too."

"Are we going to see Uncle Hank?"

"After dinner," I said. "He wants me to make arrangements with the guide; and there's some kind of a political meeting he wants me to listen in on, for some reason. I'm sure he won't mind your coming along." Actually, I wasn't a bit sure; but I didn't give a damn if he did mind. I didn't work for Congressman Priest. I glanced at my watch. "Well, maybe we'd better get started since we have to be back here before eight. He told me to come by boat and stay inconspicuous."

"Why do you call him 'admiral'?" she asked curiously.

"He never made the stars, you know. He didn't want to."

I said, "He may be captain to the US Navy, but he's admiral to me."

It seemed odd, driving the station wagon without the weight of the boat and trailer dragging behind. We had dinner at the other end of the island, in a dark supper-club kind of place I'd spotted, driving by the night before. It turned out to be passable as to food but terrible as to service. I can see why a waitress might have trouble bringing a steak before it's ready, but why it should take her most of an hour to write out a check always baffles me. Well, somebody once told me it's a theory: they think the customer will feel rushed and insulted if the bill is presented with the coffee. All I can say is that any enterprising girl who wants to try insulting me like that is going to wind up in possession of a much larger tip than the haughty serving lady who makes me wait all night before she condescends to take my lousy money.

In this case, however, it worked out pretty well, saving me from having to think of other ways of stalling. It was ten minutes of eight, and the light was fading, when we reached the new development on the way back. I slowed down as we approached the stone posts of the Priest gateway, just beyond.

"Is there a place I can hide this hearse; not too far away, from which we can reach the kitchen door without climbing any barbed-wire fences?" I asked.

Martha glanced at me sharply. "I thought you said you were supposed to come by water."

"I did. So, being a suspicious secret-agent type, I'll

come by land. Anyway, it's late and you're not really
dressed for a boatride."

"You can't possibly suspect Uncle Hank—"

"Who can't? I don't even trust me around the block…
My God, look at the limousines in the admiral's driveway!
Even if I wasn't feeling shy, I wouldn't dare park my
cheesy little six-thousand-dollar Chevy in there. Those
aristocratic heaps would snub it and hurt its feelings."

"If you turn right just around the curve up ahead,
there's an old lane leading down to the water."

I stopped the station wagon near the end of the lane,
backed it in between two trees and went around to open
the door for Martha. She led me down the lane, which
ended abruptly at a concrete embankment. Beyond was
the Waterway. I could see the Priest dock to the right,
the little outboard boat with the funny name, and the
big sportfisherman, through a chain-link fence. The
outriggers and tuna tower made a tricky, lacy pattern
against the darkening sky.

Martha made her way along the embankment to the
fence. She gathered her brief, pleated skirt around her
thighs so it wouldn't snag, with one hand, and, holding on
with the other, swung herself around the end of the fence,
four feet above the water. She waited for me to follow,
less gracefully. We stole along the Priest seawall to the
dock, and took the path that led up to the house. A slight
black man of indeterminate age, not young, not elderly,
opened the screen door to admit us.

"Why, it's Jarrel!" Martha said. "You must be the

guide we've been talking about. Matt, this is Jarrel White. He knows every local water moccasin and alligator by its first name, and I wouldn't be surprised if he'd poached a few in his time."

The black man grinned. "Now, Miss Marty, who'd waste time poaching water moccasins?"

"Where does Uncle Hank want us, Jarrel?"

"On the back porch, Miss Marty. That door over there. Well, you know. You can sit on the old sofa in the corner. There's a window open to the living room and you can hear all you want." He opened the door for us, and looked at me. "I'll be talking with you after all those folks are gone, Mr. Helm," he said softly.

"Sure."

The kitchen door closed noiselessly. Martha and I stood for a moment in the darkness, that seemed darker for the pattern of light thrown by an open window halfway down the porch, from which came the sound of men's voices. I heard Priest's quarterdeck tones greeting somebody and offering a drink.

"Doesn't sound as if they've got down to business yet," I whispered to the girl beside me. "Whatever the business of the evening may be. Doesn't your Uncle Hank believe in air-conditioning?"

"Oh, he's got it, but it's a pleasant spring evening, and he doesn't turn it on unless he has to. Deep down, I think he feels that if God had meant us to be cool in Florida, He wouldn't have made it hot in the first place." She hesitated, and touched my shoulder lightly. "Matt."

"Yes?"

"I'm sorry."

The needle went into my biceps. It was a healthy jab that must have rammed home the plunger of the hypodermic syringe she'd stolen from my suitcase with the same motion. The trouble with carrying weapons of any kind is that somebody may get hold of them and use them against you, but this is also something you can turn to your advantage if you work it right.

I had plenty of performances on which to pattern my own: Hollingshead's and Sheriff Rullington's to mention only two. I'd even had the stuff used against me before, on an assignment not too long ago. I knew exactly how it was supposed to feel and how fast it was supposed to act. I gave a little start, reached instinctively for the instrument that had punctured my skin, now being withdrawn; but I never finished the movement. Instead, I let myself slump helplessly, hoping she'd catch me, which she did, easing me gently to the floor.

"I'm sorry," I heard her breathe. "I'm so sorry, darling, but I have to do it. You understand that I have to do it, don't you?…"

For a neat ending, that should have been all, but she didn't leave. She stood beside my presumably unconscious body for interminable minutes. I realized she was listening to the laughter and chatter drifting through the open window, probably waiting for a clue to the purpose of the meeting, but like most meetings it was slow in starting. At last she made a small, irritated, breathy sound indicating that her time or her patience had run out. I heard the sound of her sandals receding, very soft and stealthy, along the porch. There was a faint, metallic rattling that after a moment I identified as the noise of a screen door hook being released. A door creaked, and she was gone.

I lay quite still. I didn't think she'd slip back to check on me, but there was no sense in taking chances. After several minutes, there was a sputtering sound from the direction of the dock: a good-sized outboard motor starting up, and moving off along the Waterway…

25

I'd been listening to the argument for over an hour, and the admiral was getting nowhere. They'd come with their minds made up and it looked as if they were going to leave the same way. I just wish they'd get on with it.

"It's all very well for you to talk like a brave Boy Scout, Hank." The voice had a hint of a Southern accent and belonged to a distinguished gent whose name I'd recognized when it was mentioned, who'd emerged as spokesman for the opposition. "The lady doesn't seem to have anything on you. Well, she has something on me. You don't stay in politics thirty years without cutting a few corners. Somehow she knows them all. It's different with you. Politically speaking, you're new and clean, if you'll pardon the description."

"You're wrong there, Senator." Priest's voice was crisp. "How do you think I learned what was going on? I have exactly the same problem as everyone else."

"Such as?"

"I haven't asked you to dump your garbage in public, have I, Senator? But very well, if it will make a difference… It involves this damned real estate development next door. All I knew when I sold to them was that I needed campaign money and had some land, and the company needed land and had some money. I'd just retired from the Navy, I was busy running for office, and I didn't take time to investigate as closely as I might have. Now it turns out that a few political palms were greased here and there; there's even a possibility that my name was used without my permission. If they fire that at me, come election time, I'll have a choice between looking stupid, which I was, or crooked, which I wasn't, So we're all in the same boat; she's got something on all of us. But if we refuse to yield to extortion…"

The senator said dryly, "Then there'll just be a lot of new faces in Washington next year."

"But one of them won't be a harpy named Love, damn it! Not if we all stick together and work to see that she doesn't succeed in blackmailing her way into the highest office in the nation."

"I still say you talk like a Boy Scout, Hank. Maybe you think that's worth your political career. I don't think it's worth mine."

Another voice broke in: "How the devil does she do it, anyway? She's dug up dirt so old I'd even forgotten it myself. She must have an intelligence system that puts the CIA to shame, not that that's so hard to do…"

It took him another half-hour to get rid of them. I

glanced at my watch, but stayed on the porch sofa where I was. At last, the door to the kitchen opened and the admiral emerged with a glass in each hand.

"I figured you could use a drink about now, son," he said, passing one over.

"Thank you, sir."

"You heard?"

"Yes, sir."

"She must have an intelligence system that puts the CIA to shame!" he mimicked savagely. "Hell, if she hasn't got the CIA, it's about the only intelligence, security, and investigating agency in the country she hasn't got. At least she's got access to their files—and it looks as if just about all of them have been spending less time and money defending the country from danger than snooping into the private affairs of a lot of private, and public, citizens. All the damned woman has to do is call up her tame chief of national security, or whatever he calls himself, Leonard, and tell him to get her something quick on Senator Snodgrass or Congressman Cartwheel—"

"Or Congressman Priest," I said.

He grimaced. "That's right. I was a damned fool, a preoccupied damned fool; and all she had to do was turn Leonard and his computers loose on me and there it was, all neatly stored in one of his agencies' memory banks or whatever you call them! And if you want to know something ironical, son, I voted for the damned reorganization bill that put him into power. I thought it was time for a little efficiency. Efficiency!" He shrugged grimly. "Of course I should have checked with Arthur, but it seemed like an innocuous and straightforward proposal, just a little streamlining of a lot of overlapping undercover empires wasting the taxpayers' money by doing the same thing twice…"

When he stopped, I asked, "What does Mrs. Love want you to do?"

"Support her nomination at the convention next week, naturally. After she's got that—and the way she's going, she'll get it, all right—she'll undoubtedly think of other little political chores for us to do, if she isn't stopped and stopped soon." He drew a long breath, remembered something, and looked around. "Jarrel said you brought Marty along to listen. I don't know as that was such a good idea, considering that there are some doubts as to the young lady's reliability."

"No, sir," I said.

"What?"

"There are no doubts," I said. "Not any longer."

He regarded me sharply. "What do you mean?"

"You can rest easy, sir. She didn't stay long enough to hear anything interesting," I said. "I think she wanted to, but apparently she was running short of time, so she just stuck me with my own hypodermic, stole your little boat, and disappeared."

His first concern, not surprisingly, was for his boat rather than my health. He looked quickly towards the dock. "She took the Whaler?" Then he frowned quickly. "If she was going to steal a boat, why didn't she take yours? It's bigger and faster."

I said, "You don't see it down there, do you, sir? I didn't bring it. I didn't figure I wanted to lose it, after hauling it clear across the country, so I came by car."

He started to speak angrily. Then he checked himself and drew another long breath. "Arthur said you were clever. And conscienceless."

"I had a good teacher in both subjects, sir."

"You seem to be in reasonable shape for a man who's had a hypodermic needle poked into his hide."

"There was plain water in the hypo," I said. "I emptied the vial yesterday—there wasn't much left—and put in half a cc, enough for one dose, from the tap. One clear, colorless liquid looks pretty much like another."

He said rather grimly, "You had it all figured out, did you, Helm?"

"Pretty close, I hope. She's a fairly predictable girl in some respects," I said. "She had three problems. The first was obtaining a certain vital piece of information. Well, we fed her that this morning, according to instructions. Your timing was very good, sir, and she couldn't possibly have missed overhearing our little discussion over the chart, although of course she had to go through the motions of pretending that she still had no idea where her daddy was hiding and it was mean and suspicious of me not to tell her. Her second problem was how to slip away from me so she could convey this information to her new friends."

"You're certain she's in touch with Leonard?"

"Yes, sir," I said. "She called a certain number in

Washington a few days ago. Obviously, she made some kind of deal with Herbie, and obviously he told her to stick with me and play it cagey until she'd learned exactly where the hideout was located down here. Having got the information this morning, she then had to keep me happy and unsuspicious until she could put me out of action long enough to give herself a good running start. I was sticking too close for her just to walk out the door; I'd have been on the trail too soon."

"How did you know she'd use the drug on you, instead of something more drastic and permanent?"

I shrugged. "I've just been through a crash course in Martha Borden, sir. I ought to be able to guess her reactions by this time. She could have tried to steal my gun or borrow one from Leonard, of course, but she doesn't believe in shooting people, and guns are pretty noisy, anyway. She could have got the billy I've been using in the boat to keep big fish from flopping all over the cockpit, but knocking a man on the head would be, I figured, another act of violence against her principles. She'd seen me use the drug kit twice. She'd seen me put it away in a secret compartment in my suitcase. There really wasn't much doubt about what weapon she'd pick if I made it easy for her. Her final problem was transportation. I gave her a choice between my car and your boat. She picked the boat. That means her rendezvous with Leonard is close to the water or on it; perhaps another boat. Unless she sinks the Whaler—"

"She'd have to fill it with rocks. They're practically unsinkable."

"Then by this time—she's been gone a couple of hours already—it's probably drifting or anchored or pulled up on shore somewhere not too far away. You shouldn't have too much trouble finding it."

"And Marty? Does your crystal ball tell you where she is, Helm?"

He wasn't liking me much; he wasn't calling me "son" any more. I said, "I'd guess she's with Leonard and his undercover army—well, navy—on the way to Cutlass Key, sir."

"Not in the dark. She knows these waters pretty well, but not well enough to run them at night."

"If you're sure of that, sir, we've got more time than I figured. I was worried that they were getting too much of a start on us."

"Well, she's been in there, but not recently, and it's not an easy area to navigate from memory. In daylight, she should be able to make it if she takes her time and kind of feels her way, but at night she'll run them aground for sure, or get them good and lost in that labyrinth of islands. I think she's smart enough to know it." Priest hesitated. "Do you really believe she'll take them there, son?"

I was back in favor again. "Yes, sir," I said.

"I can't believe she'd betray her own father!"

I said, "You don't understand idealism as practiced currently, sir. Personal loyalties and relationships simply don't count, when you're saving humanity as a whole from evil men like Mac and me and from the callous and ruthless philosophy of violence we represent."

"What about Leonard's callous and ruthless philosophy?"

"That's the big flaw in their idealistic reasoning," I said grimly. "They invariably seem to figure that if one side is bad, the other must be good. Well, we'll have to see if we can't demonstrate to Miss Borden that we're all equally dreadful in this horrible world." I drew a long breath. "Where's Jarrel White, and what kind of equipment have you got for me?"

Priest said, "There's a rifle, some cartridges, and an aerosol can of insect repellant. I can lend you a flashlight if you need it."

"There's one on the boat. Is the rifle more or less sighted in, I hope? Never mind, it's bound to be. Mac would know I wouldn't be able to do any last-minute target shooting around here." I grimaced. "There's nothing I love like taking off on a job in the dark, with a strange guide, and an unfamiliar weapon that's been adjusted by somebody else!"

"I can tell you one thing, son; no matter how much shooting you do with the gun, you'll do more with the spray can. At night, the bugs will eat you alive. I'll get Jarrel and the gear."

26

For a mild-looking, middle-aged gent, Jarrel White had some fairly violent and youthful speedboating ideas. He took us out through the pass as if our little boat were an unlimited hydroplane racing for the Gold Cup on Lake Havasu, if I have the hardware and location right, which I probably don't.

I couldn't see all the tide-rips in the dark, but I could feel every one of them through the cushioned bench on which I sat, just forward of the steering console. When we reached open water, the black man rammed the throttle all the way forward. Fortunately, it was a calm night. Even so, I had the impression that we only hit the water every fifty yards or so, and that when we did, it was hard as rock. The running lights went out.

"Shouldn't be nobody to see us without legal lights out here except the folks we're after, this time of night," Jarrel yelled over the roar of the motor, when I looked around questioningly. "You still figure they're way ahead of us?"

"They had a couple of hours' start," I shouted back, "but Captain Priest doesn't seem to think they'll head into the mangroves until they've got daylight to navigate by."

"We'll go well offshore so they don't hear us passing; then we'll swing down south and come in by the back door, so to speak." He patted the steering wheel approvingly. "Don't hold much with boats looking like guided missiles, but she handles nice. Wish she wasn't quite so deep, though. Tide's ebbing; we'll maybe have to lift the motor and pole through a couple shallow spots. Well, we'll see, cap'n; we'll see."

The title was, I knew, not a military rank. It was merely a mark of respect, indicating that I was a friend of Hank Priest, who'd given me a good buildup. There was no more conversation for a long time; just the high scream of the motor and the harsh hammering of water against the fiberglass hull. I could make out nothing but ocean—well, Gulf of Mexico—around us. Either the coast to port had dropped below the dark horizon, or it was uninhabited, or the inhabitants were sound asleep with all lights out. At last I picked up a flash off the bow. I looked up once more at Jarrel, standing at the helm behind me.

"Tortuga Light, cap'n," he said. "Off Tortuga Pass. We'd head in there if we wanted to get where we're going the quickest way. They're probably lying in there right now, waiting for light. We'll try Redfish Pass fifteen miles south. No light there, and it's not anything you'd want to tackle in bad weather, but a nice night like this we'll make it fine. Tortuga, that's turtle, cap'n. Redfish, that's what you maybe call drum or channel bass…"

Gradually, the flashing light drew abeam and fell astern. We ran on through the night. At last we swung east towards the coast, but it seemed a very long time until we picked it up. Jarrel had pulled the throttle back to half-speed, before I saw the loom of two islands ahead, low dark shadows off either bow, with what looked like an unbroken light sandbar between them.

Jarrel throttled back still more, so that the boat ceased planing over the water and, settling heavily, started plowing through it instead. Suddenly I was aware of something to starboard that wasn't water: a glistening mudbank barely uncovered by the dropping tide. The boat began to shimmy and sideslip in erratic eddies and whirlpools of current. There seemed to be all kinds of channels ahead in the darkness, a wilderness of mud and water, with patches of white here and there where the outrushing tidal waters broke in the shallows. Jarrel was dodging obstructions I couldn't see. He spoke quite calmly.

"Always remember the tide, cap'n, when you're in among the islands. Man can always find his way out if he remembers the tide. Hold on tight, now."

I saw the opening in the seemingly solid bar, but it didn't look like anything you'd want to take a boat through: a wide, angling gap of seething water moving inexorably out to sea. I felt the beat of the engine pick up as Jarrel opened the throttle once more. We hung in the entrance while he studied the situation ahead; then the rumbling vibration increased as more horsepower came into play, and we started to gain, the boat rising and planing once more, skittering over the disturbed surface, bounced and buffeted by the crazy currents. A cresting wave dropped into my lap from nowhere. The sand slid by, sometimes close enough that I could have jumped ashore. At last we broke free of the tide race and gained speed in the still, black water inside the bar.

"Used to take sailing boats through there when I was a boy," Jarrel said. "Course we had to wait for the right tide and a good westerly wind. You better use that Flit gun on your face and hands, cap'n. Like to be a few mosquitoes inshore here."

I sprayed myself and offered the aerosol can to him, but he shook his head. Apparently he was biteproof like many oldtimers. I put the can away, got out my handkerchief, and dried the rifle lying across my knees. I didn't even try to memorize our route. In the dark, with one island looking exactly like the next, black and formless, it was hopeless.

There were wide, gleaming estuaries that we traversed at high speed, and slim dark passages through which we crawled with the mangroves brushing the boat and the insects attacking in force. Once I was told to stand by with the boathook, ready to pole vigorously, while Jarrel tilted up the motor until the propeller was barely submerged and worked us over some shallow flats, disturbing a number of birds roosting on a nearby islet. Several times there were heavy splashes close to the bank as we approached; perhaps fish, perhaps alligators. I didn't ask. I didn't really want to know.

We came around a long bend, buzzed across some open water—a kind of tidal lake—and Jarrel cut the power and laid us alongside an ancient, rickety dock thrusting out from the swampy point at the end of an island that looked just like all the rest. An uneven, narrow, sagging wooden catwalk on posts led ashore over the reeds and mud.

"Cutlass Key, cap'n," Jarrel said, over the sound of the softly idling motor. "There's a deserted cabin off to the left a bit, in among the trees; nobody's used it for years. Water's low right now, but there's six feet off the end of the pier. Time they arrive, in daylight, tide'll be starting to turn. At high water, that mud'll be covered clear to the shore, but likely they won't be that late."

"We hope," I said, slapping a mosquito, "or the bugs will have sucked me dry."

Grasping the rifle, I started to rise, but Jarrel shook his head. "Not here, cap'n. You don't want to go leaving sign where they can see it. There's a place around the bend of the island, to the right there, where I can put her pretty close to the bank. I'll set you ashore there, and pick you up when you're through."

I liked the casual way he said it. It was going to be the usual, beautifully planned mission, I could see, with everything figured out to the last detail—up to the point where, having finished his job, the agent tries to get clear after kicking over the hornet's nest.

"Where'll you be?" I asked.

"There's a good hiding place for the boat alongside a little island down that way a quarter-mile," he said. "You can see it from where I'll leave you, and I can see you; but they can't see it from here. That's the point. Time they hear me coming, I'll have you back on board and be heading out again at forty-five knots."

"With bullets whistling around your ears and mine," I said sourly. "Or between them."

"Been shot at before, cap'n," Jarrel said. "Figure you have, too."

I said, "That doesn't mean I like it." I grimaced, studying the dark mass of the island. "Where will I wait?"

"Look up in the trees to the right. You'll see a kind of lump, that's an old osprey's nest. Birds haven't come back last two, three years, but the nest is still there. You'll be right under it, almost. It's a hundred and fifteen yards from your blind to the end of the dock here. Figure you'll want to let them come a little way towards you along the boardwalk, just to be sure, but that's your business."

"Yes," I said. "That's my business."

27

It looked like one of the tree blinds used for deer in the brush country of Texas; or perhaps a *machan* designed for ambushing a tiger at its kill in India—not that I considered my present quarry in the tiger class, but even a domesticated pussycat can be dangerous when you're dealing with the human variety.

As far as concealment was concerned, it was a pretty good job: a basketlike framework seven or eight feet off the ground that blended well into the surrounding tangle of branches. It wasn't the most comfortable blind I've ever occupied, but there was a sort of platform for standing and a tree limb for sitting. The only catch was that, when the time came, I'd have to rise and shoot without a rest for the rifle. There was nothing solid enough to serve the purpose. In fact, since they don't grow very big trees on those islands, the whole woven-together structure was a bit shaky. Well, a hundred yards isn't very long range for a rifle, even offhand.

"Okay, cap'n?" Jarrel whispered from below.

"Okay. Take her away and hide her," I said. "And, Jarrel—"

"Cap'n?"

"Don't be a goddamn hero, charging the flaming muzzles of the guns. If you know what I mean. I can assure you I wouldn't do it for you; don't you do it for me. If it goes sour, it goes sour, and to hell with it. Just blast out of here, tell them their fancy scheme didn't work, and hoist a beer to my memory. Okay?"

"I'm a guide, mostly," the black man said softly from the darkness below me. "I take my sports out and I bring them back. Haven't lost one yet and don't aim to, if I can help it. Good hunting, cap'n."

The world was full of high-principled lunatics, black and white, which was strange, I reflected, since you wouldn't think they'd last long, any of them. Well, I'd given him an out. If he didn't want to take it, that was his business.

I listened to him making his way back down to the shore, or tried to. He was pretty good in the woods; and I didn't really hear much until a very faint splashing told me he was poling the boat back out into deeper water so he could lower the motor. Then the hydraulic tilting mechanism whined, the starter whirred, and the sound of the big powerplant, at low speed, diminished gradually in the direction of the brushy little islet he'd pointed out to me, some four hundred yards distant.

I checked the rifle as well as I could in the dark. It was another of the bellowing, shoulder-busting Magnums that are very fashionable these days. It's getting so no hunter who values his image will even set out after rabbits without a portable cannon that will shoot through a bank vault and a couple of feet of masonry, and kill two or three innocent bystanders in the street outside, if they're lined up properly.

This was a bolt-action Winchester rifle using the .300 Winchester Magnum cartridge, a shortened and modernized successor to the old Holland and Holland .300, with a muzzle velocity over three thousand feet per second, and a muzzle energy approaching two tons. It was a hell of an artillery piece to have to fire out of a treetop, and I warned myself that I'd better make the first shot good because the goddamned howitzer might very well boot me clear out of the blind.

I made certain I had a round in the chamber and a full magazine, and that the floor plate was securely latched. Those big guns kick so hard they've been known to jar the floor plate open and dump out the contents of the magazine. It can be embarrassing to find yourself with only one cartridge when you thought you had four, particularly if, after the first shot, there's a hostile elephant heading your way under a full head of steam. At least so I'd been told. I've never met an elephant except in a zoo, but I have met some fairly hostile people and might encounter a few more tonight.

The telescopic sight was of the four-power variety recommended to beginners as the best all-round choice for hunting. I was glad they hadn't given me anything stronger, considering the shaky perch from which I'd be shooting: the greater the magnification, the greater the visible shake. I removed the protective caps from the lenses and peered through the instrument to make certain a hole ran clear through it. That was about all I could determine in the dark. I hoped no target would arrive until I had light enough so that I could actually make out the crosshairs.

The mosquitoes were the worst part of the waiting. I thought nostalgically of the pleasant hillside in Oklahoma, cool and bug-free, where I'd lain in wait for Sheriff Rullington, but it didn't help a bit. Without the dope I'd squirted liberally on myself, plus the mud I'd applied to my face and hands for camouflage purposes, I couldn't have stood it. As it was, I had to shut off part of my mind, the part that wanted to slap and scratch and, as time passed with interminable slowness and dawn approached, even scream a bit just to let me know I wasn't really having fun.

They came with the sunrise, well after it was light enough to see and shoot. Long before I saw them I could hear their motor approaching from the north and west. The sound faded for a while, and I wondered if Martha had lost her way in that swampy maze and what Leonard would do to her if she had, although I don't normally spend much time worrying about the fate of traitors—even young and pretty ones with whom I've slept. Then the motor noise came in again strong and increased in volume steadily. I saw them come into view, well out in the wide fairway to my left, too far for a shot even if I'd wanted to try such a fast-moving target from my unstable position.

I watched them through the leaves and thought I really had to hand it to Mac. The crazy, complex plan was working. In spite of lack of communications, in spite of everything, he'd stage-managed everybody to the right spot at the right time. The hidden hunter was waiting and the tiger or pussycat was coming to the bait, or what he thought was the bait.

There was the boat, a husky yellow inboard-outboard runabout some eighteen feet long with a tall whip antenna that reminded me of the houseboat, equipped with similar whiskers, that the admiral had spotted entering these waters—a communications ship of sorts, perhaps. But I didn't spend much attention on the boat, because there was the man with the white hair who'd caused everybody quite enough trouble already. Tiger or pussycat, he'd worn out his welcome. I mean, goddamn it, we do have a certain amount of professional pride, and we don't take kindly to outsiders forcing their way into our closed little undercover community, and trying to use it for their own cheap purposes. We'd tried to make this clear to Herbert Leonard the last time he'd come bucking for the title of Spymaster-in-Chief, but he hadn't taken the hint. It was, therefore, time for him to go.

He had the left hand seat behind the windshield— excuse me, the seat to port. To starboard, behind the steering wheel, sat a collegiate-looking youth in a blue yachting cap, with a pipe stuck jauntily into a corner of his mouth. Between him and Herbert Leonard, steadying herself with a hand on top of the windshield, stood Martha Borden, still in her light blue dress. How her bare arms and legs had survived the buggy night, I hated to think.

She used her free hand to point out the dock. The boat slowed and dropped off plane and swung that way, but only a little, not enough to bring it within rifleshot of the shore. It was all very cute, and I had to hand it to Leonard, too. He was almost as cute as Mac, using himself for a decoy like that. I hadn't thought him that clever or dashing, or even that brave; but I guess there comes a time for every desk officer when he feels he must go out and prove himself in the field, just once.

Anyway, this was one job Leonard would want to witness. He'd never be quite certain it had got done properly unless he saw it happen. All that now stood between him and the fulfillment of his ambitions was one man, but that man was one of the half-dozen most dangerous people in the world. Leonard would never sleep soundly until he saw Mac dead; and Mac had known this and taken advantage of it to bring Leonard here under my gun. The rest was up to me.

It was very cute, and it got cuter when they ran the boat aground out there, still well out of range, of course. They went into an act designed to show anybody watching from shore—Mac and whoever might, be occupying the cabin with him—how terribly mad they were at each other for this stupidity. The words couldn't be heard at the distance, of course, but the pantomime was clear: the college boy was obviously blaming the navigator,

Martha, who was obviously telling him hotly that if he'd steered where she'd pointed it wouldn't have happened. Leonard was obviously telling both of them to shut up and do something constructive. It was a fine diversion; and in the meantime the real attack was moving silently towards the hidden cabin—at least I suppose they thought they were being silent.

One boat was approaching along the bank just below the blind. I could hear the rythmic, liquid whisper of the pole urging it along. It landed—a large, flat-bottomed rowboat with a small kicker on the stern—and four men in camouflage clothing disembarked at the exact spot Jarrel and I had used some hours earlier. This was not surprising since a gap in the wall of mangroves made it a logical landing spot. Having them come so close was a little disconcerting, but there was an advantage: by the time they'd all got ashore, conferred together in whispers, spread out, and sneaked inland through the tangled undergrowth, the best tracker in the world couldn't have made out the signs of our earlier landing, Jarrel's and mine.

I watched the man on the right flank slip by only twenty yards distant, never looking up, of course. That's the advantage of a tree blind. Neither a deer nor a human being normally expects danger from above. He was another clean-cut young fellow in top-notch condition, educated to the teeth, no doubt, trained to break bricks with his bare hands, capable of picking the buttons off your vest with the machine pistol he carried, and totally useless in the woods.

I could follow him by ear long after I couldn't see him any longer; and the others were no better, the ones moving up the other shore of the island, presumably from another impromptu landing craft. I could trace the progress of the attack quite accurately from my elevated position by the snapping of twigs, the rustling of leaves, the clink of weapons, and the breathless curses. Well, Herbert Leonard could hardly be expected to have a squad of trained jungle fighters readily available, at least not a squad of trained jungle fighters he could trust to keep. their mouths shut about a curious operation like this.

The sun had cleared the horizon now; and out on the water the college boy with the yachting cap had managed to push Leonard's boat free. He jumped back behind the wheel and started the craft moving slowly towards the dock, as a man made his way out along the catwalk holding a bulky object that turned out to be an electronic megaphone or bullhorn—loud-hailer, I believe our British friends call it. By now, another boat was coming into view far down the channel beyond the dock, the way Jarrel and I had come. It had been a carefully planned trap; the only trouble was, there hadn't been anybody to catch in it. The man with the bullhorn confirmed this loudly.

"Cabin secure, sir!" he bellowed across the water. "Nobody home!"

Leonard produced a howler of his own, and his voice reached me quite clearly: "Repeat."

"Cabin empty. No sign of occupation. Repeat, no sign of occupation. Empty. Unoccupied. Orders?"

On board the boat, the college-boy yachtsman produced a pistol and aimed it at Martha. The man on the dock lifted his megaphone once more.

"Orders, sir?" he repeated.

"Hold everything. I'm coming in," Leonard shouted.

I watched him come. I won't pretend that my pulse and respiration remained absolutely normal as my target moved slowly into range. The college boy put the boat alongside the rickety pier, and spoke to the bullhorn artist, who put down his instrument, unslung a machine pistol, and aimed it down at Martha. The college boy put his revolver away, pulled down his yachting cap more firmly, and climbed up to secure the dock lines. Leonard, still in the boat, gestured towards the girl, and the two men on the dock reached down and dragged her up between them. Only then did Leonard move to disembark.

I guess I'd known it was coming, as Mac must have known it was coming when he gave me a gun capably of shooting through a bull moose lengthwise. The heavy, souped-up rifle was as good as a written order. It said clearly: *You will carry out your mission disregarding anything, or anybody, that may stand in your way.*

Well, it wasn't the first time I'd had this decision to make, and had made it: and this time it wasn't even very hard. I mean, the girl really meant very little to me. I find it very easy to control my passion for cocky, treacherous young ladies who make it clear that they consider me a lecherous idiot, ready to park my brains behind the door at the sight of any willing female body.

It was like watching a bad movie the second or third time, with the same old beautiful-female-hostage scene coming up. They always try it, figuring, I guess, that what works on the screen ought to work in real life. I eased the rifle forward cautiously so I'd be ready to take a clear shot if Leonard gave me the chance, but he was careful not to. He was bright enough to know that he'd been decoyed here for some purpose, and he wasn't about to expose himself until he learned what it was. That's what he'd saved the girl for, instead of having her shot at once when he learned that her information had led him to an empty cabin.

Sitting in the boat, he'd given me no target, and he offered none as he came ashore, carefully sheltering himself behind the boat's windshield pillars and a dock piling. Then he had the girl in front of him. The whole procession was moving shorewards along the catwalk. I drew a long breath. With a rifle I'd sighted in myself, and with a steady rest, I'd have tried to slip one past the girl's head into the head of the man; but this gun could be six or eight inches off at this range, and I couldn't call my shots that well from my rickety perch, anyway.

I had no choice. I rose up deliberately and placed the black crosshairs carefully on Martha Borden's body, a little to one side, figuring the angle that would center the bullet in the body behind her. They came on, still unsuspecting. I placed my finger on the trigger, and my mind gave the order to the appropriate muscles, and nothing happened. I take no credit for humanitarianism. In my mind, the girl was dead. So sorry. If you don't betray people, sweetheart, you don't get shot. If you do, you do. Goodbye, Martha Borden...

But she was still coming, and so was the man behind her, and my sentimental fingertip simply wouldn't move the necessary fraction of an inch. Then there was a sudden flurry of movement down there. The girl threw herself back against Leonard, knocking him off balance, and jumped. She landed in six inches of mud, almost fell but caught herself, and started floundering diagonally towards shore. Leonard, recovering, spoke sharply to the ex-bullhorn-artist, who raised his current instrument, the machine pistol. It was a setup shot. With an automatic weapon like, that, he couldn't possibly miss the girl struggling shorewards only twenty yards away—but Leonard was standing unprotected at last, wide open, as fine a target as any marksman could wish for.

My finger finally decided to obey the urgent orders from my brain. The big rifle roared, and recoiled violently against my shoulder. The man with the squirt gun, as I like to call them, dropped his weapon unfired into the low-tide mud below the dock and followed it limply, dead before he hit.

28

As an exhibition of unprofessional idiocy, it would be hard to beat. It was exactly the kind of mushy behavior that makes me cringe and snap off the TV set when I see it on the screen: a supposedly trained and dedicated man with a job to do upon which the fate of millions supposedly depends, turning aside from his clear duty to perform heroic rescues of totally irrelevant young ladies.

By the time I'd recovered from the outsized kick of the rifle, worked the bolt, and swung the crosshairs to where I'd last seen Herbert Leonard, he was not, of course, there any longer. The man was catching on. His behavior this morning, unlike that of some people, had been thoroughly professional. The fact that somebody might have thought him afraid, hiding behind a woman, hadn't bothered him in the least. Now, at the sound of the shot, he'd jettisoned his dignity without an instant's hesitation, throwing himself into the muck on the far side of the dock and flopping out of sight behind one of the pilings.

The youth with the pipe and the yachting cap had taken refuge in the bottom of the boat. I had a great big rifle and nothing to shoot at; then a man rose out of the brush with another squirt gun—Leonard seemed to pass them around like visiting cards—and took aim at the girl as she gained the swampy shore. I dropped him neatly: another good shot wasted on a totally unimportant mark.

The flimsy blind was kind of disintegrating from the jolting of the Magnum rifle, getting shakier by the minute. It was time to go, anyway, before the college commandos got zeroed in on my position. I wedged the gun into the fork of a tree limb, dropped to the ground, and reached back up for it—climbing around in trees with loaded guns isn't considered proper firearms etiquette. I'd barely got it loose when at least three automatic weapons started drilling holes in the blind and the deserted osprey's nest above it, showering me with twigs and leaves and splinters.

I moved off a little ways, and crouched to listen, taking the opportunity to replace the two cartridges I'd fixed. Listening wasn't much good. Every man on the island was now, it seemed, busily hosing down my recent hiding place with full-automatic fire. It sounded like 9mm stuff. The .45's used in the old Thompson choppers had had a heavier and more authoritative way of hammering at the ears. Nevertheless, the noise was impressive, and didn't give me much chance to listen for rustling leaves or stealthy footsteps.

I moved cautiously towards the landing place, stalling, hoping the girl would hold a reasonably straight line through the thick cover: she'd been aimed in roughly the right direction when she came ashore. I caught a flash of blue among the trees, and there she was. I stepped out into a small opening. She saw me, veered towards me, and stumbled up to me, muddy and breathless.

"Matt, I—"

"Down to the shore and straight out into the water," I said, pointing. "Take the first streetcar that comes along. You'll recognize the conductor."

"Matt—"

"Sweetie, you're a sneaky, slimy little bitch-Judas, and we'll discuss it later, if we live that long. Get going!"

It took them a while to reach me, as I followed her deliberately, covering our back trail. They'd heard two shots fired and seen two men fall. It was making them cautious. They were probably brave enough to charge headlong into haphazard machine-gun fire; but this kind of selective, precision marksmanship—one bullet per body—has a way of slowing down a lot of would-be heroes. I was counting on that.

One more should make the point perfectly clear, I figured, giving us time to get away. I couldn't afford to miss, however. That would spoil the psychological effect. I passed up a fleeting target on the left, therefore, and waited until a gent in the center gave me a sure shot, in a little sunlit space he'd undoubtedly have detoured if he hadn't felt obliged to show his fellow-agents and his chief what a truly courageous fellow he was. He gave a very satisfactory scream as he went down. That should hold them for a little. I turned and ran.

Down at the water, when I got there, everything was developing well. The boat, with Jarrel at the helm, was racing in on schedule, making a fine dramatic picture and producing a spectacular wake. The girl was wading out towards it. I sloshed after her, gaining by virtue of my longer legs. Jarrel held his speed until I thought he'd run us down, but when he chopped the throttle, the boat dropped off plane and squished to a stop right beside us. Jarrel checked the last of its forward motion with a touch of reverse, and jumped to the side to help Martha aboard. I was reaching for the gunwale when the black man, glancing shorewards, said quietly, "Better give that feller some discouragement, cap'n."

I pivoted, lifting the rifle, and fired as the crosshairs found a man on the shore, taking aim with a chopper. He went down, but at the same instant another submachine-gun opened up to the right among the mangroves. I slammed in a fresh cartridge and swung that way. The scope showed a face among the leaves, and a stuttering weapon. The nasty little jacketed pistol bullets seemed to be whistling and cracking and glancing off the water all around us; then my big rifle went off again, with its usual end-of-the-world bellow and kick. The face disappeared and the squirt gun fell silent. I turned, reached over the rail to lay the gun carefully in the cockpit—you don't toss around weapons that you may need again shortly—and kind of hauled and rolled myself aboard.

"Take her away!" I panted, but the boat didn't move.

There was no time to investigate. I just snatched up the rifle and threw it to my shoulder as I rose, aiming blindly at the shore. I had them well-trained by now. Three of them, all about to open up on the drifting boat, dropped flat, each one thinking the muzzle of the big Magnum was looking right down his throat.

"Matt," the girl wailed, "Matt, it's Jarrel—"

"Get us out of here!" I snapped without looking aside.

"But his face… he's bleeding…"

"Jesus Christ!" I exploded. "We'll all be bleeding in about three seconds if you don't hit that goddamn throttle, *now*!"

I heard her scramble behind the wheel. I had the crosshairs on a man who was beginning to show himself at the bow of the beached rowboat used by the attacking force, when the big motor opened up and our boat shot forward, throwing me off balance. I managed to get my finger off the trigger and set the safety, even while I was being shoved inexorably towards the stern by the thrust of all those horsepower. Something stopped my slide: a man's body.

"Zigzag!" I yelled over the screaming motor, as I crouched beside Jarrel White. There was a lot of gunfire astern. "Hard right rudder. Now left. Keep it up, but for God's sake don't run us aground. Here come the boys in the black hats, galloping in wild pursuit." The yellow runabout had just come into view around the island, throwing a wake like a junior-grade destroyer. "How fast is that bucket?" I asked.

Martha threw a glance over her shoulder. "It's fast," she shouted. "It's good for thirty-five, I think, maybe even forty."

"We can beat that, I hope," I said. "Hold it straight now; we're out of range. Open her up all the way, but watch it. You've got more power than you think. Let me get this tub trimmed right now…"

With the weight of two men concentrated to port, the little boat was racing along awkwardly with a strong list in that direction. I dragged Jarrel into the center of the cockpit forward of the steering console and everything leveled off nicely. I looked astern. The yellow boat wasn't gaining, but it wasn't falling back much, either.

"Have you got her wide open?" I yelled at Martha, who nodded. "Then that's a faster boat back there than you thought, damn it. We should be doing well over forty-five, unless…"

I looked down at Jarrel White. He was quite dead, and had been from the instant the bullet had struck him just below the right eye. His dead eyes, open, looked up at me calmly. *I take my sports out and I bring them back*, he'd said; and he'd have done it, too, if he'd lived. A good man. He would understand that I meant no disrespect by what I was about to do. I picked him up and dropped him over the side.

I was thrown off-balance once more as the boat slowed abruptly. The girl was staring at me, making some loud, outraged sounds. It was hard to believe she was Mac's daughter. Maybe her mother had slipped out one evening to dally with the executive director of the local SPCA—

but of course there were those eyebrows. Well, a dog-breeder had once told me there were weak strains in all bloodlines that should be culled as they crop out. I'd had a good opportunity to cull this one, but I'd passed it up for sentimental reasons that were looking less and less valid.

The yellow boat was coming up fast. The pipe-sucking youth was at the wheel, his yachting cap shoved back from his forehead. Leonard had the other forward seat. There was mud in his disheveled white hair. He was holding something in front of his face. I didn't have time to deter mine what it was or what it signified. There were two men aft with the usual portable automatic firepower. They were getting ready to bring it into action as the range closed.

I grabbed Martha's bare arm, yanked the girl out from behind the controls, and slung her forward. I hit the throttle lever a reckless swipe, and grabbed the wheel one-handed, barely in time to keep from being left behind as the boat took off again like a dragster burning rubber at the start of the quarter-mile strip. I spent a moment or two pulling myself into place behind the console, fighting the impressive forces of acceleration; then I risked a glance over my shoulder.

Leonard's rear-seat passengers had lowered their weapons; the range wasn't closing any more. As I watched, briefly, I saw the yellow boat begin to fall back. Jarrel's weight had made the difference. According to a boat book I'd read, boning up on my borrowed vessel, the speed of a planing hull depends mostly on just two factors: the horsepower and the load. A hundred-and-fifty-odd pounds lighter, my little craft was now a knot or two faster, enough to give us the necessary edge.

I looked ahead. We were rushing down a fairly wide, mangrove-lined channel, two waterborne projectiles churning up the calm brown surface, but ahead the fairway broke into three passages. I had no idea which one to take. Then a large white cottage came racing into sight around a slow bend in the middle passage, far ahead. At least that was what it looked like—a white summer cottage perched on top of a blunt blue scow—but it was coming towards us doing at least thirty miles per hour. I realized that what Leonard had been holding had been a microphone. He'd got in touch with his communications ship, the houseboat the admiral had told me about. It was moving in to cut us off, following radio instructions, showing a nice turn of speed for such a clumsy-looking craft. The questions were: which of us would reach the crossroads first; and if I beat them to it, which way should I turn when I got there?

The girl was huddled in the cockpit forward. I didn't even bother to ask her. With her crazy reactions, she'd be just as likely to give me the wrong answer as the right one. As I stared ahead, searching for a clue, I saw something glistening white, a dead fish perhaps, drifting slowly out of the left-hand passage towards us. I remembered Jarrel's words: *Remember the tide, cap'n. Man can always find his way out if he remembers the tide.*

The tide, that had been ebbing last night, would be flooding now, moving in from the sea. All I had to do was run against it when in doubt, and with a little luck I'd be in open water eventually. I could see that I was going to beat the houseboat to the turn by a good margin, and the yellow runabout was by now a couple of hundred yards astern. I had it made. Pretty soon I'd have lead enough, and time enough, to start firing off white flares, bringing the Boston Whaler in to meet me with a crew of armed men.

There was only one catch. The admiral had also had a few words to say, to wit: *Of course, it's expected that you'll have your job done before you signal for help.*

Still wide open, my little boat approached the watery intersection. There was a man on the roof, upper deck, or whatever you want to call it, of the onrushing houseboat. He had something shiny and metallic in his hand, a pistol perhaps, but he wasn't even trying to use it yet; we had room to spare. I saw the white object—it was a dead fish—to port, and if that wasn't indication enough, there were some pink birds wading in the right hand channel which could not, therefore, be much over a foot deep. With prop down, my vessel drew over twice that at rest; over ten inches even while planing. I drew a long breath and turned the wheel sharply to the right.

"No! Hard aport! You're turning the wrong way! Port your helm, Matt!"

That was the girl, aroused, standing forward. The pink birds rose in panic as the boat roared at them. Their legs were even shorter than I'd estimated. There was a crash astern as the big motor, striking, was pivoted violently upwards; then the hull hit hard…

29

I awoke tied hand and foot, but I was alive enough to wake up, which was the important thing. Breathing hurt my chest, but it beat not breathing. I remembered being hurled against the steering wheel as the boat came to an abrupt, grinding halt; and seeing the girl kind of sailing over the bow. Hunched over the console, gagging, with the wind knocked out of me, I'd been aware of men wading alongside and of Leonard's voice calling: "No, no, don't shoot him. Not yet. There are some questions I want to ask him first…"

Good old Herbert Leonard, predictable as always. He'd had a small, feverish touch of professionalism back there at Cutlass Key, but he was recovering nicely. Hundreds of overconfident characters have failed in their missions, many have died, from keeping dangerous prisoners alive for questioning instead of shooting them on the spot, but the message never seems to get through. People like our white-haired Herbie are never satisfied with simply winning. They want their victories and information, too.

You can count on it always, I'd reflected happily; and somebody had hit me over the head with something, probably a gun-barrel. Now I was here, wherever that was. They'd taken my gun and knife, of course, and also my belt—Leonard would know about the trick belts we're issued—but I still had my clothes and shoes on.

"Matt. Matt, are you awake? Are you all right?"

I opened my eyes and looked up at the low, white-painted ceiling of a largish cabin, at the end of which a couple of steps led up to a kind of louvered door that presumably opened—when it opened—to the main living spaces of the houseboat, if that's what I was on.

"Matt, can you hear me?"

Turning my head was painful, and the view that rewarded me was hardly worth it; although I guess it was mildly interesting to learn what a nicely dressed young lady looks like after wading through swamps, fleeing through jungles, and being pitched off a boat into muddy shallows. I noticed that, grimy and bedraggled as she was, she was practically dry, indicating that I'd been unconscious for some time.

She was lying on a bunk across the way, tied hand and foot just as I was. I caught her eye, and shook my head quickly as she started to speak.

I formed the words with my lips soundlessly: "Come here."

After a moment, cued by a beckoning finger, she got the idea and heaved herself awkwardly off her bunk and onto mine. Leaning close, she whispered, "Matt, what—"

"Figure they're listening out there," I breathed, indicating the ventilated door. "Figure they're waiting for me to come to, and for us to hold an interesting conversation about something. When they've heard enough, the fun will begin. So keep acting as if you're still trying to bring me around."

She nodded. "Matt!" she said aloud. "Oh, Matt, please wake up. I'm so scared!"

"That's the idea," I whispered. "Now, inside my left shoe you'll find a gadget looking like a short mechanical pencil, damned uncomfortable to walk on. I think you'll recognize it and know how it works. Twist the heel of my right shoe and you'll find what goes with it. Real secret agent stuff; how about it?" I grinned at her in an encouraging way. I'm not a superstitious man, and I don't believe much in ESP, but under tricky circumstances like that I prefer to avoid calling important items by their right names, even in whispers. I mean, I just don't want those particular vibrations floating around to give the wrong people ideas. Why take chances? I went on, very softly: "Thread one into the other, you know how, and hide it on you somewhere, but remember, I'm giving it to you to use when I give the word, not to wave around and threaten with like in the movies. When the opportunity comes, if it comes, our lives will depend on instant action. If you waste time talking, we're both dead. Okay?"

She hesitated, studying my face. She was smart enough to realize approximately what I was asking of her, and her face was pale under the streaks of mud. Then she nodded abruptly.

"Okay, Matt." Hitching herself back along the bunk, she raised her voice: "Matt, you've just got to wake up, they're going to kill us both, I heard them talking! They think I was in on the whole thing with you. They won't believe you and Daddy and Uncle Hank just used me as an innocent, stupid dupe to decoy Mr. Leonard to that place. They just laugh at me when I try to tell them I was quite sincere. Matt, can you hear me? Open your eyes. Say something."

It took her a while, babbling like this, to get at the concealed equipment with her bound-together hands, twisting painfully to see how the work was progressing behind her.

"I suppose I ought to hate you all!" she went on breathlessly. "Particularly Daddy and you! Think of it, my own father and a man I... I've slept with taking advantage of my... my principles and using me to set a man up for murder. But you didn't shoot. Why didn't you shoot, Matt? Just because I was in front of him? Why did that stop you? You're supposed to be the ruthless, sentimental, coldblooded manhunter, aren't you? Was it because... because we'd made love a little, or just because you're Daddy's friend and didn't want to face him after putting a bullet through his idiot daughter? Which was it, Matt? Oh, don't just lie there like a log, damn you! You're awake, I know you're awake! Say something!"

My shoes had been returned to my feet. She was

hiding something under her scanty, dirty, damaged blue dress. She bobbed her head at me to let me know she was ready for the next phase of the operation. There was a little gleam in her eyes that said she hoped her monologue had made me at least slightly uncomfortable, and maybe it had; but it was no time to discuss the question of who had been taking advantage of whom.

I licked my lips and said thickly, aloud: "Port your helm!"

"What?"

"A big girl," I said, forming the words with a difficulty that was only partly feigned, since my throat was pretty dry, "a big girl like you ought to learn right from left. Port your helm, she said, and there went the whole damned ballgame!"

She played up instantly. "But port *is* left, and that was the way we were supposed to go—"

"And helm means tiller, sweetheart; and when you shove the tiller to the left, the boat goes to the right."

"But you didn't *have* a tiller!"

"What difference does that make? You're supposed to figure the way a tiller would go and steer accordingly, even when you're using a wheel. Where did you learn your seamanship, anyway?"

Martha said, with real indignation, "But you're crazy, Matt! When you port your helm with a wheel, you go left, I'm sure you do! It wouldn't make sense otherwise!"

I said, "What really wouldn't make sense would be to have a command mean one thing on a boat that steers with a wheel and exactly the opposite on a boat that steers with a stick. Just how confusing do you want to get? What if the wheel breaks down and you rig a jury tiller, do you right away start giving all steering commands the opposite way, on the same damned ship—"

The door opened, and in they came, figuring, I guess, that they weren't going to learn anything significant from a technical argument about seamanship, and we didn't seem to be getting around to any interesting subjects. There were two of them, nice, clean-cut, American-boy types—well, actually they were in their thirties, but they'd never outgrow it. They both had smooth Florida tans. They were both wearing short-sleeved jersey sports shirts, light slacks, and the kind of expensive seagoing sneakers that are designed to get a death-grip on the wet, slanting deck of a hard-driven sailing yacht.

They were real pretty, all except the guns they kept brandishing in a very self-conscious way. They untied our ankles, set us on our feet, and used their firearms to prod us up the steps and through the low, ventilated doors into the houseboat's galley, a symphony in stainless steel. There we made a full hundred-and-eighty-degree turn and climbed another short stairway—I guess the nautical term is ladder—into a pilot house with lots of windows all around, located directly above our recent prison cell.

A big steering wheel and a lot of motor controls and instruments dominated the far end of this elevated greenhouse. To one side was a bank of electronic equipment being monitored by a young black man with less hair than most, these Afro days. He had headphones on and was perched on a stool in front of the closed sliding door, halfglass, that gave access to the deck to starboard. The mangroves were right there, just beyond the railing. We were tied up against the bank in a small cove.

To port was an L-shaped settee and a card table holding a lot of official-looking papers. The settee held my heavy, scope-sighted rifle, and Herbert Leonard. He'd washed off the mud he'd picked up diving off the dock and combed his hair. He was wearing clean light slacks and a flowered sports shirt. He looked up at our entrance, seeming annoyed.

"No, no, I don't want them up here!" he said irritably. "Take them into the rear cabin. I'll be along in a minute."

We were poked with the firearms once more, escorted back down the stairs—excuse me, ladder—and aft through the galley into another well-windowed compartment with a dinette to starboard and a kind of built-in sofa or lounge to port. Another sliding door led out to the short stern deck, but this door was also closed, presumably to keep the mosquitoes out and the air conditioning in.

Off the stern of the houseboat lay my little craft. She seemed to be floating all right, but I doubted there was enough left of her propeller, after hitting bottom at full throttle, to make her very useful for getaway purposes. There was a spare wheel on board, of course, but I'd never changed props on a motor that big, and it would take me some time to figure out the drill. Well, escape was not the immediate problem. If all I'd wanted to do was escape, I could have been safely on board the *Frances II* this minute.

The yellow runabout was not in sight, and I had seen nothing of its pilot. There were no other small craft visible, either, or any of the camouflaged pseudo-commando characters who'd participated in the attack on Cutlass Key. Apparently Leonard's amphibious forces had withdrawn, with their casualties.

"Sit down!"

That was my guard, shoving me onto the lounge. He seated himself on the end of one of the dinette benches across the way and showed me his gun once more. It was a perfectly ordinary Smith & Wesson, in no way unique. He seemed to be quite proud of it, however.

"If you want to try something," he said, "go right ahead, you dirty professional assassin! After the way you murdered Patterson down in Mexico and March and Tolley in Arizona, not to mention all the good men you shot down in cold blood this morning, all I need is an excuse, just one little excuse!"

I looked at him more sharply, alerted by his blustering voice, and realized that he was scared. It always surprises me a little. I mean, I never feel particularly scary; and I felt even less so than usual that morning, with my chest aching, the back of my head throbbing, the camouflage mud still coated on my face and hands, and my hands tied behind me. But dirty or clean, healthy or unhealthy, tied or untied, I apparently frightened him. His companion, facing Martha from the end of the other dinette seat, didn't seem very happy, either. It told me what attitude to employ. I fell into the spirit of the occasion and became the deadly, bloodthirsty old pro annoyed by a couple of ineffectual novices.

"What did you boys do," I asked lightly, "flip a coin or something?"

"What do you mean?" my guard asked.

"How did you decide who'd get stuck with the dull chore of shooting me, when the time came, and who'd get all the fun of putting a lot of holes in the pretty lady—"

"Pretty lady, hell!" said Martha's specimen. "Just because she's put a dress on doesn't make her a lady in my book, even when she isn't all plastered with mud! We saw the greasy specimens she was associating with down in Mexico. This country would be a damn sight better off if all the filthy hippie types, male and female, were lined up against a wall and used for target practice, leaving the country to clean, decent people; real Americans!"

That scared me, a little. It was the first hint I'd had of the motivation behind Senator Love's secret crusade, as abetted by Herbert Leonard and his handsome young followers. There's nothing more frightening to me than a character who thinks he knows what a real American is—mainly because it generally turns out he's convinced it's somebody just like him. It seems an odd notion to me. I certainly don't want to live in a country populated with people just like me, God forbid! Anyway, I figure there's room for a little variety in a nation as big as ours.

I said, "You know, that's not half a bad idea. At least a little practice sure wouldn't hurt you boys any, judging by the gent who tried to plug me down in Guaymas—it's too bad he couldn't swim any better than he could shoot. And how many rounds did those characters let off this morning without hurting anybody but a poor old black man; and that was an accident, a ricochet off the water. Yes, I think a little target practice would do wonders for you lads; and you might try a few driving lessons, too, while you're at it. Those two jerks near Tucson were kind of pitiful, really. I just hated to shut the door on them like that and send them out into the rocks to die. I mean, it was kind of like going around knocking little kids off their Christmas tricycles—"

"Shut up!" After a moment, my specimen said sharply: "Talking about target practice, you didn't do so well yourself back there at Cutlass Key this morning. Sure, you managed to shoot a lot of good agents, but you didn't get the man you'd come all that way to—"

"Man?" I said, thinking fast. "Who says I was there after a man? I came for her." I jerked my head towards Martha. "And I got her, didn't I? I was told she'd guide us out of there. It's not my fault the fool bitch doesn't know her right hand from her left. There was not a damn thing wrong with my part of the job, not a thing!"

30

I was aware of Martha restraining herself from casting a startled—maybe even reproachful—glance in my direction; but it was the only way to handle it. I could never convince them, any more than she'd been able to, that she'd been perfectly honest and idealistic when she led them to her father's supposed hideout on Cutlass Key. It was better to use what they already believed, and build on that.

My guard said sharply, "Are you trying to tell us—"

"Why the hell should I want to hurt your precious Mr. Leonard, if that's who you mean?" I asked.

The man shook his head. "That won't wash, Helm! Just now in your cabin, when she was trying to bring you around, your female accomplice said in so many words that you'd been planning to shoot—"

"Eavesdropping?" I said. "Tsk. Tsk. Tell me, in your outfit do you always tell every junior member of every operational team everything about the team's mission.

It must be nice to have so much faith. The fact is, Miss Borden was never informed of the exact purpose of her assignment. Maybe she thought she was setting somebody up for a touch. Maybe it made her feel better, more important, to believe she was part of a desperate assassination squad, instead of just getting a man out of the way for a few hours. If she'd known that, she might have started asking herself—maybe even aloud—why this particular man had to be distracted at this particular time; and that's a question we didn't want being asked by anybody, until our business was all taken care of."

"Then what were you doing up that tree with that big rifle?"

I glanced sourly at the girl beside me, and grimaced. "Under normal circumstances," I said, "using a trained female agent, we'd have let her make her own way clear, or not, however it worked out. Our operatives are supposed to be able to take care of themselves. If they can't, well, we're sorry about that. But in this case we had to use a girl who wasn't an agent, simply because she was the best bait available, the person most likely to be able to sell your Mr. Leonard a bill of goods. But she'd had no training, and she happened to be the boss's daughter. Therefore, I was instructed to take whatever steps necessary to make sure she got out okay." I shrugged. "Nepotism, I guess you'd call it. I'm not really in the bodyguard business, but, hell, orders are orders. And we'd have made it, too, if she hadn't got all loused up on port and starboard. Christ, what a time to get nautical. If she'd just stuck to right and left, we'd be home free!"

"But if you didn't want to kill Mr. Leonard—" This was Martha's escort, frowning thoughtfully. "If you weren't really setting him up for murder, why go to all the trouble—"

"He's here, isn't he?" I said shortly. "He isn't up north tending to business like he should, is he? He's chasing mirages through a lousy Florida swamp, or at least he was all last night. And right now he's wasting time shuffling papers up forward, instead of using his brains and trying to find out why somebody wanted him out of circulation early on the morning of June fifteenth. It must be hell working for a stupid man. I feel for you boys, I really do. The gent I take my orders from may not be so photogenic, but at least he's got something between the ears besides a wad of crumpled newspaper clippings telling him what a wonderful guy he…"

I'd figured Leonard had sent us back here so he could sneak up and listen to us, and I was right. Now he appeared in the cabin entrance, looking stern and accusing.

"Well!" he snapped. "I hope you gentlemen are having a good time comparing employers."

Our two guards had jumped to their feet. The nearest one, Martha's man, protested quickly, "Sir, we thought it best to let him talk. He claims he wasn't really assigned to murder you, as we assumed."

"I heard what he claims." Leonard laughed scornfully. "What else could he say, having failed to carry out his mission? I've met this beanpole agent before. All his mistakes are always on purpose, to hear him tell it." He looked at me. "You'll have to come up with a better story than that, Helm. I think you're talking just to keep yourself alive!"

He was perfectly right, but it wasn't really an inspired guess. What else would I be doing under the circumstances? Of course, I was also talking to throw him off guard so I could do the job I'd been sent here for.

I shrugged in a resigned sort of way. "Suit yourself, Mr. Leonard. I'm a hell of a liar. If fact doesn't suit you, I can cook up some real fancy fiction."

He hesitated. Then he said carelessly, "Oh, no let's not strain your imagination any further. Let's stick with your current fairy tale, at least for the present. But let's make it slightly more plausible. Give us some motivation, Helm. Tell us just why you're supposed to have gone to a great deal of trouble—you, and your murderous employer, and all his lackeys and accomplices, not to mention that fine little actress, his daughter—to set an elaborate trap for me, if all the time you were intending to magnanimously spare my life?"

"I told you," I said, mixing a little judicious falsehood with a lot of truth, or what I guessed to be the truth. "Anyway, I told these characters. It wasn't a trap. For various reasons it was essential to get you out of Washington for a day or two, Mr. Leonard; out of Washington and out of easy contact with your key people. My chief knew, of course, that when he went underground you'd keep a sharp eye on his daughter, hoping she'd lead you to him. He simply had her take you on a wild goose chase into darkest Florida, leaving him to carry on undisturbed up north." Leonard tried to interrupt, but I went on without pausing. "Why should we shoot you, Leonard? You're through, but even a discredited Chief of Intelligence can cause a lot of awkward questions if he's found with a bullet hole in him. I think my chief will be willing to settle for your resignation and retirement from public life—that is, of course, if you turn Miss Borden and me loose unharmed."

They were all grinning. As a comic, I was a big success. "My, that's mighty big of Arthur Borden," Leonard said playfully. "You're sure that's all he wants, my resignation and retirement? Oh, and the two of you unharmed, of course."

I said blandly, "Well, I haven't had a chance to consult him about the details, sir, but I feel he intends to be generous. Of course, you'll never hold another government position as long as you live, but at least you will live." I congratulated myself on getting the lie out with some conviction. I went on, "It's your last chance, Mr. Leonard, assuming that I'm right and he's willing to give it to you. We're getting kind of fed up with you. This is the second time you've inconvenienced us. Most people don't manage it more than once." I pulled my wrists around. "So if you'll just cut us loose now, and give us back our boat—"

Leonard nodded slightly. My guard lashed out with his pet Smith & Wesson, catching me alongside the head and knocking me against the end of the settee. It showed how much he really knew about revolvers, using one as a club. Half dazed, I felt the blood running down my cheek from a nick in the scalp. Leonard stepped forward to stand over me.

"The trouble with you, Helm," he said coldly, "the big trouble with you is that you've been allowed to get away with your arrogant bluffs so often you think they'll work on anybody. I hate to disillusion you, my man, but you're not pulling it off this time… What is it, Bostrom?"

The man who had hit me said, "Can't you hear it, sir? It's a powerboat. Probably Jernegan coming back."

"Oh."

Leonard stared at me for a moment longer, but the motor sound was approaching rapidly. He squeezed between me and my guard, not the best technique in the world even if my hands were tied, and threw open the glass door leading to the deck aft. The yellow runabout was in sight, dropping off plane as it neared the houseboat. The youth with the yachting cap, apparently named Jernegan, was at the wheel. A gray-haired woman in a blue-flowered dress occupied the other forward seat. As they coasted in to a landing, Leonard hurried forward to help the passenger make the climb to the houseboat's deck while Jernegan secured the boat and climbed aboard under his own power.

"It's a pleasure to have you here, of course, Mrs. Love," I heard Leonard say. "Naturally, when I got your emergency message, I sent the boat right away, but I wish you'd explain—"

"Explain?" the woman snapped. "I want to hear *you* explain what you're doing way out here in this godforsaken alligator park when I need you, Herbert! Oh, and did you know that your man in Denver, Colorado, just died in a freeway accident? And the fellow in Bangor, Maine, who was going to get me some leverage on that reluctant congressman, keeled over with a fatal heart attack last night? What is going on, Herbert? I thought you said you had everything under control, but when key personnel start dying like that, even accidentally—"

"Mr. Leonard!" It was the voice of the radio operator, calling from up forward. "Mr. Leonard, take a call on the blue phone, please. New Orleans is on the line."

"Excuse me, Mrs. Love."

Leonard came back into the cabin. He threw me an odd, wary glance, picked up one of the telephones on the dinette table, and identified himself. I could hear a male voice speaking rapidly in the receiver, but I couldn't make out the words. Leonard frowned.

"What?" he said. "A crazy man with a couple of guns and a grudge against policemen... What the hell do I care how many Cajun cops got themselves killed by a kamikaze maniac? Oh, you say Jack Westheimer was caught in the crossfire, kind of accidentally..." He hung up slowly, started to glance my way again, but changed his mind, and called forward. "Martin, get me Bill Frank, in Washington."

We waited. Presently, the light on the blue phone glowed once more. Leonard hesitated, picked it up, spoke, and listened. I saw his face go flat and gray. "In the hospital? Botulism, what the hell is that… Oh. They couldn't save him? I see. Thanks." He put the phone down once more, stood for a moment in thought, and called, "Martin, get me Homer Dunn, in Los Angeles… What?"

"I was just going to tell you, sir. Mr. Dunn's office just called. Mr. Dunn went boating over the weekend and didn't return. They were wondering whether to alert the Coast Guard."

Leonard turned slowly to look at me. There was a kind of scared horror in his eyes, and a burning hate.

31

He started by slapping me, which was childish. His smooth, handsome, politician's face was kind of white-pink with rage and fear; and his eyes actually seemed to bulge slightly from their sockets. He looked like a good candidate for a coronary, but I knew I'd never be so lucky. It was my job. I'd flubbed it once, but I'd have to take care of it eventually.

The trick was staying alive long enough to do it. There was, at the moment, no possibility of help from Martha, bound and guarded. I saw the lady senator standing in the doorway aft, taking in the scene in the crowded cabin. I realized that she was my best bet. She hadn't got where she was by being stupid.

Leonard gave me another peevish whack across the cheek, like an irritable mother disciplining an infuriating child.

"How many?" he demanded in a choked voice. "How many cold-blooded assassinations—"

I laughed in his face. "Says the man who sent an agent clear to Mexico to shoot me in the back with a scoped-up 7mm rifle! Don't talk to me about cold-blooded assassinations, Leonard! Who started it? How many of our people did you actually manage to have murdered, trying clumsily to wipe us out?" I laughed again. "What the hell made you think you could play the killing game with us, little man? We're pros, not political dilettantes. You never had a chance, any more than if you tried racing on the same track with the Unser brothers, or playing golf with Palmer and Trevino."

I couldn't tell whether or not my arrogant speech impressed the gray-haired woman in the doorway; but it stung Leonard to fury, which was almost as good. After all, who wants an ally who flips his lid in a crisis? He came at me with both hands, this time knocking me back against the cushions of the lounge.

"*How many?*"

I shook my head to clear it. "I don't know how many," I said. "It doesn't matter. You can be sure there were enough. Since last night, when you were playing hide-and-seek in this mangrove labyrinth, you haven't got an organization any more. All you've got is a bunch of scared civil servants waiting for lightning to strike them out of a blue sky. A runaway truck. A bullet out of nowhere. A little synthetic heart failure or plague in the morning milk. They know, little man, they know. They know that the one who takes your orders from now on, dies. Try it. Pick up your pretty blue phone. Have your radioman connect you. To anybody—of the ones still alive, I mean. See if the person you reach will snap to attention at the sound of your voice, or laugh at you. Or curse you for a bungling, ambitious incompetent who got a lot of his friends and associates killed. Go ahead. Try it!"

It was a bluff, of course. Actually, I suspected, Mac had been very careful not to let the night's operations take on the aspects of a nationwide bloodbath. The dead had, I figured, all been agency people, of one undercover agency or another in Leonard's shaky empire. Well, agents are always getting themselves killed, and the machinery stands forever ready to hush it up so as not to attract attention. It would take time before those in the know added up a freeway crash here and a drowning there and, realizing that they'd happened on the same night, came up with something resembling the right answer, which by that time would be ancient history.

Nevertheless, it sounded good, I thought; and a worried look on the face of the man guarding Martha confirmed my opinion. He looked like a man beginning to wonder if he'd bet more than he could afford on the wrong nag. I hoped Mrs. Love was having similar thoughts; but her face was harder to read.

"Well?" I said, when Leonard didn't move. "Aren't you going to call the roll of your trusty henchmen? Try the fellow running your show in Phoenix, Arizona, for instance. What was his name, now? Bainbridge, Joseph W. Bainbridge. Give him a ring. I doubt he'll answer, but don't take my word for it. Or the woman in Chicago—"

He swung a fist at my head, and connected glancingly,

and stepped back nursing his bruised hand. "Jernegan!" he gasped.

"Yes, Chief."

"Take him into the pilot house and work him over!"

"Yes, sir!"

It was the woman who stopped it last, as I'd hoped she would. By that time, they were all gathered in the pilot house watching the show; and the young boatman, a tougher specimen than either of the two who'd been guarding Martha and me, was obliging with a performance that made up in enthusiasm for what it lacked in skill. I was playing right up to him, of course. If I do say so myself, I'm pretty good at letting myself be knocked down in the way that hurts the least.

I've had lots of practice in absorbing that kind of punishment. You'd be surprised at the faith people have in the power of fists. As far as I'm concerned, beating a man up is a good way to get yourself killed—for every dozen or so you manage to intimidate that way, there'll always be one who just gets mad and comes back with a gun. I started getting a little mad myself as the ordeal went on; and I was sustaining myself by thinking of all the fun I'd have carrying out my instructions regarding Herbert Leonard, when Mrs. Love finally stepped forward impatiently.

"Stop it!" she snapped. "Herbert, you're wasting time. Call off your boy."

"We have to have the information. If it bothers you to watch—"

"My dear man, I've seen blood before. I was raised

on a farm, and when it was time for a chicken dinner, I was the girl who was handed the hatchet. This wouldn't bother me a bit if you were getting somewhere, but you aren't. I think you'd better let somebody else interrogate the man while he can still talk."

"What makes you think *you*—?"

"What makes me think an elderly female can succeed where you strong young males have failed? My dear man, it's a matter of psychology. May I have a knife, please?"

"Mrs. Love—"

"A knife, Mr. Leonard. *If* you please! Thank you." Lying on the floor, pretending to be in very bad shape— which didn't take hell of a lot of acting—I waited for her to approach, wondering if I'd misjudged her. If so, I was in serious trouble; but her footsteps went the other way, to the little group by the electronics department consisting of the radio operator, Martha, and her guard.

I heard Mrs. Love's voice. "Turn around, girl. Hold out your wrists. That's right. There you are. Now clean up your friend so I can see his expression when I talk with him. Young man, you with the gun, lend her your handkerchief and fetch her a pan of water from the kitchen. *If* you please!"

Then Martha was kneeling beside me, dabbing at my face. She was making the commiserating noises to be expected under the circumstance, but I was listening to Mrs. Love arguing with Leonard.

"You've tried your way, Herbert," she was saying. "Now let me try mine... All right, girl. He's presentable enough. Help him up... Mr. Helm, you're not unconscious. Don't try to fool an old woman. Over there on the settee. Good. Now go back where you were, girl, and behave yourself, or you'll find yourself tied up again so fast it will make your head swim... Mr. Helm?"

I wasn't unconscious, of course, but things were a trifle hazy. I looked up at the motherly figure in the printed dress, with the neatly waved blue-gray hair, and said, "Yes, ma'am."

"We've been trying to get the answers to a few questions—"

"No, ma'am," I said.

She frowned quickly. "What do you mean?"

"He's been trying," I said. "You haven't been trying."

She studied me for a moment. "Are you saying you'll talk to me, Mr. Helm? Why to me and not to him?"

"Why should I waste time talking to a dead man?" I asked. "I was kidding him along before you got here, telling him he'd be allowed to live, but it isn't true. I can't tell him anything that'll save him, and wouldn't if I could. Anyway, I can't let him go to his death thinking he can beat information out of a trained, experienced agent. He's got enough misconceptions about this racket already. There are methods, sure, but they don't involve fists."

Leonard, standing at the head of the ladder, leading down and aft, with Jernegan and my former escort, Bostrom, beside him, stirred indignantly.

Mrs. Love snapped, "Be quiet, Herbert. You've had your turn, Mr. Helm?"

"Yes, ma'am."

"Am I a dead woman?"

"Nobody's after you that I know of, Mrs. Love."

"Why Mr. Leonard and not me?"

"You're not one of us, ma'am. What you do isn't our concern. But he is, of he's trying to be, and he's sold out. He's tried to use his country's undercover services for private political purposes—"

"My purposes, Mr. Helm."

"Sure, but there are always ambitious politicians who'd like to use us," I said. "Their ambitions—your ambitions—have nothing to do with us. We're not responsible for keeping the whole world honest. What does concern us is us. Any time an agent sells out, or allows his knowledge or skill or training to be employed for private purposes, that's a black mark against the whole profession. At least I figure that's how my chief feels about it. He's spent most of his life at this business, and he has very strong opinions about the place of agencies like ours in a democratic society—strong enough for him to pass the death sentence on any agent who abuses his privileged position as Leonard has done and led a lot of others to do."

The woman was silent for a little. When she spoke again, it was on a totally different subject. "Why do you call me 'ma'am'?"

"Perhaps you remind me of a teacher I once had, Mrs. Love."

"Probably a tough old biddy," she said. "Well, we're

wasting time. Let's get to the questions Mr. Leonard was asking you. How many?"

"I don't know."

Her eyes narrowed. "I can have that energetic young man turned loose on you again."

"I don't know, ma'am," I repeated. "That's the truth. All I know is that I was responsible for a list of ten names, and I have no reason to believe they weren't taken care of by the people I assigned to them."

"Tell us the names."

"Leonard already has them."

Mrs. Love turned quickly. "Is that true, Herbert?"

The white-haired man hesitated. "Well, yes, they fed me some kind of a list through the girl, there. I didn't really believe it, of course—"

"Why not?"

"Who could conceive that a supposedly, civilized man like Arthur Borden would plan a deliberate massacre—"

"Your men have been shooting at his, I understand. What's so inconceivable about his shooting at yours? What steps did you take when you received this information?"

"I… I warned the individuals in question and arranged for protection where it seemed to be required. However, we were given the wrong date. We were led to believe that the attempt, if it was made at all, would be made on the seventeenth of the month, two days from now."

Mrs. Love regarded him coldly. She said, "But you did know, and your agents were warned, and they died anyway? I'd hardly call that an attempt, Herbert. I'd call it a successful execution of a carefully laid plan."

"We don't know that *all* the people listed—"

She sniffed impatiently. "Don't quibble. You've checked on five of your key men, and all five are dead, if we figure that Mr. Dunn in Los Angeles isn't very likely to be returning from his yacht trip." She sighed. "It's really too bad. I had faith in you, Herbert. I counted on you. I was warned that your track record in this field wasn't impressive, but you talked a very good fight. You convinced me. Obviously, I was mistaken."

"Mrs. Love—"

She ignored him, turning back to me. "If you had to guess, Mr. Helm, how many other groups like yours would you say your chief had operating around the country?"

I hesitated, then I shrugged, winced, and said, "Hell, it doesn't matter now. It's all over except sweeping up the pieces and dumping them into the trash can. If I had to guess, ma'am, I'd say none."

She frowned dubiously. "Then you think the total body count is only ten, assuming that all your agents performed successfully."

Getting smart, I refrained from shaking my head. "No, I didn't say that. You asked how many groups there were like mine. I think there was only one group like mine, operating independently. The list I was given pretty well covered the country, with the exception of a limited but important area on the East Coast. I noticed the gap when I received my instructions; and Leonard's man who died of botulism in Washington, D.C. was not on my list. I think that man and quite a few others—I have no way of estimating how many—were taken care of by agents working directly under my chief. I think Mac handled the critical East Coast area himself, leaving the hinterlands to me and my group. I figure that's why he had Leonard decoyed out of Washington, so he could have time to clean house without interference."

"I see." Mrs. Love was still frowning thoughtfully. "That would make, perhaps, twenty or thirty human beings violently dead in one night. Do you feel no remorse, Mr. Helm?"

"Do you, Mrs. Love?" I asked boldly. "You're the one who set the machinery of violence in motion. What did you expect when you started using men with guns, that nobody would ever shoot back?"

She sighed. "Well, I must say, I find it a little shocking. If I'd thought there was any chance our little scheme would meet such direct and brutal resistance, I probably wouldn't... Well, the question is academic now, isn't it?" She was silent for a moment, looking down at me; then she said, "Give my regards to the man you call Mac, if you ever see him again. You realize, of course, that I can't do anything for you here. The situation is out of my control."

As she said it, she let her eyes, touch, for an instant, the girl in the corner who had been bound and was now unbound.

"Yes, ma'am," I said.

She turned on her heel. "I'll want your pilot to take me back to civilization right away, Herbert. Oh, and under the circumstances, I think I would like another man along, armed. How about the young man beside him? I don't altogether trust Mr. Helm's assurances; they were just a little too glib."

As she started down the stairs, or ladder, with Jernegan and Bostrom in tow, she glanced back casually, and I saw one eye close in what could have been construed as a wink. She was making certain that I was aware that, having first untied my accomplice, she was now reducing the odds against me by as many men as she could plausibly take with her. She wanted to be sure this was credited to her account. A tough, smart, old biddy.

"Don't bother to see me to the boat, Herbert," she said. "Just get on with your fun and games."

There were still too many men in the room, but two of them—Martha's guard and the radio operator—were basically non-combatant types, I hoped. At least they weren't, I hoped, the kind to die loyally for lost causes. I also hoped that Martha was ready and not hampered by too many peaceful inhibitions after watching the terrible, brutal beating I'd received. I also hoped the gadget I'd given her would work after being soaked in swamp water. That was, I realized, a lot of hoping.

Leonard waited until the runabout had pulled away and the sound of its motor had faded in the distance. I got up as he came for me. He stared at me hard for a moment, his hands closing into fists, and I thought we were going to have the sock-and-slap routine some more. Then he wheeled abruptly.

"Give me that!" he snapped, snatching the revolver from the hand of Martha's nameless guard.

"But, sir—"

Leonard ignored the protest, if that's what it was. He came back towards me, deliberately, his knuckles white with the tension of gripping the pistol. It was no way to hold a gun for accuracy, but at that range he could hardly miss. There was a convincing look of ferocity on his handsome face. Even pussycats get mad.

I circled warily past the houseboat's big steering wheel towards the electronics section, aware of movement behind me as the spectators scrambled instinctively out of the line of fire. Leonard raised the pistol and took aim. I stopped, facing him.

"Twice!" he breathed. "Twice I had it all in my hands, all I ever wanted, and you, always you, took it away from me, Helm! Well, you're not going to live to gloat about it—"

"Martha, *now*!" I shouted, throwing myself to the floor.

He was an amateur to the last. He looked quickly towards the girl instead of doing his shooting first and his sightseeing afterwards. There was a sharp crack behind me, like the report of a firearm. An intense white light filled the pilot house, brighter than the sunshine through the big windows. The light seemed to envelop Herbert Leonard's face, and his hands as well, as he tried to claw away the fiery, incandescent thing that had struck him. He screamed and fell to the floor, rolling back and forth in agony.

Nobody moved except the thrashing man on the pilot house floor and I. I hitched myself over to pick up, with my bound hands, the gun he'd dropped. I struggled to my feet, moved to stand over him and, by twisting and craning, managed to aim accurately enough to put a bullet into the back of his head and stop the noise. After a little while the flare burned itself out.

I looked at the two men. Martha's guard raised his hands in a gesture of submission. The black radio operator spread his wide, with a little shrug, indicating that his field was electronics, not violence. Martha looked at me blindly for a moment. Then she threw the little flare gun away from her, turned, snatched the door open, and stumbled to the houseboat's rail, very sick.

It took me a while, unassisted, to cut my hands free with Herbert Leonard's pocket knife, find the signaling device again, reload it, and go out on deck to fire another flare straight up into the blue Florida sky.

32

Mac hadn't changed much. He still looked, if you didn't look too closely, like a banker strayed from the financial fold, in a neat gray suit that, in deference to the local climate, was a little lighter than his customary working uniform. His black eyebrows still made a striking contrast with his gray hair. His cold gray eyes hadn't changed much, either; but his voice was a little different, here in the admiral's living room, from the crisp, business-like tones I was used to hearing over the phone or in his Washington office. It occurred to me that this was the first time in our long relationship that we'd met socially, so to speak, in a private house.

"I haven't had an opportunity to speak with you, Eric," he said.

"No, sir," I said.

He'd been waiting on the Priests' dock when the *Frances II* brought us in. I'd given him the mission-accomplished sign as I stepped ashore, and with that off his mind, he'd turned his attention to his daughter. What the two of them had found to say to each other under the circumstances, I didn't know; but they'd apparently worked out some basis for coexistence, and it was none of my damned business anyway.

"I want to thank you," Mac said.

I looked out the window of the bright room at the dark screened porch from which I'd once eavesdropped on a political meeting. That had happened only twenty-four hours ago, but it seemed like the distant past. Through the wire netting of the porch, I could see the big sportfisherman lying at the flood-lighted dock as if she'd never left it, the shovel-nosed Whaler that had brought me armed help that I'd no longer really needed; and my own little craft, well, I still thought of her as mine, although actually she belonged to Uncle Sam and always had. The chewed-up prop had been replaced, and she was ready to go again, but the assignment was completed, and there was nothing more for her to do here or myself either.

I turned to look at Mac. It was the first time I could recall that he'd ever thanked me for anything. Well, I guess it was the first time he'd had anything to thank me for. You can commend or reprimand a subordinate for the way he does his job, but you don't generally thank him for it.

"*Por nada*," I said.

He said, "I couldn't in good conscience put a sniper in a situation like that hampered by orders not to harm, particularly when a member of my own family was involved."

"No, sir."

"The other solution would have been acceptable. You understand that."

"Yes, sir."

He smiled faintly. "Of course, as the head of a government agency, I'm obliged to point out that your behavior was sentimental and reprehensible, but… Thank you."

"Yes, sir," I said. "The fact is that we've worked together for a hell of a long time. I couldn't shoot a kid of yours, job or no job. I hope you couldn't shoot one of mine. Where the hell does the admiral hide his liquor, anyway?"

It was an undigestible mixture of personal and business relationships, and I walked away from it. If he didn't like it, he could go for tarpon in the morning and take it out on a fish. I found the liquor cabinet by tracking down the sound of glass clinking against glass. Martha was pouring herself a stiff concoction involving, mostly, vodka. She'd washed off the mud of the morning's adventures, but as some kind of protest, I suppose, she was back in her grubby pirate costume: the striped jersey, the white pants, and the frayed sneakers. She was talking with the admiral. When I came up, I reminded her of something.

"Uncle Hank," she said, "when you port your helm, does the boat go right or left?"

"Right, of course," he said, "but who ports any helms around here? What are you trying to do, impress somebody with how salty you are? The Navy command to the wheel is 'right rudder,' and that's what I taught you, young lady… Excuse me. Laura seems to want me in the kitchen."

When he was gone, I said, "Now you know."

She made a face at me. "I wasn't trying to impress you with how salty I was! I was just… It happened so fast, and I didn't know what commands you were used to."

I said, "Hell, I'm an old Annapolis man, didn't you know?" I grinned at her unbelieving look. "I spent a couple of weeks there once, taking a course in small-boat handling for spooks who might be put ashore on strange coasts. I learned to do things the Navy way, on the water, at least."

"You're a surprising man," she said. "And a terrible one. But I'm glad you're here."

"Why?"

"I can count on you not to be sweet to me. Everybody else is being so goddamned sweet and understanding and forgiving I could urp." I didn't say anything. After a moment, she continued, rather bitterly: "Code double negative!"

I grinned once more. "Cute, wasn't it?"

"Does it always mean two days early, like the fifteenth instead of the seventeenth?"

"Two days," I said, "or two hours, or two minutes, depending on how the time is given. It's just a little understanding between your dad and his more senior operatives. You won't find it in the official manual of procedure, so even if you'd mentioned it to Leonard— apparently you didn't think it important enough—it wouldn't have meant anything to him!" I gave her my nasty grin still one more time. "It also means that the bearer of the code is untrustworthy and should be utilized accordingly."

She flushed. "Like you utilized me, you and Daddy between you!"

I said, "If you'd played it straight, you wouldn't have got utilized, would you?"

"I had to do it!" she said. "I had to do something. It was all so *wrong*." She stopped. I said nothing. After a little, she said, "But I'd like you to know that before I told Leonard about Cutlass Key, I made him promise—it sounds naïve as hell now—but I made him promise that Daddy wouldn't be harmed." I made no comment on that, either. She gave me a sharp, sideways glance and went on defensively, "How could I know? After watching you and your cold-blooded friends in action, I had to believe that somewhere there were normal, decent people with a sane regard for human life! And Mr. Leonard seemed so civilized. How could I know he was just as bad as the rest of you?" She shivered. "I keep seeing his face," she said, looking at me. Her eyes were wide and dark.

"It'll fade," I said.

Martha shook her head minutely. "I don't know. Why aren't you telling me what a brave girl I was, saving the day by my heroic... I didn't care about saving any days. I just knew that after he killed you, he'd shoot me, too. I did it simply because I didn't want to die. I did it, in spite of my... convictions, simply because I was scared, that's why! That's how much my... my ideals are worth, Matt! How am I going to live with that?"

I said, "Cut it out. Everybody's scared. It's a perfectly natural—"

"You weren't scared."

I said, "Hell, this is the first time I haven't been petrified in twenty-four hours."

"No, don't lie to me!" she breathed. "You don't know what fear is, that kind of fear. We were safe, and then you… You didn't really get mixed up about port and starboard, did you, Matt? That's what you told them, so they wouldn't know you'd deliberately let them catch you. You ran that boat aground on purpose when you could easily have got away, because you hadn't carried out your mission. Well, I suppose that's very admirable, in a way. But you'll excuse me if I find it just a little sick, considering what your mission was!"

I looked at her for a moment longer. We'd come a long way around, but we seemed to be back just about where we'd started one evening in Mexico; and it was a circle we'd never break. Anyway, she was Mac's daughter. He was a good man to work for, in his field, but I had no desire to become a member of his family, even by association.

I got out of there, out the front door, and headed towards the big station wagon I'd parked on the other side of the driveway, after cleaning up at the lodge. Then I stopped and stepped back into the shadows instinctively as a sedan turned in from the highway and pulled up behind the parked vehicle. A lean, feminine figure in pants got out. I moved forward. Lorna stopped and squinted up at me in the dark.

"I can't make out your features, mister, but the elevation is familiar," she said. "Agent Lorna reporting, sir. Mission accomplished, sir." She drew a long breath. "Well, we pulled it off. I hope the man is happy. What happened to Carl, going suicidal like that and getting himself shot by a cop?"

I said, "It's too hard to explain. Anyway, he got the man he was sent after, didn't he?"

"Don't snap at me. You look as if you'd been taking a beating, both physically and psychologically. I think you need a drink and a woman."

"I need a drink," I said. "I've had a woman."

Lorna glanced at the house, as a youthful shadow showed briefly on a drawn blind. "Hell, that's not a woman," she said. "You can do better than that."

As it turned out, I could.

ABOUT THE AUTHOR

Donald Hamilton was the creator of secret agent Matt Helm, star of 27 novels that have sold more than 20 million copies worldwide.

Born in Sweden, he emigrated to the United States and studied at the University of Chicago. During the Second World War he served in the United States Naval Reserve, and in 1941 he married Kathleen Stick, with whom he had four children.

The first Matt Helm book, *Death of a Citizen*, was published in 1960 to great acclaim, and four of the subsequent novels were made into motion pictures. Hamilton was also the author of several outstanding stand-alone thrillers and westerns, including two novels adapted for the big screen as *The Big Country* and *The Violent Men*.

Donald Hamilton died in 2006.

ALSO AVAILABLE FROM TITAN BOOKS

The Matt Helm Series
BY DONALD HAMILTON

The long-awaited return of the United States'
toughest special agent.

Death of a Citizen
The Wrecking Crew
The Removers
The Silencers
Murderers' Row
The Ambushers
The Shadowers
The Ravagers
The Devastators
The Betrayers
The Menacers
The Interlopers
The Poisoners
The Intimidators
The Terminators
The Retaliators (August 2015)
The Terrorizers (October 2015)
The Revengers (December 2015)
The Annihilators (February 2016)
The Infiltrators (April 2016)
The Detonators (June 2016)
The Vanishers (August 2016)
The Demolishers (October 2016)

TITANBOOKS.COM

ALSO AVAILABLE FROM TITAN BOOKS

Helen MacInnes

A series of slick espionage thrillers from the New York Times bestselling "Queen of Spy Writers."

Pray for a Brave Heart
Above Suspicion
Assignment in Brittany
North From Rome
Decision at Delphi
The Venetian Affair
The Salzburg Connection
Message from Málaga
While Still We Live
The Double Image
Neither Five Nor Three
Horizon
Snare of the Hunter
Agent in Place

TITANBOOKS.COM

ALSO AVAILABLE FROM TITAN BOOKS

Lady, Go Die!
BY MICKEY SPILLANE & MAX ALLAN COLLINS

THE LOST MIKE HAMMER NOVEL

Hammer and Velda go on vacation to a small
beach town on Long Island after wrapping up the
Williams case (*I, the Jury*). Walking romantically
along the boardwalk, they witness a brutal beating
at the hands of some vicious local cops—Hammer
wades in to defend the victim.

When a woman turns up naked—and dead—
astride the statue of a horse in the small-town
city park, how she wound up this unlikely Lady
Godiva is just one of the mysteries Hammer feels
compelled to solve…

TITANBOOKS.COM

ALSO AVAILABLE FROM TITAN BOOKS

King of the Weeds
BY MICKEY SPILLANE & MAX ALLAN COLLINS

THE PENULTIMATE MIKE HAMMER NOVEL

As his old friend Captain Pat Chambers of
Homicide approaches retirement, Hammer finds
himself up against a clever serial killer targeting
only cops.

A killer Chambers had put away many years ago
is suddenly freed on new, apparently indisputable
evidence, and Hammer wonders if, somehow,
this seemingly placid, very odd old man might be
engineering cop killings that all seem to be either
accidental or by natural causes.

At the same time Hammer and Velda are dealing
with the fallout—some of it mob, some of it federal
government—over the $89 billion dollar cache the
detective is (rightly) suspected of finding not
long ago…

TITANBOOKS.COM